JACK
AND DJINN

JASINDA WILDER

DJINN:

"Jinn or djinn (singular: jinn, djinni, or genie; Arabic: al-jinn, singular al-jinn) are supernatural creatures in Islamic mythology as well as pre-Islamic Arabian mythology. They are mentioned frequently in the Quran (the 72nd sura is titled *Sûrat al-Jinn*) and other Islamic texts and inhabit an unseen world in dimensions beyond the visible universe of humans. The Quran says that the jinn are made of a smokeless and "scorching fire," but are also physical in nature, being able to interfere physically with people and objects and likewise be acted upon. The jinn, humans, and angels make up the three sapient creations of God. Like human beings, the jinn can be good, evil, or neutrally benevolent and hence have free will like humans and unlike angels. The jinn are the analogue of demons in Christian tradition, but the jinn are not angels, and the Quran draws a clear distinction between the two creations."—Wikipedia

Chapter 1

Carson

Present Day

A maintenance worker found the body—if it could even be called that—on the lowest level of the parking garage at MGM Grand Detroit. Completely immolated, the body was burned beyond recognition. All that remained was a charred pile of bones and teeth. Detective Carson Hale knelt beside the pitiful remains of what had once been a person, prodding a femur with the tip of his pen.

"Damn," he said. "There's just nothing left. I mean, *nothing*." Carson stood up and wiped the pen on his pant leg, wishing he hadn't just poked a dead body with it—he had a tendency to chew on his pens.

"I know," the responding DPD officer answered. "What I can't figure out is, what could have happened to do this to a body? I mean, I'm not even sure how we'll get a positive I.D. on this person."

"Not only that, but there's no other evidence of fire. Look around. For it to get hot enough to do *this* to a body, there should be other evidence of the fire, right? But there's nothing. No scorch marks on the floors, the walls, or even on the ceiling, which isn't that high."

"Maybe the body was torched? Like, with accelerant or something?" The officer was a young woman, only two years on the force, and seemed queasy looking at the remains.

"I don't know, though. If that were the case, wouldn't there at least be burn marks on the pavement here? Also, if a person is on fire, they panic, you know? It takes time for them to die, so they run around, knock into things. There should be smears on the wall where the victim slammed into it, but there's nothing. It's as if the victim was lit on fire where they stood and then instantly they were virtually vaporized into this little pile."

"Okay, let's forget the body for a second." The officer glanced around at the taped-off crime scene. They were in a distant corner of the garage, a dead end where few cars ever parked. "What else do we know? Anything?"

"Well, for one thing, there's that pool of blood over there." Carson pointed to a spot a few feet away from the skeleton where the forensic team was taking samples. "It's a big pool of blood, but I don't think it's from this guy here, though."

They walked over, and the officer examined the blood more closely. It was partially dried and still tacky in places, likely several hours old, but not more than twenty-four. "You're right about that. I agree that this blood is definitely from a second person."

"And, number two, there's the matter of the four shell casings and the 9mm pistol near the body. It almost looks as if the gun was dropped when the victim was torched. However *that* happened." Carson pointed to a third area, nearer the burned skeleton. "We're probably looking for a second body, based on the amount of blood that's here. I'm guessing we have a double homicide. The pistol and the casings are near the burn victim, which makes me think he or she was the shooter." Carson was conjecturing out loud, trying to piece together a scenario based on the few facts they had.

"I don't know," the officer objected. "If someone is shot four times, they won't be setting anyone on fire. If you ask me, I think you're looking for another body *and* a third person, the killer."

"I agree," Carson said. "Either way, the next step is to fingerprint the gun and the casings, and see where that leads us."

The casino manager was standing nearby, giving his report to a patrol officer. Carson didn't like the manager on sight. He was an older man, short and agitated, with a sharp nose, beady, shifting eyes, and nervous fingers. He avoided eye contact, and he shuffled his feet as if he'd like to run away. *Ratty*, Carson thought, *Mr. Rat*. The man even had a squeaky voice.

"I don't know nothing," Mr. Rat exclaimed. "I swear it. I wasn't here 'til mebbe five o'clock this evening, and you're telling me this all happened late last night or early this morning. The shifts've all changed since then. I can't tell you nothing but who was on schedule last night and when they'll be on again. But you gotta remember, we got dozens of waitresses, plus security and janitors. This place is huge, officer. You know that. We got a staff that runs in the hundreds. Getting any of 'em to tell you a straight story, even *if* they saw something, well, that's gonna be quite a chore, not to mention tracking 'em all down. I'll tell you what I can do is, I'll put the word out to the staff that if anyone knows anything to tell me, and I'll pass it along to you. The thing is, like any parking garage, that one's open to the street, so anyone could've wandered in and my staff wouldn't've seen nothing anyway."

Carson hated to admit it, but Mr. Rat was right. There was simply no way they could spend the time hunting down all the people who might have seen something, especially when there was no evidence the victim or victims had ever been inside the casino in the first place. As he swung his muscular, six-foot-three frame into the unmarked Impala, Carson had a feeling that this was going to be a tricky case. Some were like that. You started out with very little to go on, and got no further. The boxes full of unsolved cold cases back at the precinct were proof of that.

There was something about the way the body was burned that kept turning over in Carson's head. No matter which way he looked at it, he couldn't make sense of it. Had the body been burned somewhere else and dumped in the garage? That made no sense whatsoever; the body had obviously fallen *in situ*. The way the bones were arranged suggested the body had toppled over dead on the spot, some bones still touching where they had been joined by tissue. If the remains had been dumped, the bones would be a jumbled mess. Besides, why would someone dump a dead, burnt-to-a-crisp body in a casino parking garage? A gambling debt? That was one possibility, but until they had a positive I.D. on the body, it was mere conjecture.

The security cameras had a few images that might be connected to the crime, but there was no footage of the crime itself.

"I'm gonna need the surveillance tapes for the whole garage," Carson said, "going back forty-eight hours. Officer Nagle, you can handle that. Go through the footage and see if you can find anything."

He went back to the precinct and immediately went to the forensic lab. The pistol and the casings were dusted for fingerprints, the results from the FBI database coming back a couple of hours later: The prints belonged to Benjamin Wade, twenty-nine years old, two tours of duty in Afghanistan with the U.S. Marine Corps. No priors except for a few parking tickets and a speeding ticket. Wade rented an apartment in downtown Royal Oak. A day spent digging produced Wade's military records and resulted in dental records matching the body found in the MGM Grand parking garage.

It wasn't much to go on, but it was a start.

As soon as the positive I.D. on the body came back, Carson drove up to Wade's apartment complex in Royal Oak and spoke to the apartment manager. The apartment manager claimed he'd only met Ben once, when he signed the lease. Out of all the residents, there was only one neighbor who had any pertinent information, Matthew Hackett. Matt was a retiree, a portly older man with yellow, nicotine-stained teeth and long, unkempt hair and a grizzled beard.

"Yeah, I know Ben a little," Matt claimed in a rough grumble tinged with a thick Southern drawl. "Not well, but some. He's nice enough to me, when

I see him in the hallway. Spent two years fighting that war in Afghanistan, you know."

"Does he have a girlfriend?" Carson asked. "Anyone who comes over on a regular basis?"

"Oh, yeah," Matt answered, "Miriam, I think her name is. Nice girl. Mebbe five-five, real long brown hair, nearly down to her waist. Beautiful girl, that Miriam. Had a real nice set of—" Matt trailed off with his hands cupped in front of his chest. "Er. Yeah. She's real pretty."

"Do you know if she and Ben get along?" Carson asked.

"Most of the time, I guess. I hear 'em arguing a good bit, mostly him yelling at her. She don't stay over, though—she usually leaves late at night. I don't sleep much, you know."

"So you watch your neighbors?" Carson asked.

"Well…." Matt shifted uncomfortably, flushing red. "I ain't done nothing—I just watch her go, make sure she gets out to the street okay. I feel bad for her, a bit. Why she stays with Ben, I don't know."

This got Carson's attention. "What does that mean, Mr. Hackett? Does Ben mistreat her?"

"Well…I—I've seen her leave with a black eye once or twice. These walls, they ain't too thick, you know? So I hear things, but I ain't *tryin'* to listen in, you know?" The more agitated he got, the thicker his Southern drawl became. "So, yeah, I've heard him smack her a few times. Say, what's this about, any-ways? He finally went too far, is that it? Come to think of it, I ain't seen him in a while."

"We are currently investigating Mr. Wade's death," Carson said.

"He's dead?" Matt was shocked. "How'd he die? You think Miriam did it?"

"I can't divulge the details of the case, Mr. Hackett. Is there anything else you can tell me?"

Matt thought before answering. "Well, they both worked at the Taproom a couple miles down the street. I think Miriam lives right near the bar. I heard 'em talking about that a few times. Try the bar. You might find something useful there."

"Okay, well, thank you for your time, Mr. Hackett," Carson said, handing the older man his card. "If you think of anything else, call me."

"I'm headin' down to Florida tomorrow," Matt said. "But I'll think on it."

After getting the key from the manager Carson checked Ben's apartment and found it almost spartan. An expensive but faded leather couch and love seat, a huge flat-screen TV, no artwork or decorations of any kind, except a single picture of Ben's Marine unit on a side table. There were a few bills lying on the din-ing room table, with a box of 9mm shells and spare clips next to them. Ben's apartment seemed like it was somewhere he slept and that was about it. Other than the shells and clips, there was nothing else. The search had yielded little new evidence. But the real lead was the interview with Matt Hackett regarding Ben's girlfriend, Miriam.

He needed to find Miriam, but the burning question was whether he would find her dead or alive.

CHAPTER 2

Miriam

One month earlier

MIRIAM WATCHED BEN POUR THE TEQUILA INTO THE shaker, trying to gauge his mood. He seemed calm enough, but that didn't always mean anything. She placed the last highball on the round black tray, hefted it to her shoulder, and moved out into the bustle of the bar. She navigated the crowd carefully, holding the tray above her head. The Taproom was bustling, full of drunks watching the Tigers game. She felt a hand grab her backside, and she halted in her tracks, cursing the jerk. He just leered, winked, and reached for her again, but Ben was there in an instant. He latched onto the guy's arm with crushing force. Miriam winced in sympathy, knowing exactly how painful Ben's grip was.

"Keep your filthy hands to yourself, asshole," Ben growled, leaning down over the customer, a sweaty, round-faced man of about forty, wearing a green and yellow John Deere trucker hat and a flannel shirt. "If I see you touch my waitress again, I'll throw you out on your ass, you understand me?"

"Yeah, sure. I getcha, pal," the man said, trying to tug his hand free. Ben clamped down harder, until the man squirmed. With one last glare, Ben released him and sauntered back to the bar. Miriam delivered the rest of her drinks and went back to the service bar with her new orders.

"Thanks, Ben," she said.

"Yeah. You okay, baby?" Ben snatched a ticket from the printer.

"He just copped a feel, no big deal."

"It *is* a big deal. Not in my bar. Not my girlfriend." He mixed the drinks and slid them to her. "If he does that again, tell me. I'll beat the shit out of him."

"Ben, you don't have to do that. I'm fine."

Ben glared at her. "Just tell me if he does it again."

Great, Miriam thought. *He'll be in a bad mood for the rest of the night.* A good mood with Ben was mercurial, coming and going like clouds drifting across the sun, but a bad mood would linger, and very little could lift him out of it. A bad mood for Ben meant a bad night for Miriam.

The rest of the night passed without incident, and closing time finally arrived. Ben bellowed out the last call and cashed out Miriam and the other servers. By the time they were done with their sidework—refilling salt and pepper shakers and the other condiments, and rolling silverware into napkins—Ben had shooed the last stubborn drinker out and was counting the cash register drawers to make the evening deposit. Ben shut off the lights, locked the doors, and exited out the back, the other waitresses scattering to their cars, leaving Ben and Miriam standing in a pool of flickering orange light coming off the fixture over the back door.

"You coming over?" Ben asked.

"I don't know, Ben. I'm tired, and I work a double tomorrow." Miriam hoped he would take the hint, but she knew better.

"Just come over for a little bit." Ben grabbed her hand and rubbed her knuckles with his thumb in idle, annoying circles.

Miriam sighed. "Ben…I'm exhausted. I've been on my feet all day, and tomorrow is going to be worse."

Ben's eyes narrowed. "You've always got some excuse. You're tired. You have a headache. You have a long day tomorrow." His touch turned to a warning squeeze, not enough to hurt her just yet, but with enough force to remind her who was in charge. "It's almost like you don't love me anymore. Like you'd rather be somewhere else."

"Ben, you know that's not it—"

"Somewhere else, or *someone* else? Is that it?" His voice was low and threatening, sharp with latent rage. "*Is* there someone else?"

"No, Ben. There's no one else. No one but you, you know that."

"Then come over. Prove it to me."

Miriam didn't have much choice. He was calm and in control right now despite his earlier dark mood, but if she resisted any more, his temper would turn. Bad things would happen. She sighed and let him lead her to his ancient, battered Chevy S-10. His hand rubbed her thigh the whole way back to his apartment, his palm moving in circles around the same spot until she wanted to bat his hand away in irritation. She didn't, though, because that would piss him off.

He was kissing her neck as he unlocked his door, and by the time they got to his bedroom, he had her shirt off and her pants unbuttoned. She was tired and her feet hurt, and this was the last thing she wanted, but it was better to just let him do what he wanted. Safer.

Ben was as self-centered in bed as he was in everything else. As soon as he had her naked and in bed, he pushed into her and started thrusting hard and fast. Miriam squeezed her eyes shut, clenched her teeth, and waited for him to finish. Normally, he'd thrust and grunt for a few minutes, finish, and then flop to his side and fall asleep. She was just there, not really participating, and certainly not enjoying it. But he didn't care.

This time was a little different, though. She felt him inside her, his hard body above her, his breath on her shoulder. She felt a loathing, a rife, dark disgust. For Ben, yes, but mostly for herself, for being too weak to get away from him. Tonight, her senses seemed hyper-attuned—she felt each individual thread of the sheets beneath her back, the hair on Ben's chest tickling her, the day-old stubble on his chin rasping over the round of her shoulder, his legs pushing to give him leverage for his thrusting. She felt the dry, painful tug of his manhood inside her, the brief punch of his hips slamming into hers.

Bile hit her teeth. She hated this. When she first met Ben, she'd enjoyed it. He'd been kind. Pretending to be, at least. Back then he pretended to care whether she enjoyed sex. Now he'd stopped pretending, stopped caring.

But now other sensations assaulted Miriam. Her skin tingled. Not from Ben, not from pleasure, or even pain. No, this was a tingling of heat, as if her skin was tightening from the presence of a nearby flame. She tried to ignore it, but the sensation of heat was all-pervasive. Ben's tempo increased as he neared his release, and the pain of his body slamming against her became fierce; as the pain increased, so did the heat coming from somewhere deep within her.

She felt the pain, but with each passing second she felt the heat even more. Heat. Fire. Anger. Disgust.

She felt him quicken, felt his hips pound against hers and hold there as he finished inside her. Then she felt another bolt of disgust and hatred and self-loathing roll through her, accompanied by an explosion of heat. It was as if she was standing too near a campfire now, the heat baking her, washing over her in thick, roiling waves. Ben drew back and pushed in once more, and Miriam felt his seed inside her, and the knowledge that he never thought about protection hit her like a hammer.

She was on birth control, of course, and had been since she realized he'd never bother caring whether she was protected or not. She had herself tested regularly as well, but that was more reactive than anything else and no protection from disease. And now, the anger inside her that Ben just didn't care, never had and never would, became something more than mere anger. It became rage. White-hot and bitter. The bizarre sensation of heat emanating from within her became hotter as her anger increased, until she was sure she could feel it crisping the skin and hair on her arms. She couldn't understand how Ben didn't notice it. He grunted once more, then finally rolled

off, turning away from her to his side, already unconscious, snoring as soon as his head hit the pillow. He
could fall asleep instantly, anytime, anywhere. She
envied him that; she would sometimes lie awake for
hours, waiting for sleep to come.

The heat and the anger continued to billow off
her, but as she tried to focus on it, she realized it
wasn't just heat, wasn't just…physical sensation. It
was something more, something deeper, as if some
circuit in her soul had been tripped, as if the slow
buildup of anger and disgust had triggered an explosion inside her.

Miriam sat propped up with the sheet around her
chest, wondering about the odd sensation she'd just
experienced. Maybe she'd only imagined the physical
heat, the feeling of fire crackling inside her.

Eventually she pushed the mystery away and
dressed as quietly as she could. Ben was snoring, but
he was a light sleeper. As she slipped her shoes on, she
noticed a cell phone sitting on the bedside table.

She picked it up, puzzled; this wasn't Ben's phone.
His was an older-model Blackberry. She knew his
phone all too well since he was always on it, sending a text or checking sports scores. He was always
complaining about it, too, saying he couldn't wait to
upgrade because it was obsolete. The phone sitting by
his bed, however, was brand new, a next-generation
iPhone, just released. She checked his pants pockets,

but they were empty. *No,* she thought, *the night table is where he always puts his phone.* She knew his routine: walk in, keys on the microwave, shoes in the front closet, phone on the bedside table. It never varied, even when he was drunk. She thought back to earlier that evening, visualizing him standing behind the bar, leaning back and tapping on the keys of his Blackberry with one thumb. She searched the kitchen, the dining room table, all the various places he might have left his old phone. Nothing. Just the brand-new phone she knew neither of them could afford.

Miriam shook her head, convinced she must be mistaken. But where *was* his old phone? He hadn't left the bar the entire night. There was no way he could have gotten a new phone, especially considering they'd been on the closing shift and all the stores would have been closed hours before. There it was, though, and no rational explanation for it. Glancing at the time, she dismissed it and left his apartment.

She had a long walk back to her small place above the bar, so it was past four in the morning by the time she made it to the now abandoned parking lot beside the bar, empty except for Miriam's ancient Volvo. She smiled at the rusted gray sedan, remembering she'd lived in it for a long time after her mom had left. It was old and ugly, and had over two hundred thousand miles on it, but it had been her home and her only possession for more than a year. She didn't drive it much anymore, since she lived above the bar, but she loved the old car.

As she let herself into the apartment above the Taproom, she thought back to what had happened at Ben's place that night. Something odd, something unexplainable, and just a little frightening.

Ben showed up at ten-thirty the next morning, rapping on her screen door. "Miriam! I know you're awake in there. Lemme in!"

Miriam stood up from the table where she'd been sipping her coffee and trying to wake up. She stretched, trying to delay letting him in. He'd be pissed that she'd left last night. He never understood why she insisted on going home to her own apartment, no matter what time it was. She didn't know how to explain it, either, which only frustrated him more. Sex was one thing, but sleeping together? That was totally different. The idea of sleeping next to Ben, vulnerable and unconscious…no way.

For some reason, she couldn't seem to find guys who were stable. Any guy she dated seemed nice enough at first, but he invariably turned out to be moody and dangerous. She'd seen a therapist once, and had been told she suffered from severe lack of self-esteem and intense abandonment issues, stemming from her father's death and her mother's abandonment. Knowing the psychological reasons for her choices didn't exactly enable her to change, however.

When she was awake, she had some kind of control over what happened. Asleep, she was vulnerable and helpless. She'd learned that the hard way. Her ex-boyfriend, Nick, had a psychotic episode one time in the middle of the night when she had stayed over. She had woken up with a hand over her mouth, a kitchen knife to her throat, his eyes wide and crazed. She'd managed to grab hold of the lamp bedside the bed and she'd brained him with it, buying her enough time to scramble out the door and into her car. Since then, she'd never slept over at a boyfriend's house.

Nick had been violent and unpredictable. He'd called her names when he got mad, cursed at her, called her a fat slut, a bitch, a whore...all the names he could think of just to hurt her. He'd hidden it well at first, but, as time went on, his true nature finally revealed itself.

Just like Ben.

Ben, whose fist pounded on the screen door now, his voice harsh and angry. "Let me in! Come on!"

She pulled open the door, saying, "Calm down, Ben. I was in the bathroom." A lie, but it was the easiest way.

He brushed past her and went straight for the cabinet and grabbed a coffee mug, helping himself.

Typical. Never asked, just took what he wanted. "Why do you always leave?" There it was. Every time. "I don't get it, Miri. I'd really like it if you stayed sometimes." He sounded like a little boy who hadn't gotten what he wanted, petulant and whiny.

"I've told you a hundred times—I'm not ready for that. Just let it go, *please*. I'll stay over when I'm ready."

Ben lit a cigarette, "So you can fuck me, but you can't sleep with me? That's messed up." His fingers tightened on the mug.

Miriam refilled her coffee, standing with her back to the counter. "Maybe so, but that's my decision. If you care about me, you'll respect it."

She was tired of this conversation, sick of explaining herself to Ben again and again. She knew this was dangerous ground, but she couldn't handle the same argument all over again.

"Respect it? How about you respect *me* for once, and do what I ask."

"If you're going to be like this, then leave." Miriam pointed to the door. "I don't want to argue."

"I'm not trying to argue. I'm just trying to figure your crazy ass out," Ben said.

That touched a nerve, and Miriam felt anger welling up inside her, hot and close beneath the surface. "Get out, Ben. Get out *now*."

He narrowed his gaze, set down his coffee mug, stood up. His brown eyes were focused on her, angry and dangerous. He loomed over her, his muscular, six-foot two-inch frame blocking her in. A vein in his forehead throbbed beneath his close-cropped black hair. Miriam clutched the coffee in her hands, ready to throw it at him if he lifted his fist. It wouldn't have been the first time.

"Fuck you, then," he muttered, and turned on his heel, stomping out and slamming the door so hard it rattled the windows. Tires squealed and his engine roared, and horns honked as he peeled out into traffic. Miriam breathed a sigh of relief and locked the front door. At least he'd been sober this time. She finished her coffee and got ready for work.

The double shift dragged by slowly, and by the time it ended at eleven that night, Miriam was thoroughly exhausted. But she was grateful that Ben was off tonight. She simply didn't have the energy to fend him off—all she wanted to do was collapse into bed and get a good night's sleep. She hurried through her side work and left through the back, breathing in the fresh, cool night air after the heat of the bar. She shuffled up to the entrance to her apartment.

Ben was sitting on the stairs to her place, smoking, his new phone in his hand. "Hey, baby, I know I should have mentioned it this morning, but I just wanted to say thanks for the phone. That was nice gesture," he said.

Miriam gave him a quizzical look. "I didn't give it to you. I thought you'd bought it yourself. I noticed it myself last night. I couldn't figure out where it came from."

Ben glanced at the phone and then at Miriam. "These are brand new, just came out at the beginning of the month. I had my old one when we left work last night. I know I did. I thought you'd left it for me before you went home...or something like that." He took a drag off his cigarette and shrugged, dismissing the subject. "Anyway, I thought you might wanna come over for a bit," he said.

Miriam cursed under her breath. "Look, Ben," she began, "I really don't. I'm sorry, I'm exhausted. I've been on my feet since eleven this morning, and I barely got any sleep last night. I just want to go to bed."

"I've been waiting here for you for almost an hour, Miriam. Just come over for a little bit. Please? Just watch a movie with me."

"Have you been drinking?"

"What the hell does that have to with anything?" He stood up, staggering slightly, slipping his phone in his pocket and tossing the butt of his cigarette to the ground.

"Well, have you?"

"A little. Coupla beers."

"Then I don't want to come over. You're mean when you've been drinking."

"I'll be nice, I promise." He stepped toward her, and she backed away. He grabbed her arm in a vise-like grip and pulled her to his car. She wanted to jerk free, but there was a couple getting out of their car nearby, and if she resisted, he would pitch a fit, causing a scene. And he'd blame her for that when he finally got her alone, and then he'd take it out on her.

She got into his truck, making herself as small as she could, sitting close to the door. Rap buzzed from the speakers, the bass cranked loud enough to rumble in her gut. His hand wandered over and clutched her leg, wandered up to her crotch, and fumbled there. She took his hand in hers and moved it lower down. He turned to glance at her, swerving on the road in the process. *Shit,* Miriam thought, *he's been drinking more than I thought.* Sometimes it was hard to tell with him.

"Ben, you shouldn't be driving." She tried to ignore her fear and sound calm. "Why don't you pull over and let me drive? I'll take us to your place, okay? I'll come over and we'll watch a movie. Just let me drive, *please?*"

"Shut the fuck up. I'm fine." Ben blinked, peering sideways at her and then back to the road.

"You're drunk, Ben. Just let me drive. *Please.* I'm begging you." She touched his forearm and looked at him pleadingly. "Just pull over. Let me drive."

He knocked her hand away, and the truck swerved, angling across the centerline and into the oncoming traffic. Horns honked, headlights flashed. "See what you made me do, you stupid bitch? Almost got us killed."

"Ben—"

"Just shut the fuck up, will you?" Ben turned the music up even louder, so loud her ears throbbed. Then he rolled down his window, letting the cold wind blow over them.

Miriam huddled against the far side of the cab, her seat belt pulled tight, hands gripping the armrest on the door. Finally, after a nerve-wracking twenty minutes, they pulled into the parking lot and Ben swung his truck into his designated spot, threw the door open, and lurched out. Miriam sat in the cab, not wanting to get out.

"Less'go," Ben slurred, wavering on his feet.

Shit, shit, shit, Miriam thought. He was hammered. When she didn't immediately get out of the truck, he lumbered over to her door and wrenched it open, yanking her out. She fell to the ground, scraping her hand on the grit of the asphalt.

She straightened and snatched her arm free, shoving Ben away. "Leave me alone, Ben," she warned, backing away from him as he took another step toward her.

He grabbed for her, nostrils flaring like a bull's, eyes rage-blurred and booze-hazed. "Don' tell me what to fuckin' do, bitch." He lunged at her, hard fist cracking against her cheekbone. Stars exploded in her head and she fell backward, slamming into the ground, bruising her tailbone and smacking her head. Ben was standing over her, one hand bunched up in her shirt front, beer breath sour and overwhelming, fist cocked to strike again.

A lance of heat washed through her gut and set her blood alight. *No, not again.* She was standing up somehow, pushing Ben away despite his greater strength. She was burning up, her mind an inferno of rage, her skin on fire. She struck Ben in the chest with a flattened palm and he stumbled backward. Her handprint was seared into his skin through his shirt, a blackened palm-shaped brand burned deep in his flesh. He was cursing, pulling at the shirt to keep it away from the open wound, glancing up at Miriam in shock and fear. Before she could register what had just happened, Ben was across the intervening space, his huge fist slamming into her gut. She stumbled backward, gasping for air, eyes watering, hands clutching her belly. Another blow, this one to her side, followed immediately by a third to the same spot. Agony blew through her, leaving her breathless and limp, leaning back against a car door, blinking, trying to breathe, trying to see, unable to even plead for the mercy she knew she wouldn't get. His fist cracked against her face, knocking her head backward, stars flashing like sunbursts. Another wicked punch to her ribs, and she felt something crack inside her. She braced herself for another blow, slid to the hard grit of the asphalt, stifling whimpers behind clenched teeth.

The blows stopped abruptly, and she heard a voice, distant and muffled. "Hey! Leave her alone, asshole!"

Through tear-blurred eyes, Miriam saw a man wearing a motorcycle helmet pulling Ben away, throwing lightning-fast punches to Ben's torso, followed by a vicious uppercut that left Ben laid out on the asphalt. Miriam clawed at the car, struggled to her feet, blinking to clear the tears of pain.

Her rescuer rushed over and wrapped a gentle arm around her shoulders.

"Come on!" His voice was kind and deep and musical.

He gently guided her to his motorcycle and helped her on, pulling her arms around his waist. The bike rocketed forward, the back tire stuttering sideways. Miriam clutched at his stomach with frightened fingers, feeling his rock-hard abs through his thin T-shirt. She laid her head against his back, barely breathing through the throbbing pain. Her ribs were broken, she was sure of that, and at least one eye was going to be black within minutes. Her savior twisted the throttle, and the back tire squealed as he guided the motorcycle out of the parking lot and onto the main road. Once they were away from Ben, her rescuer slowed down, obviously trying to be considerate of Miriam's possible injuries. As carefully as he drove, however, the slightest motion of the bike sent spears of agony through her, and Miriam closed her eyes, focused on pushing down the tears of pain and anger.

He pulled into the empty parking lot of an office building and skidded to a stop, helping Miriam off the bike. She stumbled away from him and leaned back against the lamppost illuminating the parking lot. She doubled over and focused on breathing, trying not to vomit.

He pulled his helmet off and held it under one arm, brushing hair away from his face with the other hand. "I didn't know where else to bring you."

"It's fine," Miriam breathed, not looking up, pain making it hard to talk.

"Are you okay?" He laughed out loud, a bark of sarcasm. "I guess that's a stupid question. What I mean is, should I take you to a hospital?"

Miriam shook her head and straightened. "I'll be fine." She hated hospitals. There was nothing they could do to help her anyway.

"Do you want me to take you home, then?"

"No! Not home." Miriam shook her head again, not wanting to be alone in an empty apartment.

"Actually, I'm hungry, but I can't go home yet. He'll look for me there."

She looked at the man who had rescued her, really seeing him for the first time, and she found her breath catching. He was over six feet tall, with angular, attractive features, messy light brown hair and liquid, vivid blue eyes. He wasn't brawny or muscular like Ben, but toned and wiry, exuding confidence and kindness. He wasn't physically imposing, tough-looking, or intimidating, but there was still something about him that was intensely masculine and sexy.

He nodded. "There's a National Coney Island not far away." He thrust his hand at her, saying, "I'm Jack, by the way."

"Miriam," she told him, shaking his hand in hers. "Thank you for helping me, Jack."

"Of course." Jack eyed her curiously. "Are you sure you're okay?"

She shrugged, holding back a wince as the motion sent a ripple of pain through her. "I'll be fine."

Jack looked skeptical, but nodded. "Okay, then." He gave her his helmet to put on, swung a leg over his bike, and held his hand out to her. Getting onto the bike behind him hurt but, strangely, not as badly as she thought it should, considering how hard Ben had hit her, and how many times.

National was crowded, even at twelve-thirty in the morning. But they were able to get a booth near the back, and they each ordered coffee and food. As she sugared her coffee, Jack tilted his head and leaned forward, looking at her curiously.

"What?" Miriam asked.

"Well, it's just that I saw your boyfriend hit you in the face, like, a couple of times. You should have a black eye by now."

"I don't?" She prodded her cheek where Ben had hit her, expecting to feel a twinge of pain where the bruise should have been.

"Nope. Nothing at all."

Miriam pulled a compact out of her purse and examined her face in the mirror. He was right—she didn't have a mark on her. Nothing. She stretched her torso and felt only residual pain as she twisted to test the ribs she'd known from experience were at least bruised, if not cracked. She'd felt them break; she distinctly remembered feeling the bones snap. She remembered very vividly the piercing pain, the breathlessness of agony.

"It's odd, but I feel fine."

Jack shook his head, confusion written on his handsome features. "He was beating the hell out of you, Miriam. I *saw* it. I watched him hit you at least three times before I could get to you. You shouldn't be fine. I mean, I'm glad you *are,* but it's just… weird."

Miriam thought about the handprint on Ben's chest, the rush of heat she'd felt. Had Jack seen that? She didn't think so, but she didn't want to ask.

She could only shrug. "I don't know how to explain it. Maybe he didn't hit me as hard as I'd thought?"

Jack shook his head decisively. "No. I saw him punch you. I saw you fall. He wasn't holding back. And even as wasted as he was, a guy his size can hit *hard*."

Miriam didn't need Jack to tell her that; she'd felt the truth of it before now.

"I don't know what to tell you," she said finally.

Jack didn't respond right away, clearly suspecting more than he was saying. "Well, whatever the case," he eventually said, "I'm glad you're not hurt."

Conversation was stunted after that, thick with the knowledge that something unusual had happened, but neither of them was willing to conjecture any further. Eventually they finished their food, and Jack took Miriam back to her apartment. They lingered on the steps, the black of night tinged with gray.

"Thanks again for...you know, saving me and all," she said. She was standing a step up so she was level with Jack's intense blue eyes. She found herself unable to look away.

"Anyone would have done the same," he said, running a hand through his messy brown hair.

"Not in my experience," Miriam said, watching the wind toss a thick tendril of his hair back across his face and wanting, absurdly, to brush it away.

"I know it's none of my business," Jack said, his eyes flicking to hers and then away again, "but…why do you put up with an asshole like that?"

"It's complicated." The stock answer was meant to push him away. It was impossible to describe her situation to anyone who hadn't lived through something similar himself.

"Complicated." His flat tone told her he knew a brush-off when he heard it. "Right. Well, you deserve better."

"What makes you say that?"

"No one deserves that. Getting beat up in a bar fight or something, that's one thing." Jack seemed to struggle for words, for calm. "Letting your boyfriend just beat the shit out of you? That's *not* okay." He shook his head, a lock of brown hair slipping down to brush his temple.

"It's not like I just *let* him. It's not that easy, Jack. I can't just—" She shook her head, cutting herself off. "You know what? Never mind. You wouldn't understand."

"Maybe not." Jack took a step forward, hands on the railing on either side of her. Not touching, but close. Too close. She should want him to back away. She should turn away, go inside. But she didn't. She couldn't. He was inches away, far too close, but she stayed where she was. He smelled of engine oil and deodorant and male sweat, a masculine combination of scents that had her heart hammering, had her wanting to bury her face against his T-shirt. "I might not understand why you stick around a cocksucker like that, but what I do understand is that you *shouldn't*. You're beautiful, Miriam. You deserve better. You may not believe it, but you do."

Miriam's breath caught. She *didn't* believe it, and Jack somehow knew it. Every guy she'd ever been with had treated her the same as Ben. It was how men were.

But Jack was different. She knew it, deep down.

She stared at him, unable to fathom her own reaction to him. Normally, when someone started in on how she should just leave whoever was giving her the black eyes and sore ribs, she would clam up and shut down. If you've never been caught up in the cycle of violence, you can't understand it. Even if you know you deserve better, even if you know you should just leave, it just isn't that easy. Guys like Ben, they don't let you leave. And if you tried, there would be hell to pay.

As Miriam got to really know Ben, she had felt herself closing up, emotionally, mentally, physically. She pulled in, put walls up, hardened herself. She went into survival mode, thinking of nothing but getting through whatever new hell came next but unable to free herself from him, from his hold on her.

But Jack, standing on the stair one below hers... he inspired a different reaction in her. He made her wonder if, maybe, there could be someone out there better than Ben. Was there a way to break the cycle? To get away from Ben and find someone who would treat her better? Jack made her want to open up, to allow someone in who would care for her heart, for her body.

He made her wonder what would happen if she kissed him right then. It was a crazy thought. Totally insane. She couldn't. She wouldn't. Ben would know. He'd smell it on her. And she just couldn't. She couldn't kiss a man she'd known for less than three hours. But she wondered, nonetheless, what it would be like if she did.

The crazy desire to find out pestered her, nagged at her, dug at her. He was right there, inches away, his messy, sweaty hair hanging around his face and in his stunning blue eyes, his strong hands on the railing just below her own hands, his body angled forward, his eyes searching her. His lips were right there; all she had to do was lean down and touch hers to his.

Scant inches narrowed to scarcely a hair's-breadth, their faces so close she could feel his breath, feel the heat from his body mingling with her own.

Before the impulse took over, Miriam backed away, up a step, two, three. "Thanks again, Jack." She turned around and went up the rest of the way, feeling his gaze on her. She turned back around as she opened the door. "It was nice meeting you."

Jack nodded. "No problem. Nice to meet you, too, Miriam."

He was watching her, one foot on the first step, as if he was about to follow her up. She half-hoped he would. She felt an attraction to him that was dangerous in its suddenness and intensity. She'd known him for a matter of hours, and she wanted to feel his strong, gentle hands on her body, kiss his lips and tangle her fingers in his hair. She wanted to feel things with him that she'd never had before. Not with anyone.

She shook herself. It was impossible. But god… she wanted it.

Pulling open the tautly sprung screen door, then pushing open the interior door, Miriam heard a boot on the steps. "Miriam, wait."

Jack lunged up the steps, reached into his jacket pocket, and pulled out a business card for an auto repair garage in downtown Royal Oak. He pulled a pen from the same inside pocket and scribbled his first name and a phone number on the card. "If you ever need anything, call me. Okay? Anything, anytime."

Handing her the card, he didn't wait for a response before turning and tripping quickly down the steps, stuffing his helmet on his head.

Miriam let the door slam shut, then threw herself on her couch and listened to the roar of his motorcycle recede, thinking of his eyes on hers, dreaming of impossible things.

The next day came all too early. Miriam worked a mid-shift, which she hated. Opening was fine, closing was fine, even doubles were okay, but mids were the worst. Showing up at one in the afternoon meant there wasn't enough time to really *do* anything before work, and by the time she got off at eight or nine, the day was mostly gone. She'd rather just close and be done with it. Closing meant she could avoid Ben, who tended to work primarily day shifts. He'd been texting her and calling her nonstop since first thing in the morning, but she couldn't make herself answer.

She did listen to one of the voicemails, though: "Miriam, it's me," Ben's voice said. "I'm sorry if things...got out of hand. I must've had too much to drink and blacked out or something. I'm not entirely sure. I don't remember much of last night, and what I do remember...it doesn't make any sense. I don't know. Just...call me when you get off work, okay? All right, 'bye." Miriam felt a rush of hope when she heard that. He thought he'd blacked out, so he might not remember seeing Jack at all, which would make things a *lot* easier. She'd spent the entire morning trying to come up with an explanation he might believe; maybe now she wouldn't have to.

Miriam dragged herself through the day, her thoughts returning to Jack more than they should have. She found herself waiting for orders at the service bar, staring at the liquor bottles, and wondering how she could arrange to see him "accidentally." She had the card he'd given her in her server book, tucked behind the order pad.

Larry, the general manager, was cutting her a few minutes before six, since the bar was dead. Miriam sat on the stainless steel counter in the kitchen, counting her cash, staring at Jack's scrawled name and phone number. She told herself to go home and catch up on *The Bachelor*. But...her car did need brake work.

It couldn't hurt anything to just see him, could it?

Yes, it could, the logical side of her brain answered. *You won't just go see him. You'll end up going somewhere with him, and he'll be charming and perfect, and you'll think he'll be different. But he's not. All guys are the same. Don't go down that road. Just don't. Go home. Watch* The Bachelor.

Logic lost the argument when she thought of Jack, remembering the warmth of his blue eyes, the feel of his hard abs through his thin T-shirt, his strong back against her face as she'd held on to him for balance.

She thought of how close she had come to kissing him. It was crazy, and she knew it. She'd just met him, had spent barely three hours with him, and yet she couldn't stop thinking about him. And about what he'd said. How he thought she was beautiful. She would just go home. She pocketed her tips, changed out of her uniform, and continued to tell herself to be sensible and stay home.

When she did get home, though, the TV stayed off. She took a short shower, just to wash off the smell of the bar. When she got dressed, she found herself putting on a low-cut top, because it made her feel sexy. A girl needed to feel good about herself, right? She curled her hair so the long dark brown spirals hung at her shoulder blades and framed her face. She wasn't doing her hair for Jack, she was just...doing her hair. And the makeup she put on, the eyeliner, the lip stain, and the hint of mascara...that was for....

Oh, hell, she thought. *I want to see Jack, and that's what I'm going to do. No sense in pretending.*

She Googled the address of Jack's garage on her phone as she pulled away in her rattling old Volvo. Miriam found the place without a problem, a mere fifteen-minute drive away. The front office smelled like oil and old coffee, a pile of tires stacked in one corner, a few cracked plastic chairs lined along one wall on either side of a small table holding a coffee maker and a couple of *Auto Trader* magazines. A thickset,

balding man in blue mechanic's coveralls sat behind
the counter, wiping his hands on a rag and staring at a
computer monitor. He looked up when the little bell
attached to the door tinkled.

"Can I help you, darlin'?" He had a slight Irish
accent and brown eyes. A name patch on his coveralls
read *Doyle*.

"Well, I need my brakes looked at," Miriam said,
trying to peer past him into the garage, hoping for a
glimpse of Jack.

"Okay, well, what's wrong with 'em?" Doyle
tossed the rag onto the counter, digging in his ear
with a pudgy forefinger.

"They're squealing when I stop, and shuddering
when I get off the freeway." She didn't really care
about the brakes, but now that she was here, she was
finding it hard to come right out and ask for Jack. She
shifted to one side, seeing a flash of blond hair from
underneath a car.

Doyle glanced behind himself and back to Miriam.
"Are you lookin' for someone?"

Miriam blushed, nodded. "Is Jack here?"

Doyle laughed, an uproarious belly laugh, as if
she had said something hysterical. Miriam just stared
at him, unsure how to respond.

"Why, sure he is! Why didn't you ask in the first
place? I ain't gonna bite you, you know. Hang on a

tick, I'll get him." He leaned backward in the chair, tipping over so far Miriam was sure he'd fall over.

"Jackie!" he bellowed, loud enough that Miriam flinched. "Hey, Jackie-boy! There's a girl here to see you."

She heard Jack's voice call out, "A girl? Who is it?"

"Well, I don't know, do I? A pretty one!"

Jack entered the office, wiping his hands on his pants leg. "Miriam! I wasn't expecting to see you...I mean, I'm glad you're here, but—" He cut himself off, grabbed the rag, and wiped his face with it, smearing grease across his forehead and eliciting a laugh from Miriam.

"Well, I needed brake work...." Miriam gave the excuse, hoping he'd see through it.

"Yeah, sure," Jack said, coming around the counter and walking her out into the early evening sunlight. "You know you just came to see me," he teased. If only he knew how true that was. Now that she was here with him, she wasn't sure what to do next.

"No," she protested, "I really do need my brakes fixed."

"There's only, like, a hundred garages closer to you than this one." Jack was rubbing his hands on his coveralls, but they never seemed to get any cleaner.

"Yeah," Miriam said, "but I was hoping you'd cut me a deal. And the mechanics at those other garages are all ugly. And rude."

"And that makes me…what?"

"Nice. And…not ugly?"

Jack laughed. "Thanks?"

Miriam went for broke. "You know what? You're right—I really did come just to see you. I can't thank you enough for what you did the other night."

Jack's eyes hardened. "Anyone in their right mind would've done the same thing."

Miriam shook her head. "Not everyone. It's happened to me before, just like that. There was a guy walking out to his car, and he started to say something, but Ben just glared at him and the guy left."

"Well, he was a fuckin' coward, then." Jack shook his head. "Listen, I'm off in, like, twenty minutes. I just have to finish one last thing. Do you wanna grab a burger or something when I'm done?"

Miriam told herself she shouldn't. *Just go home.* "Sure, sounds good," she said, feeling butterflies in her stomach.

Jack was as good as his word, emerging a little more than twenty minutes later, the top of his coveralls unzipped and thrown back, revealing a white tank top and hard, toned arms, a Celtic knot tattooed on his left bicep with what she guessed was Gaelic script underneath it. Miriam left her car at the garage and sat behind Jack on his bike, enjoying the ride immensely, trying not to think about how much she was liking the feel of Jack on the bike in front of her, how intoxicating his scent was, the sweat and the engine oil and faint deodorant.

He took her to his apartment, an aging red brick two-story building in the Ferndale area. "I've gotta clean up real quick. Come on up." Miriam just nodded and followed him to a second-floor apartment, a neat and sparsely furnished one-bedroom. It smelled of oil paint and turpentine. A canvas sat on an easel in a corner of the living room, where a TV might usually go. There were faint pencil sketches on the canvas, but nothing Miriam could identify.

Jack followed her gaze and shrugged. "I love to paint. The garage pays the bills, but the painting is where my heart really is." He swept an arm at the apartment. "Make yourself at home. I'll be out in a minute."

He stepped into the bathroom, pulling his shirt off on the way, and her gaze followed the rippling muscles in his back, the shift of his biceps. He closed the door, and Miriam turned to a stack of canvases leaning against the wall near the galley kitchen. She flipped through them carefully. He was talented, she realized, although she was no artist herself. There were landscapes, still lifes, portraits. One painting in particular caught her eye, a depiction of a candle flame seen from close up. It looked completely real, the candle and the wick just barely visible at the bottom of the canvass, the wax caught mid-drip and pooling near the wick. The flame was hypnotic to Miriam, as if she could feel its heat, see it wavering and dancing in the darkness. Staring at the painted flame, Miriam felt some coiled energy deep in her core expand and unleash, sending waves of heat from her in distorting shimmers.

The thrust of the power was consuming her, burning her, pressing on her chest so hard she couldn't breathe; she had to get it out, had to release it somehow. Miriam extended a finger to touch the image of the flame, and at the moment of contact the painting began to dance and waver, becoming impossibly real. She felt heat coming from the painting, so hot she thought it might scorch her skin and catch her clothes on fire. When her hand left the surface of the canvas, the dancing candle flame went still, returning to its painted image.

Jack spoke then, and she jumped, gasping. "Like it?" he asked, his voice at her ear. She could feel the heat radiating from his body. She didn't have to turn around to know he would still be wet, his hair mussed and damp, a thin towel wrapped around his angular hips, looking like it might fall off at the slightest touch. She took a deep breath and turned to face him. She forced her gaze upward, keeping her hands at her sides.

"It's amazing," she said, not certain whether she was talking about him or the painting.

"You can have it if you like it that much," he said. He seemed to have picked up on her unintentional double entendre, returning its meaning in the tone of his words and the smile in his eyes.

"Really? I would love it. It would go great in my room." She was sure she was blushing. She hadn't blushed since high school. She was almost thirty, and blushing. What was wrong with her?

"I'll bring it over sometime, then." He was inches away, looking down at her. Miriam's hands were lifting on their own, tracing the lines of his abdominal muscles, drifting toward the "V" where his torso met his hips and groin. Her fingers followed the rolled rim of the towel, inching it farther downward, loosening it. She hadn't meant to touch him, but where her fingers brushed his skin she felt an electric tingling, a flutter of wings in her belly.

She withdrew her hands, but Jack's fingers pinioned her wrists in a gentle but implacable hold. His eyes roamed her face, flitting from side to side, down her neck, and down to the expanse of her cleavage. She had no memory of moving, but somehow she was pressed up against him, her breasts crushed to his bare, damp chest, her chin tilting upward, her eyes on the hard angles and planes of his face. Jack released her hands, but she couldn't bring herself to move them—she couldn't pull her palms away from the hot skin of his sides. Her lips parted, and she watched as he slowly bent over her, one of his hands cupping the curve of her lower back, pulling her flush against him, and the other palming her cheek, his thumb grazing across her lips just before he angled his mouth over hers.

Miriam sighed into the kiss, letting her palms skate up his bare back to clutch his shoulders, lifting up on her toes to meet him, and when his tongue traced the seam of her lips, she let her mouth fall open, let his tongue slide between her lips and touch her teeth and tangle with her tongue, and she tasted toothpaste, smelled fresh soap and shampoo.

She felt his desire thickening between them. She stepped away before her hands helped the towel fall off, pushing him toward his bedroom. "Go get dressed," she told him. "I'm hungry."

Jack complied slowly, stepping backward without taking his eyes from hers. After half a dozen steps, he let out a sigh and turned, vanishing into his room to get dressed. He emerged a few minutes later wearing a pair of tight, faded jeans and a plain gray T-shirt that hugged his torso.

As they walked out, Miriam noticed a candle flickering on the counter in the kitchen. She was sure it hadn't been there before. It was a plain white candle, thick and round, with wax pooled near the wick and spilling over to drip in clumps down the length of the candle. The drips had not yet reached the countertop.

Miriam dismissed it from her mind, or tried to, but the image of the dancing candle flame on the canvas stuck in the back of her mind.

"Should I blow out the candle?" Miriam asked.

Jack stopped in his tracks, confused. "What candle?" Miriam pointed at the candle, and Jack shrugged, then crossed the room to blow it out. "That's weird. I've never bought a candle in my life. I wonder where it came from?"

Miriam had an idea where it might have come from, but she pushed the thought from her head. No way. Could she have just imagined the painting coming to life? Really? It must be her imagination. Maybe it had been a gift, and he'd just forgotten about it. That had to be it.

Jack took her to Mr. B's, then got them a pitcher of Killian's and a plate of cheese sticks, waiting for Miriam to order before he did. She was used to Ben ordering for her, taking her to fancy restaurants neither of them could really afford and buying bottles of wine, freaking out about every little thing she said, getting offended at everything, and always talking, talking, talking, just to fill the silence. Jack was calm and confident, able to sit and peruse the menu in companionable silence, not needing to fill it with endless chatter. He kept the conversation light, and Miriam was grateful.

Halfway through their meal, his cell phone rang, and he answered it. He spoke briefly and ended the call. "Sorry," Jack said. "That was my older brother. We're having a get-together next weekend, and he was finalizing the plans. Hey, you should come."

"You have a brother?" Miriam, having been an only child, was always curious about people with siblings.

Jack laughed. "Yeah, I have...two brothers and two sisters." He paused for a split second before he said "two"—a slight thing, but Miriam noticed it. She tilted her head in a silent question.

Jack shook his head, as if wishing she had missed it. "Well, technically, now I have three siblings."

"Technically?"

There was sadness in his eyes, and Miriam wished she hadn't broached the subject. "My oldest brother, Joe...." Jack hesitated, then took a drink from his beer. "Joe hung himself when I was fifteen. It was weird, though. I'd fallen asleep during history class, and I had this intense dream where I came home from school and found Joe in the garage, strung up with a noose around his neck, a chair kicked over beneath him. I woke up halfway through class, sweating, almost crying. It had been...just so *real*. It didn't feel like a dream. It felt like...like a memory that hadn't happened yet.

"I cut out of school and ran all the way home, knowing what I'd find. And I did find him, exactly as

I'd dreamed it. So now I only have two brothers." He waved his hand, as if dismissing the memory.

"Oh, god, Jack, I'm so sorry! I had no idea," she said, wishing she could comfort him somehow. It was obviously still a raw, painful memory for him.

"Of course you didn't. How could you? It was a long time ago." Jack took a drink and changed the subject. "What about you? Any siblings?"

Miriam shook her head, "No, I was an only child." She hoped he wouldn't ask for details. There was a lot about her childhood that she didn't want to explain. At least not yet.

He nodded, his eyes searching her expression for something. As if he felt her unspoken desire to talk about something else, he changed the subject. "Ah. Well, you should come to the party next weekend. It'll be fun. My family is a riot at parties, lemme tell ya." A hint of Irish crept into his voice. "My sisters always wanted an extra girl in the family anyhow."

Miriam tried to imagine what it would be like to have that much family. She couldn't wrap her brain around it. "I'd like that. It sounds like fun."

"Oh, it will be. These family get-togethers are always a right crazy ruckus, as my grandpa says."

They continued to linger over dinner, their conversation easily meandering from topic to topic, but never touching on anything deep or painful. When they finished their pitcher, Jack paid the bill, and they left Mr. B's to wander around downtown Royal Oak, walking close together, their hands brushing. More than once Miriam nearly took his hand in hers, but she couldn't quite summon the courage to do so.

Eventually Jack brought her home, well past midnight, and once again she found herself standing a step up from him, staring into his wide blue eyes, wondering what he was thinking. They were at that awkward distance, not quite close enough to kiss, but almost. She hesitated, her eyes locked on his, not pulling away, but not moving closer. Jack broke the tension by kissing her. His lips were soft, and he kissed her gently, giving her the chance to pull away if she wanted.

His arms were around her waist, at the small of her back. Her shirt was hiked up in the back, exposing a strip of skin above the waistband of her pants; his fingers found this gap, exploring tentatively, warm palms sliding up her spine, and she couldn't resist anymore. She leaned in against him and tangled her fingers in his hair and kissed him back, pressing her body against his. She could feel his heart hammering wildly, feel his exploring hands tremble against the flesh of her back near her bra strap. He was as nervous as she was, and this endeared him to her all the more. Time slowed and stilled, and Miriam felt the same odd rush of warmth in her gut, heat spreading throughout her, setting her skin alight, making her scalp tighten and every sense heighten so she could hear Jack's heart beating and feel every brush of his hands on her skin like arcing electricity. She could smell him—aftershave and paint and leather. Miriam was breathless, she was drowning; no, not drowning, but burning up, she was being consumed by the fires within her....

Jack was the first to pull away, suddenly hissing between his teeth. "God, you're...you're hot, like, physically *hot* to the touch." He looked at his palms as if expecting to see melted skin. He grinned at her. "I mean, you're hot, too, in another sense—like, beautiful." Miriam laughed, glad he wasn't bolting in fear. She had thought for one crazy moment that she might actually burst into flame. He was looking at her with obvious hunger, visible desire, his hands resting on the swell of her hips. She knew it wasn't fair or right to compare them, but she couldn't help it: Ben had never, ever looked at her like Jack was looking at her now, had never touched her the way Jack was touching her now, had never kissed her so passionately.

Ben touched her as if he owned her, as if she was his and she had no rights or needs. Ben kissed her as part of foreplay, but just so he could sleep with her. Ben looked at her... how? Miriam tried to categorize how he looked at her, and couldn't. With ownership? Contempt? Smug possession seemed to be the most apt term.

"What are you thinking?" Jack asked. He was perceptive. Her face must have betrayed her thoughts.

"Just…." She couldn't tell Jack what she was feeling. He'd want to continue this—this whatever *this* was, and that would only get him hurt. "Just that I'm sorry. I can't do this. I shouldn't have—I'm sorry." She turned and ran up the stairs, leaving Jack standing at the foot of the stairs.

"Did I do something wrong?" he called. She could hear the hurt and confusion in his voice.

Miriam paused halfway up the steps. She couldn't let him think this was his fault. "You didn't do anything," she said, turning around but not descending. She didn't trust herself to get near him again. "I promise, Jack, you didn't do anything. Bad, I mean. Or wrong, or whatever. You stopped Ben, and I'm thankful for that. You've been so nice to me…too nice. I just—I shouldn't do this with you. I mean, I just met you, and…." She tried to think of a better reason, but he was coming up the steps toward her, and the desire in his eyes washed away her logic.

"I know what it is," Jack said. "You're trying to protect me. You're afraid of him finding out about us, and what he'll do to me." He was two steps below her now, and she felt her will to turn away weakening. "And to you."

"I–no, I mean, yeah. A little, I guess." She wasn't making any sense. She took a deep breath, tried again. "Listen, Jack. You're right. But it's not that I don't think you can take care of yourself. I just know Ben. He's…you don't want to mess with him." She backed up a step. "You're amazing, Jack. I mean that. I don't want to see you get hurt. Not for me."

"I'm sure he's a badass," Jack said, a wry edge to his voice. "He looks like he could rip my arm off and beat me with it. I'm sure if I knew him, I'd be pissing myself. You're his girl, and he'd kill me for even looking at you. I get it, Miriam. But what if I don't care? What if I'm willing to take that risk?"

"Don't be stupid, Jack. You just met me. You don't know me." He was getting too close. He had burrowed under her walls somehow and found her vulnerable heart, saying exactly what she had always wanted to hear, and it scared the hell out of her.

"Yes, I do. You may be his girl, but you don't belong with him. You deserve better."

"And you can give me better, I suppose?" She was getting defensive now, and she felt her walls going up. Not because she didn't trust him, or believe he could and would treat her better, but because she *did*. She wanted to trust him, desperately, and that was dangerous for both of them.

"Yes! I can. And I will," he said.

Bang, the walls were up, the gates closed. She wanted him more than anything, but she knew how it would go. He'd be all nice and charming now, but if she left Ben for him, he'd change. Assuming Ben didn't kill him beforehand, of course.

"It won't work, Jack. I'm sorry. You should forget you met me." Miriam turned and ascended the steps, refusing to look back.

"Yeah, right." Jack actually laughed at that. "You can't push me away that easily, Miriam. I know what you're doing, and it won't work."

She stopped but didn't turn around. "What am I doing, then?"

"You're shutting me out because you're scared. I get it. I really do." She was walking away, and he was raising his voice, not yelling, not desperate, only insistent. "You can't scare me off, Miriam, and you can't push me away. Just give me a chance."

Miriam wanted to, more than anything. She wanted to rush back down to him, but she refused to let herself. She unlocked her door and closed it behind her, leaned against it and tried not to sob. *This is stupid*, she told herself. She'd just met him. He didn't know what he was talking about.

All men are assholes, she reminded herself. *No matter how perfect they might seem at first.*

The trouble was, Miriam didn't believe herself.

Chapter 3

Carson

The present

JOHN DOUGLAS LOOKED EVERY INCH A MARINE. PERFECT posture, muscular, confident. He sat in a plush red chair, sipping coffee. He stood when Carson approached, shook his hand in a crushing grip.

"So, what happened to Ben?" John asked.

"Well, we're still investigating that," Carson answered.

"Well, how did he die? Was he shot? Hit by a car?"

"We can't discuss details of the investigation at this time. I'm sure you understand that. All I can say is that we suspect it was a homicide." Carson delivered the standard *do-not-discuss* lines with practiced ease.

"So, what do you need from me?"

"We're trying to get a sense of the guy and have a few questions for you," Carson replied, then continued, "Did he have any enemies? Anyone who would want him dead?" Carson took out his small notebook and pen, and prepared to take notes.

"Not that I'm aware of." John glanced up and away, thinking. "I mean, he wasn't the easiest person to know. Especially after he got back from his first tour. He got fucked up over there. A lot of guys did. He handled it, but maybe not as well as he could have. Drank a lot." Douglas paused. "But did he have enemies? Like, people who hated him, wanted him dead? No, I don't think so. He got in a few bar fights here and there, but I don't think they were anything that would lead to him getting murdered. He liked to scrap. You get to miss the rush of a fight after a while, you know? Maybe you don't, I don't know."

"He liked to knock girls around, huh?"

John shifted, uncomfortable. "I don't hang out with him all that much…."

"Answer the question," Carson pressed.

"I'd heard that he would get a little nasty after he'd had a few. I know he went after me a few times, drinking off-base. But that's different, you know? I don't do that shit. I don't hit girls. Ben, he got messed up in the head pretty good, but he tried to hide it."

John leaned forward. "What does that have to do with his murder?"

Carson decided to change tack a bit. "Do you know anything about any of his girlfriends?"

"Well, Ben was…a player, I guess you could say. Always seemed to have a couple of girls around. Lately, he'd been seeing a girl named…god, what was it?…Mary? Miriam? That's it, Miriam. Beautiful girl, but a little odd, though. From the few times I met her, she wasn't any easier to get to know than Ben. Like I said, Ben and I didn't hang out all that much."

"What can you tell us about Miriam?"

"Not a whole lot. I think he knew her from the bar where he worked—the Taproom. She seemed like a really quiet, self-contained person. Closed off, maybe. I only met her a couple of times, and I couldn't get a good sense of her."

"What's that mean?" Two people who had met Miriam more than once, but neither of them could say much about her. Carson found that interesting.

"I'm a pretty good judge of people," John said. "I can usually get a feeling for what a person is like the first time I meet them. You know, whether I'd like them, whether I'd instinctively trust them, that kind of thing. Miriam was someone I just couldn't figure out. Like she didn't want to be known, almost. If that makes any sense."

Carson nodded, closed his notebook, and then stood up. "No, I get what you mean. Well, I think I've got what I need for now. If you think of anything else, give me a call." Carson handed John a card and left. Carson's instincts told him that interviewing Miriam would be the next best step to look for clues. Something about her raised his suspicions. He couldn't have explained why, but he knew he had to talk to her for more reasons than the obvious ones.

CHAPTER 4

Miriam

Three weeks earlier

IT WAS BEN AND MIRIAM'S ONE-YEAR ANNIVERSARY. BEN had reservations at Ruth's Chris Steakhouse in Troy, which was where he always took her for special occasions. But she hated it. She hated steak, she hated expensive wine, and she hated the stuffy, buttoned-up servers and the fancy atmosphere. She liked things simple, for the most part. She didn't mind expensive dinners every once in a while, but something about the place just set her on edge. She'd told Ben this, of course, but he'd brushed it off. Special occasions always equaled Ruth's Chris, no matter what. So here she was, sitting in the passenger seat of his truck, wearing a dress and wishing she was at home in her yoga pants.

She knew how the evening would go: He'd order the most expensive wine he could afford and drink at least one bottle, if not two. He'd splurge like crazy on himself, but he would never ask her what she liked. He wouldn't consult her on the wine, and he'd behave like a total dick to the wait staff. She was just supposed to go along and keep her mouth shut. And sleep with him when they got home, of course. Normally, she'd keep herself in her shell, sip on one glass of wine, and nod in all the right places.

Tonight, for reasons she couldn't have explained, Miriam decided to go a different route. When Ben poured the wine—$120 a bottle—she drank it as fast as he did. He didn't seem to notice right away. She'd finished her third glass before the entrees had arrived, and she was feeling loose and unafraid for once.

"Good to see you finally relaxing a little," Ben remarked, refilling her glass.

"Hey, a year is a long time. Something to celebrate." The words were tumbling out of her mouth without any forethought, and she was grateful for it.

Maybe if she got drunk enough, she wouldn't remember anything the next day. Ben would want to have sex, but she just couldn't make herself do it anymore. It had been okay when they first started dating. Better than Nick, at least; that, more than anything, had made Ben seem like a decent guy at first: He was better than Nick. She could even pretend that he loved her, that he cared about her...sometimes. But the longer she dated him, the more she came to realize that his drunken rages were going from an occasional explosion to a regular part of their relationship, becoming ever more frequent and ever more violent.

He used to slap her every now and then, yell at her, curse her out. Eventually he'd pass out, and that would be it. Then, one night, he got really drunk with his buddies from the Corps and showed up at her door with anger in his eyes. She'd tried her best to keep him calm, but he had memories of the war in his thoughts, and when that happened, there was no avoiding the hurt. He'd cracked her with a fist that night and nearly broken her jaw. The next time he hadn't been as drunk, but he still slugged her in the stomach for no good reason. It was always the little things that would set him off. A misunderstood question, a reply too long in coming. Eventually he didn't need a reason. Of course, he'd feel bad the next day, take her out for dinner, buy her flowers or jewelry, charm her into bed. Sober, he was the man she'd known when they first started dating.

But he wasn't sober much anymore.

She chewed her steak slowly, each bite tasting like sawdust. If she refused to eat it, or complained about it, or ordered something different, he'd fly into a rage and blame her for making him mad and making a scene. So she ate the steak. She washed it down with more red wine, becoming dizzier by the moment.

But there was another reason she was getting drunk.

Jack.

She kept seeing his face every time she closed her eyes. She felt his hands on the skin of her back, his lips on hers. Ben was across the table from her, chattering about some basketball game, but she didn't hear a word he said. Instead, she was hearing Jack tell her she deserved better. She also wondered if Jack was all he seemed to be. She found herself hoping he was, and tried to think of innocent reasons to see him again.

"Miriam!" Ben's voice cut through her reverie.

"What, Ben?" She tried to focus on him, but his face was wavering and splitting into two.

"I said, I'm sorry about the other night."

"You did?"

"I said it, like, three times. You were staring off into la-la land or something."

"Oh, sorry." She didn't want to talk about that night. "It's…just…don't let it happen again, okay?"

"I won't, I promise," Ben said. "So. How do you like your steak?" He always asked that, and she always told him she didn't like it. Tonight, she was more interested in getting home.

She forced down another bite, wishing Ben's face would come into focus. She was looking at him, but somehow it was Jack's face that would slide into view, looking at her with his wide, kind blue eyes. "He's great—I mean, *it's* great." *Oh, shit,* she thought. *He'll catch that slip.* Too much shiraz was catching up with her.

"He?" Ben asked, the suspicion apparent in his voice.

"I meant *it*. The steak. The cow. He, the cow, is what I meant." Her words were coming slurred.

Ben burst into laughter. "You're drunk!" He seemed to think this was funny. "Oh, god, you're wasted. I don't think I've ever seen you this drunk."

"Yeah, I may have had a bit too much wine." Miriam set down her fork and wobbled to her feet. "I want to go to the ladies' room. Then we can go?"

Ben chuckled again. "Yeah, sure. You gonna make it to the bathroom on your own?"

"Yeah, I'll be fine."

"You sure? I can help you, if you want." He waggled his eyebrows and winked.

She just shook her head and concentrated on taking one step at a time, wishing she'd worn flats instead of heels. She didn't have to pee; she just needed a few seconds away from Ben. Miriam touched up her makeup, more for something to do to pass the time than because she cared whether she looked good for

Ben. When she ran out of stalling tactics, she stood at the mirror and stared at her reflection, hating Ben, hating herself for being stuck with him. Wishing, more than anything, that she was with Jack.

She wasn't, though. She had to leave the bathroom; she had to go back out to Ben and try to keep him calm until she could escape home.

Taking a deep breath, Miriam returned to the table, keeping thoughts of Jack firmly out of her mind.

Ben's apartment was always too hot, and it smelled like cheap cologne and old coffee. They'd gone back to his place, of course. He hated her apartment. It was too small, he said, and he didn't like being right above where he worked. It was three miles from his place to the bar, and Miriam had walked those miles more times than she could count. She often ended up stranded at his place without a ride home.

Now they were back at his place, and both of them were tipsy; Ben was fumbling to untie his shoes, tossing his keys on the microwave, peeling his shirt off. He swayed across the room to where she sat on the couch. Miriam felt his hand on her knee, his lips on her neck. She swallowed in an attempt to fight back the sudden rush of nausea in her throat.

"I'm not feeling so good right now, Ben," she said.

He either didn't hear her, or didn't care. His hand slid farther up her thigh, under the hem of her dress, and his lips found hers. She couldn't kiss him back. All she could do was keep her eyes closed and push away the urge to vomit.

But no go.

She lurched to her feet, tripped, stumbled, and kicked her heels off as she ran to the bathroom. For several long, painful minutes, Miriam heaved into the toilet, acid burning her throat, her stomach lurching in protest. She felt Ben's hands holding her hair back, heard his voice murmuring something meant to be comforting. Finally, the nausea passed, and she felt better. *Strange how that works,* she thought. She hated throwing up, but she always felt better afterward. She rinsed her mouth and brushed her teeth with the extra toothbrush Ben kept for her.

Maybe he'd take her home now.

No such luck. He was waiting for her in his bedroom, stripped down to his boxers, sending a text.

"Come on, baby, come lie down with me," he said, setting down the phone.

"God, Ben, give it a rest. I just threw up." It would have been better to remain sick. Maybe she could vomit again.

"Don't you feel better, though? Anyway, it's our anniversary, and I switched shifts with Eric so we could be together tonight." He stood up and took her by the hand, pulling her to the bed. He kissed her chest between her breasts, unzipping her dress with one hand, the other exploring upward from her knees, his fingers clumsy and rough.

She was still drunk, and she couldn't summon the energy to resist him, so she stood unmoving, eyes closed. His fingers looped through the hem of her panties, pulling them down, and then his fingers continued their exploration upward. Her dress was on the floor now, and he was unhooking her bra and kissing her throat; her body was responding, not quite against her will. She had once wanted to love him. Well, not exactly. She had *wished* she could love him, and tonight that would have to be enough. She had to get through this somehow, after all.

She was lying down on her back, and he was kissing her breasts, playing with her nipples, moving downward, kissing her thighs and between them, and all she wanted was to push his head away, but she didn't dare. He rarely put this much effort into sex, so maybe she should try to enjoy it while it lasted.

She closed her eyes and let go, let herself pretend she liked it. Then, suddenly, Jack's face appeared in her thoughts. He was gazing at her, and she couldn't help but dream, but wonder, how he would feel pressed up against her, warm skin to warm skin, his hands tender and gentle on her body, his eyes watching her with real love. She lost herself in the dream, muzzy, still-drunk thoughts mixing reality with imagination. She felt someone push inside her and move above her. She knew it was Ben, but she just couldn't help wishing, wishing, wishing it was Jack. She had to keep herself from crying out for fear she'd say Jack's name by mistake. Her body was with Ben, but her heart was with Jack, and her mind was too confused to make sense of anything.

Again she felt her blood begin to boil, and this time it didn't build up slowly. No, this time it was abrupt and full of force. She was alight all at once, feeling a pool of power grow within her, burgeoning into a well of magma that had to be released, but she didn't know how, didn't know what it was that she was feeling. It wasn't sex; it was something else, something new. It was a fire in her blood, painful in its intensity, and it was growing hotter by the moment. She *had* to release it. She imagined an explosion in her mind, visualized a bomb going off, put all of the heat in her blood into the imagined detonation. Time stopped for a fraction of a second, and then she felt a rush of nova-hot heat run through her. She was no longer Miriam; she was fire, she was heat.

Suddenly, Ben rolled off her, cursing. "Shit, Miriam!" he shouted. "What the fuck is wrong with you?"

She felt drained now. "What's wrong, Ben? What happened?"

"You burned me!"

"What? What do you mean, I burned you?" She peered at him blearily and noticed the skin on his torso had reddened, as if he'd been sunburned, or scalded by boiling water.

"I don't know! Your skin, it was…hot, like, *burning* hot. I don't know what the hell is wrong with you, but it hurts like a bitch. You sick or something?"

"I don't know, Ben. Maybe. I'm sorry, I didn't mean to hurt you."

"Sorry isn't gonna make it hurt less, you crazy bitch." He was angry now. He hated showing pain.

"Well, I said I'm sorry. I don't know what else you want from me. I don't know what happened." She slid off the bed, wary of his rage.

"You're a goddamn freak is what happened." He lashed out and slapped her, open-palm, across her face.

Something inside her snapped, and she hit him back with a closed fist, as hard as she could. Ben stumbled backward, clutching his jaw in surprise. Rage filled his face, flushing his tanned skin darker. He stood up, his fists clenching at his sides. Miriam wanted to run, but refused. She wanted to scramble away from him, jump through the window stark naked and flee, anything but let him hit her again. But she refused to show him fear. She glared back at him, fierce, defiant. He took a half-step toward her, and she tensed, waiting for the blow. But it never came. He turned away with a growled string of curses, put on a pair of gym shorts and a tank top, grabbed his keys, and left. He'd never left before. She felt relief, but she also knew that he would keep his rage pent up, releasing it later, twice as bad.

Miriam turned to the window above his bed and watched him leave. He was looking down at his phone, texting as he walked. Almost at his parking space, he looked up and stopped, almost dropping his phone. A red Maserati sat in his designated parking spot, his truck nowhere to be seen. He sorted through his keys and seemed stunned to find not the Chevy key, but a different one.

Ben turned to look at Miriam through the window, then back again at the car, a calculating expression on his face. He pressed a button on the key fob, and the headlights flashed, accompanied by a brief horn blast. Ben trailed his fingers across the hood, stroking the lines of the car, an affectionate gesture. He rested his hand on the door handle, hesitated, and , with one more glance at Miriam, he slid down into the driver's seat and turned on the ignition. He rubbed his hands together with glee as the engine rumbled to life. The door closed, the engine roared, the tires shrieked, and Ben was gone.

Miriam scanned the parking lot, but all was still and silent. Ben's beat-up S-10 was truly gone, without explanation. With no *logical* explanation, at least. Ben had just looked at her as if thinking she had something to do with it, and Miriam found herself wondering the same thing. Twice now something odd had happened, either during or after sex. Both times something Ben wanted appeared out of the blue, and both times she felt as if she were going to catch on fire, literally and physically.

Was *she* making these things happen?

Miriam shook her head, refusing to entertain the idea. Freak coincidences. Hot flashes, maybe. A prank by one of Ben's Corps buddies? But none of his friends could afford a car like the one Ben had just driven off in, so that couldn't be it. She didn't know how it had gotten there since they'd come home from the restaurant. She honestly didn't. Magic? Magic wasn't real. There was no such thing as magic. And certainly not in any way connected to *her*. She didn't even know why the word "magic" had come to mind.

There was no such thing as magic.

It was all nonsense. Coincidence.

But, yet again, Miriam was trying to convince herself of something she didn't believe.

As she walked home, Miriam tried not to think about the strange business with the car and the cell phone. She tried not to think about Ben. Or Jack. Instead, she turned her thoughts inward, to herself.

Her memory wandered back in time, to the time before her dad had died. Her dad had been her hero, her rock, and when he was alive, it had been the only time she'd ever felt truly loved. Her mother was a difficult person, betrothed to Miriam's father when she was barely more than a girl herself. Miriam suspected that her mother had never accepted the match, or even tried to like her husband, much less love him. Khadeeja al-Mansur was a cold and distant woman who had never wanted children. She had treated Miriam like a nuisance her entire life, and then when Miriam's father died, things only got worse. Miriam had been relegated to servanthood, forced to cook and clean and stay silent, lest her mother's short temper explode.

Miriam tried to remember her father's face but found it difficult. She was only eleven when he died of a heart attack. She tried to push that memory away as well, but it was stubborn. The day he died, she had been in the bathroom, curling her hair before school. She heard her father grunt, and then she heard the thud of a body hitting the floor. Khadeeja hadn't screamed or cried. She had watched with a detached expression on her face as her husband had clutched his chest, gasping for breath, eyes wide and frightened. Miriam had been the one to dial 911, to hold her father's hand as the tears formed in his fearful, wrinkled eyes. By the time the ambulance arrived, Aziz had gone still, and Miriam was alone in the apartment. Her mother sat on the front step of their Dearborn home, smoking a Virginia Ultra Slim, conversing desultorily on the phone in Arabic with her sister.

Later, Miriam had wept alone in her room; her mother had never cried, even at the funeral. She never talked to her daughter about death, or tried to console Miriam.

Six years passed, uncomfortably and slowly. Miriam stayed at school longer and longer each day, joining clubs and teams simply as an excuse not to go home. Then, a week before her seventeenth birthday, Miriam had come home to a silent house. This was not unusual; her mother spent much of her time at her sister's house across town, or with the neighbors. This time, however, something had felt…off. Wrong. Miriam hadn't been able to put her finger on what it was, but a tension in her belly told her something had changed.

She searched the house carefully, half-expecting to find her mother's body in the bathroom. Instead she had found a stack of money on the kitchen table—two thousand dollars in twenties and fifties—along with a curled yellow Post-it note in her mother's crabbed scrawl: *You're on your own.* No signature, no "I love you." Just two thousand bucks and four words. Six months later, the house had been foreclosed on and repossessed, leaving Miriam with no home, no family, and no income.

Her father's family was still in Iraq, so there was no help from them. Her mother's sister claimed that she couldn't take in another mouth, not with four of her own children to feed. Miriam's aunt had allowed her stay with them for one night, and then the next morning she'd given her a couple hundred dollars and sent her on her way, refusing to answer the door if Miriam came by after that.

Miriam's only real friend from school, Yanira, had begged her father to let Miriam stay with them for a few weeks. Yanira's father had agreed, and Miriam had found a job waiting tables at a Leo's Coney Island. That had been the start of Miriam's independence. She saved enough money while living in Yanira's basement to buy a car, and that beat-up old Volvo had been her home until she could afford an apartment of her own.

The day she moved into her own place changed Miriam's outlook on life. Up until then she had simply been trying to survive, one day at a time. She had spent nights lying awake, wondering what she had done to make her mother abandon her, and what she could have done differently. When Miriam laid her head on the pillow that first night in her new place, she realized that she hadn't done anything wrong, and couldn't have done anything different. The pain of that knowledge didn't go away, and the hole in her heart hadn't vanished, but it was a start.

Then she met Nick, and things had changed on her again....

Glancing at the time, Miriam shook herself, refusing to think about Nick. Down that road a world of bad memories waited...memories she did not want to relive. Besides, she was almost home and could hardly wait to get into bed.

"Miriam." Jack's voice startled her so much she yelped and put a hand to her chest to still her hammering heart. Jack just laughed. "Sorry, I didn't mean to scare you." He was outside her apartment, sitting on the bottom step, waiting for her.

"What are you doing here, Jack?" She wanted her voice to sound harder than it did, and wished it sounded less relieved.

She didn't want to be so glad to see him. She didn't trust herself around Jack. His eyes delved too deeply into her, and his hands on her body had excited her in a way she'd never felt before. She wanted him, but she couldn't let herself have him. If she got too close, Ben would find out and hurt him. Or else Jack would change, as men always did. They would seem nice at first. And the nicer they were at the start, the nastier they became later. That was a truth Miriam had learned the hard way, through black eyes and broken ribs and excuses no one ever believed.

"I wanted to see you," Jack said. He made it sound so natural, and the sound of his voice, the sincerity in his kind blue eyes, pushed all her concerns away, making a lie of her fears.

Damn it, Jack. He was making it hard on her. *I don't want to see you.* The words wouldn't come out. "Well, here I am," she said. It was better than throwing herself into his arms, but not by much. She kept her eyes down. If she let him see her eyes, he'd ask what was wrong, and she'd tell him....

His fingers touched her chin, tilting her head up. Oh, lord, there they were, those bright blue eyes that seemed to see into her heart, past her defenses and into the soft core of her soul. "You're upset," he said.

"I'm fine." She didn't even believe herself as she said it.

Jack rolled his eyes. "If by 'fine' you mean upset, then yes, you're fine," he said.

How the hell could he know how she was feeling just by looking at her? She had always thought she had a pretty good poker face, but Jack saw straight through her to the real emotions she tried to keep hidden.

"I'm fine, Jack. Leave me alone." Her only defense was anger.

Jack didn't seem bothered. "You didn't even see me until I just said your name. That's not fine. And why the hell are you coming home at one-thirty in the morning, on foot? Is something wrong with your car again?"

Questions…so many questions. Each answer would lead to more questions, and then he'd get all *sensitive* on her, and she'd let him in to her kitchen to talk, and then she'd kiss him, and then she'd wake up and he'd be gone. Once they get into your pants, they're as good as gone. Or they stick around just to get *back* into your pants, and then you can't get rid of them, and once they're tired of you, they leave. And *that* was the preferable outcome.

"What does it matter to you?" She knew she sounded bitchy, but that was the only way to get Jack to leave. It would be for his own good.

"If you need a ride, you can call me. You shouldn't be walking around alone in the middle of the night."

Oh, hell. He was protective, too? "Jack, just go. We can't do this."

"Do what? Talk? I'm not even touching you. I'm just worried about you, Miriam."

"You don't have to worry about me. I've been taking care of myself my whole life."

Jack finally stood up and put his hands on her waist. He barely knew her, but he knew how to touch her, how to hold her, how to make her feel like she was his. She hated that she didn't mind him touching her. She hated that she didn't knock his possessive, gentle hands away, even though she knew she should. She despised herself for wanting to belong to him.

"Maybe you shouldn't have to take care of yourself," he said.

She tried to exert the will to move out of his embrace. She couldn't. She only managed to lean in closer. "You don't know me."

"Yes, I do." His lips were close, and his eyes were fixed on hers. His hands were at the small of her back, brushing up the hem of her shirt again and seeking the warmth of her flesh. An innocent touch, there on her back, but his hands on her skin ignited sparks in her blood, lit fires in her heart.

"You just met me," she said, trying again to break free. He held her against him, gentle and unrelenting.

"So? Maybe I did just meet you, but I *know* you. I may not know *much* about you, but I know you. I don't need to know where you went to school, or who your parents are, or why you're so sad all the time. But I *do* know you deserve love, and you're not getting it. You're getting the opposite. That Ben guy, he's an asshole, and it'll only get worse." Jack kissed her jaw, midway between her ear and her chin. Her last bit of resistance melted. "And I know you know that. You've resigned yourself to being with Ben. As if that's all you deserve. You won't even consider anything else. You're scared of being alone, and more than anything, you're scared of me."

Miriam opened her mouth to argue but couldn't. He was right, and she knew it. Damn it, he was so right. Miriam wrenched herself free, stomped up the steps, and fumbled with her keys, slipping the key into the lock and opening the door. Jack was right behind her. He grabbed her shoulders, turning her around. He wasn't violent or rough about it, and that didn't help her efforts to resist him. He was gentle and possessive and insistent, pulling her against his body. Miriam was pressed up against him, her breasts crushed against his chest and her hands on his shoulders and in his hair, his lips pressed against hers, moving on her mouth, his tongue slipping between her lips. He tasted like spearmint gum, smelled like paint and leather; his scent was familiar, comforting, and began to mean *Jack* in her mind.

His hand slid up her back, under her shirt, and her doubts were erased by the tantalizing fire of his touch. Her will to resist fluttered away on the night breeze.

She felt herself growing hot again. The back of her mind, where her thoughts never stopped, was making a connection between the fact that all Jack had to do was kiss her and she would be lit on fire. Ben had to hurt her to get that reaction.

Jack was pushing open the door and they were inside, the door kicked closed. Miriam leaned back against the kitchen counter, slipping Jack's motorcycle jacket off and running her hands over his chest. Her shirt was on the floor somehow, and his hands were unhooking the eyelets of her bra one by one, his palms caressing the line of her ribs from back to front and pressing up against her breasts, fingers brushing her stiffened nipples; their hips were pressed together, and she felt his hard length against her. Oh, god, she wanted him. She couldn't help it—she unbuckled his pants, slipped her hand against his stomach, under the elastic band of his underwear, and—

Miriam ripped herself free and put the counter between them, leaning over it with her head in her arms. She was stuck somewhere between a sob and half-crazed laughter. She heard Jack hiss in frustration and buckle his pants.

"I'm sorry, Jack," she said, not looking up. "I know it's not fair. I want you, so bad. I do. It's not that, believe me."

"Then what? What is it, then?" For the first time, a tinge of anger crept into his voice. She didn't blame him. She was yanking him around, and he had every right to be angry.

"God, it's so hard to explain."

"Try." He was staring into her, as if he could see every crack and crumbled shard of her oft-broken heart.

Miriam took a deep breath and stood up with her arms crossed over her chest. Her shirt and bra were on the other side of the counter, and she knew if she got too close to Jack, she'd be right back in his strong, tender arms. "You're everything I could want. You're sexy, kind, and you obviously like me—"

Jack laughed, a bark of disbelief. "Yeah, I obviously *like* you, Miriam. That's all this is, clearly—"

Miriam cut him off. "Let me finish, please. I want you, so bad. God…why do you think I'm over here, with the counter between us? If I get too close to you, it'll all be over. I'll have you in my bed within seconds."

Jack tried to round the corner of the counter, but Miriam skittered back to thump against the cold surface of the fridge, her hands not quite touching his chest as he stood a few inches away.

"No, please. Just listen. We can't do this, not this way. We can't be together behind Ben's back. I can't and won't do that. I've been cheated on more times than I can count, and I hate it. I won't do it to someone else. I've already been dishonest just by kissing you. By going out with you. If you want to be with me, then you'll wait, and you'll help me figure out a way to break up with Ben.

"I know you don't want to hear this, and it'll probably piss you off, but it's just the facts. If Ben catches a whiff of this, if Ben sees you with me, he'll kill you. I mean that literally. He did two tours in Afghanistan, and he just didn't come back the same. Something inside him just...didn't survive the war, even if he did come back physically intact. The drinking and hitting me, all that...he was like that before, just not so bad. It's gotten worse in the last year since he's been back. His dad knocked his mom around, and that's a learned thing, I think. If you see your dad hit your mom, you either do the same thing, or you do the complete opposite. What I'm talking about with Ben, it's hidden deep inside. You don't see it, but it's there. I've seen glimpses of it, in the worst moments. A cold kind of craziness."

Jack handed Miriam her bra and shirt, then turned around to face away from her. "I guess that makes sense," he said.

"Why did you turn around? You've already seen me," Miriam said.

"Yeah, but if I look at you now, it'll make it harder to keep my hands to myself. So put your shirt on, if this is how you want things." He wasn't angry anymore, but he was frustrated.

He turned back when Miriam gave the okay, and she could see that the evidence of his frustration still bulged against the zipper of his jeans. She forced herself to look away. She took a pair of Bud Light bottles from the fridge, opened them, and gave one to Jack. They went outside and sat on the bottom step, drinking as they talked.

"It's not how I *want* things, Jack. It's how they have to be, for right now at least. There's literally nothing I want more in the whole world than to be with you. In every way, I would love to be with you. Please believe that. I can't get you out of my head. I want you. I swear I do. But not like this, not in secret."

Jack seemed perfect in every way, and she didn't want that to change, as she knew it would the second she slept with him. All men changed after they got what they wanted. It was just life as far as Miriam knew.

The thing that scared Miriam was how inevitable it all was. As if she had no intention of *not* sleeping with Jack. She examined her thoughts with ruthless honesty: It *was* inevitable, she realized. She wanted him, and she would have him. She just hoped she wasn't setting herself up for worse hurt.

"I'm really sorry, Jack," she said.

He was quiet for a long moment. "For what?" he asked, resignation in his voice. "You're right. You're absolutely right. I've been cheated on, too, and I don't want it like this, either. I don't want to start a relationship on the wrong foot. I've done it before, and it... it sucks."

She laughed, a little nervously. A relationship? "Well, yeah, but that's not what I meant." Jack glanced at her quizzically. "I meant I'm sorry for leaving you... frustrated."

Jack laughed, shrugging, and took a long drink. "Oh, that," he said. "I'll be fine. I mean, it sucks, yeah. But I'll live. Just promise me one thing."

"I hate making promises, Jack. But I'll try." Promises made only led to promises broken.

"Until we can be together, let's not let things go that far." Jack drained the beer and set it down.

"Hey, you started it," Miriam said. "I won't promise, but I'll try." Jack put the lie to his own words by kissing her, so lightly it was almost a breath of wind against her face. "No fair," she whispered. She started to say something and then froze, listening; she was sure she heard the revving of a powerful engine and the squealing of tires not far away. It was Ben; she could feel it in her belly and in her bones. She jumped up and pushed at Jack, panic in her eyes. "Go! He's coming. I know it. He can't see you here."

"Maybe we should just confront him," Jack suggested, all but being shoved onto his bike, helmet in hand.

"No. That's not the way to do this. I'll think of something. Just go." She watched him reluctantly put on his helmet and ride away, waving once as he pulled out onto the road. She left her unfinished beer next to Jack's and went back inside the apartment, locking the door, thinking of Jack and preparing for the worst.

Ben pounded on the door, growling curses when she didn't answer. Eventually he gave up and descended the stairs, assuming Miriam must be out. He stopped and looked back up at her door, a sly smile forming on his lips. He pulled out his phone and sent a text message: *I'm coming over.* While he waited for a response, he lit a cigarette. As he smoked, he noticed a pair of beer bottles sitting on the ground near the bottom step. One of them was less than half-finished, and it had the sheen of Miriam's lip gloss coating the bottle top. The other bottle was empty, with a thin layer of foam at the bottom, the way a beer looked after it had been chugged hurriedly.

Ben stood up, flicking the butt of his Marlboro Light away with an angry snap of his fingers. "Fucking bitch," he muttered.

His phone vibrated: *Okay, sexy. Waiting for u. Hurry.* Ben smiled to himself. There was more than one fish in the sea. He got behind the wheel and roared out of the parking lot, not seeing Miriam looking out behind the blinds.

Chapter 5

Carson

Present Day

Carson stood outside the Taproom, waiting for the manager to arrive. Over the last couple of days, he had tracked down a few other people Ben had known, but all of them had basically said the same thing: Ben had been a decent enough guy, but the war had scarred him. No one could think of any compelling reason that anyone would want to kill Ben Wade. None of them knew much about Miriam, and some of them had never even heard of her.

As he stood waiting, Carson considered yet again the manner of Ben's death. He'd been set on fire, but that fire had been localized to him, and only him.

Nothing else was damaged. Not even singed. The ME had said the fire that killed Ben had been unnaturally hot and intense. The fillings in his teeth had melted. His bones had been charred to a crisp, nearly turned to ash, as if he'd cremated. The ME had said she'd never seen anything like it, and had not been able to offer any explanation. She said that even bodies recovered from the very hottest fires weren't that destroyed.

A few minutes later, the manager of the Taproom showed up, a pudgy, balding man sorting through his keys. He didn't see Carson standing there and almost bumped into him. "Oh, excuse me," he said.

"Larry Genosi?" Carson asked, flashing his badge.

"Yes, can I help you?"

"Detective Carson Hale, Detroit PD. I have a few questions for you about Miriam al-Mansur."

Larry shifted uncomfortably. "I haven't seen her in a couple of days. Honestly, I don't know where she is."

"I see. But you know her?"

"Well, yeah, of course. She works for me. Great waitress."

"Do you know where she lives?"

Larry licked his lips, flipping his key ring around. "Uh, well...she lives up there." He pointed at the apartment above the bar.

"Is she still there?"

"Well, I dunno. Like I said, I haven't seen her in a few days. It's not like her. I'm worried about her.

She always shows up for work. Always. Never missed a day in six years. Then she just vanishes without a word. Is she okay?"

"We'd like to ask her a few questions with regard to another employee of yours, Benjamin Wade."

"Oh, Ben. Yeah. I haven't heard from him in a few days, either."

"That's because he's dead, Mr. Genosi. He died under rather strange circumstances, and we'd like to talk to Miriam. Are you sure you don't know where she is?"

"Yeah, I'm sure. How'd he die? He was a rough guy, and I know he and Miriam had their issues, but Miriam ain't the sort to do nothin'."

Carson stepped closer to the bar manager. The man was hiding something. "Larry, you want to tell me the truth. Where is she?"

"I don't know, I swear!" Larry lit a cigarette and puffed on it rapidly.

"Then why are you so nervous?"

"I...listen, I paid her under the table, okay? And I rented her the apartment up there off the books."

"Why, Larry? What was she hiding from?"

"Not *what*, Detective, but *who*. She has a way of attracting the wrong guys. She started working for me *on* the books about six years ago, and then she came to work one day with a black eye and broken ribs. She made some stupid excuse, but no one believed it. I

know what a beat-up girl looks like, okay? I'm not stupid. But she claimed it was nothing, and I let it go. She
was just a girl who worked for me, you know? What
could I do?

"And then the guy showed up here late one night
after closing, and waited for her outside. She kept
finding reasons to stay in the bar, and he was getting
real angry. I was watching him through the back door,
and he was mad. Finally, I had to lock up, and asked
her if she wanted me to walk her out. She wouldn't
let me, but I could tell she was scared shitless. She
didn't come to work the next day. I visited her at her
apartment, and she wouldn't let me in. She had the
little chain locked, but I could see enough to know
that he'd beaten her up real bad. I convinced her to
come with me, and I took her to my place. My wife
helped her get cleaned up. I've had that little apartment up there for years, just used it for storage and
stuff. I emptied it out and got her a bed and stuff, and
let her stay there.

"Me and some of the guys would take turns keeping an eye on her, making sure that Nick fella didn't
come back." Larry shrugged, waved a hand. "Well, he
did come back, and Ben lit into him. I had to pull Ben
off to keep him from killing Nick. Took me and three
of the cooks to do it, too. Miriam felt she owed Ben
something, I guess, and she's been with him off and
on ever since. Only now Ben's the one knocking her

around. He wasn't the same when he came back from deployment, you know? Used to be a decent guy."

Carson was starting to get the larger picture. He felt for Miriam. As a kid, he'd watched his own mom get knocked around. He had no patience for wife-beaters. He'd become a cop to stop shit like that from happening. To stop people like his dad. Carson shook his head, refusing to think of his father. He put his notebook in his pocket. "So where do you think Miriam would go?" he asked.

Larry shook his head. "I dunno, Detective. I swear. She don't have any family around here—not that I know of. Like I said, she tends to stick around this place, not doing much but work and spending time at home. Sometimes she'd go to Ben's place, but if he's dead and she ain't there, then I dunno *where* she'd go. I hope she ain't in no trouble. She's a sweet girl. Just has shitty taste in men."

If that shitty taste in men had led to an argument, Carson could see it going too far. If Miriam had gotten fed up and finally snapped, anything could have happened.

That provided motive, but it still didn't answer the two biggest questions: What had caused the fire? And where was Miriam?

CHAPTER 6

Miriam

Two weeks earlier

MIRIAM'S PHONE BUZZED IN HER APRON. SHE TOOK THE pair of Coors to the two businessmen at table forty-five and then retreated to the kitchen to check her phone. Some vague intuition told her it was Jack, and she was right.

Are u still coming to the party tonight? I'll keep it kosher i promise. Pick u up @ 7?

Miriam had already agreed, hadn't she? She couldn't very well ditch him at the last second. See you at 7 then, she texted back. He'd keep it kosher. The part that worried her was that she didn't want him to keep it kosher; she wanted him to touch her, to kiss her.

The thing that worried her was: *Where's Ben?* He hadn't been to work, and the last time she'd seen him had been a few nights ago, when he'd left her place thinking she hadn't been home. She felt relieved and scared at the same time, secretly hoping he had taken off for good.

Right now, however, what she was feeling was confusing, even to her. She wanted, more than anything to see Jack. This would be their second date, which meant she was now technically cheating on Ben. Actually, she'd cheated on him when she'd kissed Jack. Did thinking about Jack count as cheating? If so, then she was cheating every five seconds.

Ben would freak if he knew. Like, he'd actually kill them both. There were times when his eyes went dark and evil, when the Ben who was still in Afghanistan hunting down terrorists showed up, and that Ben scared her shitless. The thought of telling Ben *that she wanted to see someone else* actually made her blood run cold. She wouldn't tell him—she *couldn't* tell him. She would find a way to break things off, and he would never have to know.

Yeah, right. Because *that* would work.

At the end of her shift Miriam cashed out, said goodbye to Larry, and went upstairs to change. What should she wear to a family party? She'd never been to one before. It wasn't a one-on-one date, so nothing too sexy, but she wanted to leave a good impression.

Eventually, she decided on an arabesque-patterned maxi-dress, not too low-cut, but still clingy in all the right places. She was finishing her makeup when Jack knocked on the door. She went out to meet him, thinking as she locked the door that a dress might be tough to manage on a motorcycle.

"You look amazing," Jack remarked. "Like, totally stunning. It's gonna make this whole keeping-my-hands-to-myself thing even harder."

Miriam ducked her head, unused to compliments. "Thanks," she said, "you look great, too." He *did* look hot in a pair of khakis and a tight black sweater that hugged his muscular torso, the sleeves pushed up just beneath his elbows, his hair tousled in its usual brown tangle. Ben never told her she looked nice. His way of complimenting her was slapping her ass or squeezing her tits. Not exactly the same thing.

Miriam was contemplating suggesting she should change when she realized his bike wasn't in the parking lot. "Where's your bike?"

"Oh, I thought an actual car might be more appropriate. I figured you might do your hair or whatever, and a bike would mess it all up, right?"

Considerate, too? He needed to stop being so amazing. He followed her down the stairs to an older but well-cared-for black Jeep Wrangler with oversized tires. He opened the door for her and lifted her up. His hand was warm and dry, and he left it in hers for a moment longer than strictly necessary. Not that she minded.

Jack's parents' house was a modest two-story Colonial not far from Jack's apartment. When they pulled up to the curb, there were already several cars lining the street, and Miriam could hear voices laughing and talking from the backyard. She was more nervous than she'd ever been, if such a thing was possible. Jack took her by the hand, twining his fingers in hers. She squeezed his hand, realizing that she was more than just nervous...she was outright terrified. This was more than a family party—she was meeting his parents. Oh, god. What had she gotten herself into? She'd been on one date with Jack, maybe two. Why was she here?

She stopped and pulled back. "Wait, Jack...I don't know about this...."

He halted with her. "What? Are you nervous or something? Don't be. It's just a party."

"I don't know. This is, like, your family. Your parents. I don't know if I'm ready for this." She wasn't even really his girlfriend. She had a "boyfriend," for god's sake.

Jack seemed to understand her trepidation. "Look, you're my friend, okay? There's more than that, sure, but that's between us. My brothers and sisters bring friends to these parties all the time. It's no big deal, okay? Just relax." Miriam nodded, a little reassured, but not completely.

Jack pushed open the front door and led her in. Inside was a madhouse. There were, as Jack had promised, dozens of people, all of them with drinks in their hands, milling and chatting. Not letting go of Miriam's hand, he led her through the crowd, most of whom greeted him with a hug and a slap on the back.

She leaned in close to his ear, asking, "Who are all these people? Is this *all* your family?"

"Most of them are family—cousins, uncles, and aunts—and some friends as well. We're a big family. This isn't even half of us. You should see this place during the holidays!" Miriam tried to imagine double the amount of people, and she just couldn't. Holidays, when she was growing up, were quiet affairs, to say the least. Jack led her outside to the backyard, going straight through the house, past the kitchen and living room, both of which were packed as well. He sat her down on a rocking swing on the back porch and disappeared. Miriam was rigid, hands folded on her lap, back straight, breath coming in short, shallow, scared heaves. Everyone seemed to know everyone else, and there seemed to be many conversations going on between people—some from across the yard. Everyone was drinking, but no one seemed to be drunk, just loose and genial. An elderly man tottered up to Miriam and sat down next to her, sipping whiskey and Coke from a red plastic cup.

"Hello there, girlie," he said in a thick Irish accent. "I saw Jackie sit you down here, and thought ya might need some company, hey? I'm Séan, Jackie's grandfather. He treatin' you well, then, my boy Jackie?"

"Hi, yeah, I'm a friend of Jack's. I'm Miriam."

"Miriam, you say? Why, ain't that a pretty name, then." Séan leaned in close and peered at Miriam with bright blue eyes set deep in a tanned, wrinkled face. He seemed to be searching Miriam's face for something, exactly as Jack had done before, not looking at her so much as looking *into* her. He nodded.

"Aye, you'll do, then," he said, cryptically.

"I'll...do?" Miriam had no idea what to make of his words.

"Oh, aye. You'll do." Séan tapped the side of his nose; a gesture Miriam didn't quite know how to interpret. "You're Jackie's *friend*, you say, but old Séan, I know better. No need to hide the truth from me, no, ma'am. He's a good boy, my Jack. He'll take good care of you. Just promise me one thing, will you?"

"I'll...I'll try, I guess."

"He loves quick and hard, that boy. The other one, the mean one you've been seeing? He's trouble, he is. Best make your move quick, or you won't make it a'tall." Séan nodded sagely, sipped his drink, patting Miriam on the knee. Miriam's head was spinning. He seemed to know exactly what was going on. Had Jack talked to him?

Jack returned with two bottles of Corona, wedges of lime stuffed into the tops, as well as a bag of tortilla chips and a bowl of salsa. "Ah, you met Gramps, I see. You aren't scaring her, are you, Gramps?" Séan moved over and Jack sat between them, handing Miriam one of the bottles.

"Oh, no. We just chatted a wee bit. Didn't tell her none of your secrets."

"I don't have any secrets, Gramps. Don't be weird."

"Everyone's got secrets, boy-o." Séan glanced sideways at Miriam as he said this, winking at her. "Yours are just more boring than most."

Jack laughed, crunching a chip. "Oh, yeah? So what's an interesting secret, then?"

Séan pulled a cigar from his shirt pocket, clipped it and lit it, puffed on it. At length he answered. "I'll tell you a secret, Jackie. One of my very own. Just 'cause you're my favorite grandson, and this here Miriam of yours seems a right corker." Miriam didn't know what a corker was, or whether it was good thing or not, but she didn't interrupt.

"This goes back, oh, to when I was sixteen or so. Before the war, this was. Me and my two best mates were off to the river, fishin' on a Sunday mornin'. Mass was over, and we had nothin' to do but laze about all the day, and that's what we did. Well, on about noon come these two girls, strollin' down the road pretty as you please. They sees us, me and my mates, and they come over to us and they ask us what we're doin'. Well, we thought it were fairly obvious what we was doin', so I says, 'We're fishin' ain't we?' and the prettier of the two, 'cause you know whenever there's two girls as friends, there's always one who's the prettier, I dunno why, but there it is. Anyway, the prettier of the two lasses says to me, she says, 'Well, I've got a dare for one of you, if you're brave enough.'

"This was a serious thing, you know. You don't never back down from a dare, most especially at sixteen you don't. So I puffed up me chest and said, 'I'll take your dare,' and threw my pole to my mate Bill. The girl takes me by the hand and starts pullin' me back up the road, away from my mates and her friend and the fish, and I says, 'What's the dare, then? Where're we goin'?', and the girl, she don't answer, just yanks me into a run. I can't back down, can I? So I run with her, and she takes me right over the hill and down the other side and around a corner so we're alone as can be, and she comes to a stop behind a bush, and she says, 'Are you sure you want to take the dare? No backin' out if you promise now.'

"And I tell her of course I'll do it, even though I got no idea what the silly girl has in mind. So she pushes me down to the ground and starts tuggin' at me pants, and I'm wonderin' if the girl has gone and lost her silly damn mind. I say so, too, I ask her, 'What the bloody hell are you doin', girl?' And she just says, 'Well, I took a dare from Emily that I wouldn't get married still a virgin, didn't I? And I'm gettin' married tomorrow, so I can't stay a virgin.' And with that, the girl, whose name I didn't know, who I'd never met, why, this girl pulls up her dress and shows me her bubbies, and away we go. And it were my first time, that was, right there in the grass behind a bush, with a girl I ain't never met in my life. And you know what? I still don't know her name, to this very day. I saw her next day, ridin' in a wagon with a strapping young lad, and she were dressed all in white with flowers and the whole bit, just married. She passed right by me on that wagon, sittin' next to her brand-new husband, and she smiles at me, nods, as if we had only spoken in the pub or somethin'. Damnedest thing ever, that was."

Jack was coughing, having aspirated his beer. "Gramps! You can't go around tellin' stories like that!"

"Why ever not, Jackie? It's all true, every word, and don't no one know that that's livin. 'Specially not your grandmother, and I'll thank you not to repeat it. She'd skin me alive if she knew, though it happened 'fore I ever met her."

"Gramps," Jack said, "that never happened, did it?"

"Why, of course it did! Would I lie about that?" Séan grinned, and Miriam saw a glint of roguish humor in his eyes.

"Gramps, you tell the biggest fish stories of anyone I know."

"This ain't a fish story. You need more details, to prove it? The girl, she had red hair, all braided up, and she wore a blue gingham dress, with black shoes. And she had a big old freckle, right near her nose, and another one on her ribs, just below her great, big—"

"Gramps! Okay. I believe you."

"She did have the biggest, roundest bubbies I ever saw, though," Séan muttered into his cup. Miriam actually laughed out loud at that. Jack just shook his head and finished his beer, then stood up to get another.

When he was gone, Miriam asked, "Was that story really true, Séan?"

Séan nodded. "Oh, aye, mostly. I did know her, though. Kate O'Hara, her name was. And we'd been flirtin' all summer. I'd been tryin' to get up the nerve just to kiss her for weeks. But I really was fishin' with my mates on a Sunday after mornin' mass, and she came up and took my pole from me and dragged me off and we really did…you know…without so much as her sayin' nary a word. I guess she got tired of me hemmin' and hawin' about it. It was a dare, that's true enough, and she did get married the next day, as I said."

Miriam heard Jack just inside the kitchen, and it sounded as if he was angry about something, his voice raised. Jack threw the screen door open and stormed out, followed by a younger man who looked enough like Jack that she assumed it was his brother. He was an inch or two shorter than Jack, but wider and more muscular, wearing a white tank top and black jeans, his massive arms covered in tattoos. "I said I don't want to talk about it," Jack was saying. "There's nothing to discuss, okay? Just let it go, Jimmy."

"You've never let me explain, though," Jimmy yelled. "She came on to me! She was throwin' herself at me—what was I supposed to do?" They were now out in the middle of the yard, standing face to face. Jack pushed Jimmy, hard.

"You were supposed to say NO! You were NOT supposed to sleep with my *fiancée!*" Jack was furious, the veins in his neck standing out, the muscles in his arms corded and bulging, fists clenched.

Jimmy shoved Jack back, shouting, "Well, I did, didn't I? She was a slut! She was sleepin' around on you behind your back the whole time you were with her. You were just too damn stupid to see it. She slept with your friend Brian, too. Did you know that? And I slept with her again, after you broke up. The day you dumped her, she came back here, and I fucked her in my car."

Jimmy was poking Jack in the chest, spitting his words, goading Jack, who half-turned away, rubbing his forehead. Then he whirled around and hit Jimmy in the jaw. He struck so fast Miriam wasn't even sure what had happened until Jimmy stumbled backward, staring at Jack with anger in his eyes. Getting to his feet, he then bull-rushed Jack, swinging both fists. Jack took one to the gut, but the other missed, and then Jack was dancing away, Jimmy following, head down between his shoulders, fists low, bouncing on his heels. Miriam stood up to stop it, but Séan pulled her back to the swing.

"Nah, let 'em go, lass. They're Irish boys—that's how they solve things. And those two have had this comin' for a while now. Best for them to get it out rather than stay angry."

"So no one's going stop it?" Miriam was horrified.

Séan shook his head, waving a hand at the fighting brothers. A crowd had formed around them, cheering them on. "It ain't a family party without a scrap, is it? Oh, I know you're worried for your boy. You can relax, girlie. Jackie can take care of himself. I know Jimmy is a rough-lookin' sort, and he is, right enough. He fights in those, what do you call it, cage matches. Disgraceful, if you ask me, fightin' for money like that, tearin' apart people you don't know, just for show. But Jackie, now, he's a canny scrapper, he is. Don't look it, but he is. Jimmy loves the fight. He's got the warrior in him. Jack ain't that way—he only fights if he has to, and he fights to get it over with.

"Watch him now. See how he don't let Jimmy in close? He's seen Jim fight, he knows he can't go in close. Jimmy will tear him like paper if he lets him get his arms on him, but Jackie's got the longer reach, so he stays back, fights smart. THERE! Get him! Use your LEFT, Jackie!" Séan was standing up and shouting now, and Miriam looked from Séan to the crowd, and back, not quite understanding. Jack was bleeding from his mouth and nose, but he didn't seem much slowed, and Jim was shaking his head like a confused bear, not bouncing on his toes as much as he had been at first. Jimmy charged again, and this time Jack swiveled out of the way and hit him on the cheekbone with a hard right, and Jimmy went down. Jack slumped back against the fence, and Miriam rushed over to him, a napkin in her hand, dabbing at his face. Jack stripped off his shirt, pressing a palm to his ribs. Miriam couldn't help admiring his physique, shining with sweat and still heaving from exertion.

"What the hell was that, Jack?" she demanded.

Jack shook his head, too winded to speak. He leaned over and held a hand out for Jim, who took it and let Jack pull him upright. The brothers exchanged a glance, and Miriam could tell it was fraught with unspoken meaning, though she couldn't tell what it meant. Jimmy nodded, dabbing at his lips with his wrist, and then he went in the house.

When he had caught his breath, Jack said, "That's just my asshole brother being an asshole. It's an old story that's not worth telling. It happened a long time ago, and now it's over."

"But you had to fight him over it?" Miriam asked.

"Well, yeah. He'd have hit me, so I had to hit him first." Jack said this as if it were obvious, like two plus two equals four. Miriam pressed the napkin to his nose, standing closer to him than she should if they were supposed to be just friends.

"Are you okay?"

Jack nodded, straightening. He hissed, though, and put his palm back to his ribs. "I think he bruised one of my ribs, but I'll be fine." Miriam watched him trying to ignore the pain, and she felt the coil of power in her belly unfurl, a feeling that was becoming familiar. The energy rushed through her body to her palm, and she pressed her hand against Jack's side. She felt the heat buzz from her hand to his ribs, felt the break under her palm knit back together, the bruise fading and vanishing. His nose stopped bleeding, and his split lip healed. Jack looked from Miriam to his side, pressed a finger to his nose and lip, and looked back to Miriam. His eyes held a thousand questions, and Miriam didn't have answers for any of them.

"I don't know," she whispered to him, although he hadn't said a word.

Walking back into the house, Jack finally asked a question, although it wasn't the one she had been expecting: "Did Gramps say anything…odd to you? Anything that…didn't make any sense at all, but yet made perfect sense?"

"Actually, he did. He came over and sat down next to me, and said I didn't have to hide the truth. He told me you love quick and hard, and that the mean one—which is Ben, obviously—was trouble, and that I should make my move soon or I wouldn't be able to." She turned and caught Jack's arm, searching his eyes. "You didn't say anything to him?"

Jack sighed and rubbed the back of his neck. "Of course not. Gramps…sometimes he just knows stuff. He calls it 'the second sight,' and don't ask me what that means. Some old Irish legend, I think. But he really does know things that he shouldn't be able to know. He had the look on his face that he gets when he's had the second sight. However he knew it, what he said was right. You need to do something soon, or it'll just get worse."

Miriam knew it, too, but she wasn't sure what she could do. Thinking about it only made her realize even more how completely trapped she was, and how much she was risking just by being at this party with Jack. He must have picked up on her thoughts, because he introduced her briefly to his parents and the rest of his family, and then took her home.

He was as good as his word, dropping her off at her apartment and giving her an awkward goodbye hug, brushing the side of her face with his hand. "Be careful, Miriam," he said.

Miriam gave him a long, sad look. "You, too."

CHAPTER 7

Carson

The present

CARSON WAS FLOUNDERING. AFTER TWO WEEKS, THERE was just no evidence to go on. No witnesses, no weapon, no clear motive, and no sign of Miriam. A girl getting knocked around didn't mean she'd resort to murder. Maybe it *should*, but that was a different story. Carson blew out a long breath, stretching his back, sore from sitting at his desk too long.

He closed the file, shut down his computer, and left the precinct, intending to go home. His thoughts wandered over the case as he drove, and he found himself pulling into the parking lot of his favorite watering hole, the Old Shillelagh. He hesitated in the car, knowing he should just go home. But he was here, and he might as well have a drink. Just one or two, to loosen up his thoughts. He sat down at the bar, scrolling through his email on his phone, and ordered a gin and tonic without looking up. The bartender mixed it, set it in front of Carson, but didn't leave.

"Thanks," he muttered. He wasn't in the mood for a chatty bartender. He wanted to be left alone to drink and think.

"No problem." The bartender's voice was smooth and feminine and sultry; something about her voice piqued Carson's curiosity. He glanced up into a pair of smoky black eyes, friendly and expressive.

"You must be new here," Carson remarked. He'd remember a bartender as beautiful as this one.

"Yeah, just started yesterday, actually," she said. "I just moved here from Chicago."

"Chicago, huh? I've got friends on the force down there. What prompted the move?"

The bartender glanced away, hesitating before answering, just a beat of silence, but enough for Carson to notice. There was a long story hidden in that brief pause. "I needed a fresh start, I guess. I grew up in Chicago and just...needed a change. I have a cousin up here, and she's letting me live with her for a while." She chewed on a nail, took a ticket from the printer, and mixed the order for the service bar. "You're a cop?"

Carson nodded, set his badge on the counter. "Yep. Homicide." He offered his hand, and she shook it gently. Her hand was trembling slightly, he noticed, and she seemed uncomfortable somehow. "I'm Carson, by the way."

"Leila. Nice to meet you." She turned away, another service ticket in her hands.

Carson watched her mix the drinks, wondering what her story was. You don't just up and leave the city you grew up in for no reason. There was a depth to her eyes when she looked at him, a tiredness, the heaviness of old memories buried beneath the skin. Carson recognized that look: He saw it every time he looked in the mirror.

He finished his gin and tonic, ordered another, and found himself bantering inanities with Leila, light, meaningless bar talk. The rest of his mind, the critical part, was running through the case, a constant process for him. The detective in him never quit; he was always turning the case over in his head, seeking cracks in the smooth façade of the wall between himself and the truth. He'd pick away at the wall, circle it, examine it endlessly, over and over again, until the surface of it was as familiar as the wrinkles in his palm, until he could recite every piece of information by memory. It was then, when the facts were automatic, that he began to make progress and catch the irregularities, the inconsistencies, and the slight breaks in the mortar.

A third gin and tonic, and Carson's thoughts wandered to his own childhood, to a small ranch-style house in Farmington Hills, the yard uncut and scraggly with crabgrass and rioting dandelions, a cracked sidewalk out front where Carson had spent most of his time as a boy. Outside was a refuge, away from the constant tension in the house, away from the raised voices, from his cursing, quick-fisted father and his shrill, nagging mother. She never defended herself, and that's what had always bothered Carson. She didn't just take it; she seemed to invite it, to bring it on herself somehow.

This brought him back around to Miriam. Carson wondered what kind of victim she was. Did she suffer in silence, applying foundation to cover bruises and offering lame excuses? Or did she strike back and curse and scream and invite it on herself because she knew it was coming? Had she pent up years of pain into a ball of rage and then finally snapped? He had no sense of her, and that blinded him to the reality of the case. She was an enigma, this Miriam. No family, no known friends or relatives, very few people who'd even heard of her. Almost a nonentity, it seemed. The only picture he had was a driver's license from when she was sixteen.

Carson stumbled from the bar after more gin and tonics than he could remember. The bartender with the black eyes…Leila, that was her name…she had called him a cab. He rode to his apartment a few blocks away, dizzy memories of his father's belt and fists coalescing with thoughts of a Miriam cloaked in shadow. And then there was Leila's face, with her deep, dark eyes that seemed to whisper familiar secrets to him.

The next day, nursing a considerable hangover, Carson reviewed Miriam's files, then checked out a police-issued sedan. He was going to Dearborn, Michigan. Based on state records, he knew that Miriam al-Mansur had been born at St. Joseph Mercy Medical Hospital in Ann Arbor in 1983. Parents were Aziz and Khadeeja al-Mansur, Iraqi immigrants who moved to Dearborn in 1982. Her father died in 1994, cardiac arrest. Dearborn home repossessed in 1999. No records after that of any kind, just a blank. Only known relative was Fatima Afridi, still living in Dearborn.

Hence the trip to Dearborn.

Fatima was a short, stout woman with alert brown eyes that regarded Carson from within her black hijab. After seeing his I.D., she invited Carson inside. She was polite, but she refused to shake Carson's hand.

"What is this about, please, Detective?" Fatima's voice matched her eyes: sharp and clear.

"I'm looking for information on Miriam al-Mansur. She's your niece, correct?" Carson sat on the edge of the tan microfiber couch, a yellow legal pad balanced on one knee.

"Yes, she is my niece. But I haven't seen her in many years. At least ten years, I think. Is she in trouble? It wouldn't surprise me if she was—she became very western once she was on her own. She doesn't wear the hijab, and she associates with men."

"At this time we're trying to locate her, and we're pursuing all possible avenues, Mrs. Afridi." Carson scrawled something on his pad. "Miriam's father passed away in…1994. Is that correct?"

"That sounds about right. It was an awful time for my sister. She was devastated. More than anyone knew, I think. Such a kind man, Aziz. Too kind. He doted on his daughter, gave her everything. Never disciplined her. Didn't hold her to the faith. I always said no good would come of that girl."

"What happened after Mr. al-Mansur passed away? Their house was repossessed, wasn't it?"

Fatima shifted uncomfortably, plucking at the edge of her hijab. "Yes, it was. Very sad. My sister couldn't control her daughter. Miriam was too wild, out of control. Staying out all hours, worrying her poor mother. They had a falling out. After Aziz died,

Khadeeja…she met a man, a good man. He would take care of her, she said. Aziz spent all his time in his store, ignored his poor lonely wife."

Carson heard something hidden in the story Fatima was telling. "So, she remarried, then? Can we speak to her?"

Fatima wouldn't look at him, obviously not wanting to answer. "I—no, I don't actually know where they are. She calls me sometimes, but I don't know where she lives."

"Then where is Miriam? You're her aunt—wouldn't she come to you if she was in trouble?" Carson let a little edge slip into his voice.

"Well, as I said, she was a very headstrong girl. I couldn't do anything for her. Her mother, Khadeeja, left so suddenly, and I have children of my own, four mouths to feed and…another would have been too much. I just couldn't. I gave her what I could, truly, but…."

"Wait, go back, Mrs. Afridi. Your sister left? What do you mean, she *left?*"

"Oh, well…I mean—" Fatima chewed her lip, hesitating, and then the words tumbled out in a rush. "I had no idea she was planning to leave, you know. She didn't tell me her plans—she just vanished with that Peter character, and Miriam showed up so upset, poor girl, but I just couldn't take her in, my husband barely brings in enough for the six of us. I wanted to help her, but all I could do was give her some money."

"So your sister vanished, but didn't take Miriam with her? When was this?" Carson was frowning as he scribbled notes.

"Miriam was…sixteen? Seventeen? So maybe… nineteen-ninety-nine? Yes, that sounds about right."

"And you haven't seen or spoken to Miriam since?"

"Well, I've wanted to send her a card or something, but I wouldn't know where to begin looking—"

"I see." Carson freighted those two words with disapproval. "Well, I think you've given us some valuable information, Mrs. Afridi. Thank you for your time. I'll be in touch if I have any further questions."

CHAPTER 8

Miriam

One week earlier

JACK SHOWED UP AT HER DOOR A LITTLE BEFORE NOON ON a Saturday a week after the party.

Miriam had just woken up, having closed the night before, so she was wearing nothing but an extra-large Red Wings T-shirt and panties.

"Do you work tonight?" he asked, looking her up and down with an admiring grin.

"Jack! What—what are you doing here?" She pulled the edge of the shirt down, but no matter how she tugged it, the shirt still barely covered her thighs.

He held up two tickets. "I've got a pair of tickets to tonight's Tigers game. Thought maybe you'd like to go with me."

"Tigers?"

"Yeah, like, baseball?"

Miriam slapped his arm. "I know who the Tigers are."

"Have you ever been to a game? It's a lot of fun."

"I haven't, actually, and I'm off today. When is it?"

"The game starts at four. I thought we could grab some lunch in Greektown before the game." Jack came in and hopped up on the kitchen counter, peeling his jacket off and setting it beside him. Miriam fought the urge to run her hands over his chest, his toned physique visible through his thin, black, skin-tight Led Zeppelin shirt.

"That sounds fun. You'll have to wait while I get ready, though."

"Okay." He hopped down and plopped himself on her couch, grabbing the remote for her little TV.

Miriam showered quickly, trying not to think about Jack sitting just a few feet away, trying not to hope that he'd let himself into the bathroom. He didn't, and she moved quickly from the bathroom to the bedroom, a towel wrapped loosely around her torso. She felt Jack's eyes on her for the split second she was visible in between the two rooms, and wondered if he'd been waiting for that one glimpse.

While Jack watched TV, Miriam got ready, choosing her outfit carefully and taking time with her makeup. She hadn't seen or heard from Ben for almost a week, which was worrying her, making her nervous. She'd tried to keep herself busy with work, and she'd made up her mind to enjoy this day off. She'd texted with Jack a few times, but she hadn't seen him since the party.

Pretending she didn't miss him was exhausting.

Jack had his Jeep again, and this time he had removed the canvas top. With the radio blaring, they pulled out of the parking lot and headed to Comerica Park. They didn't talk much on the drive over, and Miriam didn't mind the silence between them. In fact, she found it comforting and refreshing to be with someone and not *have* to talk. With the wind blowing between them, tangling her hair, Miriam was as close to being happy as she'd ever felt. Jack's hand rested on the gearshift, flecks of paint on the backs of his knuckles, grease permanently caked into the creases, a couple of knuckles still split from his fight with his brother. Miriam slipped her hand in his, and twined their fingers together, feeling the electric brush of excitement thrill through her, even at so innocent a touch.

He took her to the New Parthenon, where they had saganaki and gyros, and shared a pitcher of beer.

"Do you drink much, Jack?" The question just popped out. Miriam hadn't even been aware she was thinking it, but once it was out, she was glad she'd asked.

Jack seemed unsurprised. "No, not really. When I'm out with friends, I'll have a few beers, or maybe with Doyle after work sometimes." He leaned forward and took her hands in his. "Listen, Miriam. I want you to understand how much I'm *not* him. Okay? If you want to ask me something, just ask. I won't be offended."

"It's not like I'm comparing the two of you—"

"You should, Miriam." He rubbed her knuckles with his thumbs. "Seriously. Compare me to him. I don't want to be anything like him. At *all*. If there's *ever* even the slightest similarity between me and him, you should drop me like a bad habit, okay?" He was exuding intensity, his eyes fixed on her.

"You're nothing like him, Jack. I've never met anyone like you. You're so different from him, from anyone I've ever dated…. It's kind of scary, honestly, how different you are."

"Scary? What do you mean?" Jack asked.

"I don't know…it's—I'm used to one kind of thing, you know?" Miriam said. "All the guys I've dated have been similar—"

"Assholes?" Jack interjected around a swig of beer.

"Yeah, I guess so. I don't know why, but I just seem to attract the assholes."

"Well, I'm not an asshole, and you attracted me," Jack said with a smirk. "But seriously, though, I don't think it's a matter of you attracting them so much as you choosing them. You don't think you're worth a real man, a good man."

Miriam felt kind of insulted by that. "What the hell is that supposed to mean?"

Jack raised his hands, palms out, in a pacifying gesture. "No, listen to me. I have this cousin, Bridget. Her dad, my uncle, he's an alcoholic. He used to beat Bridget and her mom. Called her all sortsa names, kicked her out of the house when she was eighteen.

"She always ended up dating these guys that were just…god, *assholes*—" He said the word like it was the ultimate epithet, the worst thing he could think of calling them. "I mean, real douchebags. They treated her like I wouldn't treat a dog. Hit her, called her names, just like Uncle Danny had. One even pimped her out to his friend, and she just went along with it, god knows why.

"She stayed with these guys no matter how badly they treated her, and no one could talk her out of it, even *after* Uncle Danny left. I think she just didn't understand that there was any other kind of guy, that she had any other options. It's what she'd grown up with, you know? All she knew. And if that's all you know, you stick with it. If your dad didn't love you, if he didn't treat you right, then you keep trying to fill that hole where his love should've been. You fill it with men who are like him, and that will never work.

I don't know about your dad, if he was like that or not."

Jack touched her chin with a finger, tipping her head up to look at him, but she wrenched her face away and withdrew her hands, staring down at the table. She couldn't look at him, not with the welter of emotions boiling inside her. She scraped the table-top with a fingernail, and where her nail dragged across the surface, a hissing noise and a thin trickle of smoke followed. A line of scorched black was incised in the table. Jack noticed it, lifted an eyebrow, but said nothing.

There was silence between them, and an unusual tension. "It's not like that, Jack," Miriam said, trying not to sound sullen and angry. She knew her anger was surfacing because he *was* right.

"Well, there *is* a reason you make the choices you do, Miriam. You know there is—you just won't admit it. I'm telling you the truth as I see it, and I'm not gonna apologize for it, although I will say I'm sorry if I hurt you."

Miriam didn't know how to respond, so she simply nodded. Jack brushed her hair aside, lowering his face so that he could meet her gaze. He looked so worried that she had to laugh. Damn him and his puppy-dog eyes. "It really wasn't like that, exactly," she said eventually. "My dad did love me, just not...

not for long enough. I don't want to talk about that right now, though. I want to have fun."

"Fair enough." Jack poured the last of the pitcher into their glasses, letting the subject go. He really did seem to respect her privacy, and that was hard to resist in itself. She wished he didn't seem to understand her so well. It made her feel vulnerable, and that made her walls come up. She didn't want walls between her and Jack, but they were there, ingrained from habit, maintained out of the need to protect herself at all costs. Yet...he always seemed to find a way of getting around them.

Miriam enjoyed the baseball game, even though she hadn't expected to. She had only agreed to go because it meant being able to get out of the house and spending time with Jack, not so much caring about the game itself. The fans were energetic and excited, and their ebullience was infectious. She didn't really know the finer details of the game, but it didn't matter; that wasn't as important as the experience itself: swilling overpriced beer from clear plastic cups, eating buttery popcorn, standing to cheer whenever the fans got to their feet.

There was camaraderie in the atmosphere, a kinship shared by everyone in the stadium, and that was a new feeling for Miriam. She clutched Jack's arm, watching him get excited as the game progressed.

He held her hand, sat with his arm around her shoulders, showed her affection, for which she was starved. She felt something burgeoning inside her, a sense of contentment, strong and warm and all-enveloping, threatening to overwhelm her, filling her heart to bursting.

Her instinct, when faced with such strong, positive feelings, was to shut down, to run away: Such things never lasted. Jack would turn on her. There would be a moment of frustration, and he would scream at her, or raise his hand, maybe not actually hitting her, but the threat would be there. She fought the urge to create a situation where it would happen, just to get it out of the way. Once he turned, she could go back to her life as it was—painful and difficult, but familiar. She knew what to expect and how to deal with it. But Jack never responded the way she expected, never treated her in a way she understood. It scared her. The unfamiliar was scary to her, not knowing where things stood or where they were going. *That* was terrifying.

Jack must have sensed her introspective mood, for he sat down despite the standing, cheering crowd around him. "What's up, buttercup?" His tone was light, but his eyes conveyed a serious concern.

"Nothing."

He smirked and rolled his eyes. She should have known better than to think he'd buy that.

He leaned close, his arm around her shoulders. "If you don't want to talk about it, then say so. If you want to go, we can go. But don't feed me the 'it's nothing' B.S. when I can clearly see it's not nothing."

She searched his face for signs of frustration or irritation. The crowd around them was going crazy, but Jack seemed to have forgotten the game entirely. "You'll laugh. You'll tell me I'm being ridiculous."

"You probably are being ridiculous, but that's no reason to discount how you're feeling." He finished his beer, tugging her hand to lead her up the steps and out to the concourse. The roar of the crowd was still loud, but distant. Groups of people came and went through the concourse, buying snacks and beer, balancing cups and bags, laughing and talking, all of them oblivious to Miriam and Jack. She watched the people come and go, trying to sort out what she was feeling and how to communicate it.

"I'm not used to having a good time, I guess. I mean, I've had fun. It's not like I live every day moping around and hating my life. And it's not like Ben is always horrible all the time, either. He *can* be charming—it's just getting less and less frequent these days. He's changing. The good times used to outweigh the bad, which is why I've stayed with him for so long. But recently he's been drinking more, and that always leads to things getting bad." She looked down. "Listen to me, dragging on about Ben. I'm sure this is the last thing you want to hear about. I'm sorry."

Jack shook his head, squeezed her hand. "No, please, keep going. This is important to you. It's part of you. Do I like hearing about Ben? No, of course not. I wish I could just…snap my fingers and make him go away, so I can have you all to myself. But listen, you have to make your own decisions for yourself. I'm not just assuming you'll dump Ben and be with me. Obviously, I'm hoping you will, but even that is complicated. I want you to leave him for *you*, not just because I want to be with you."

Well, there was transparency for you. Miriam pinched the bridge of her nose, feeling the hooks of affection and desire dig deeper into her heart. "I don't know what to do, Jack. I honestly don't. You're so…I don't know…so much more than I know how to deal with. I never know what to expect with you. You never act like any guy I've ever known, and it's confusing."

"Well, I'll take that as a compliment, then. But I'm not trying to confuse you, I promise."

"I know. And it is a compliment. I've been thinking about it this week, and I realize I can't just break up with Ben right now. It's very complex. He won't let it go. I'm honestly afraid of what he'll do when I tell him. I've said all this before. I *want* to be with you, please know that. But I can't just wave a magic wand

and make it all easy and simple." Miriam watched Jack process this, thinking about it before responding.

"Okay, listen. Lemme put it this way. I'm here for you. No matter what. I want you to be happy. If you decide to stay with Ben"—this was hard for him to say, clear in the way he spat the words out as if they tasted bitter—"then I'll respect that. But if you need time to figure things out, I'll wait. I want as much time with you as I can get, in any way I can get it. And if you decide to leave him, I promise I'll protect you, no matter what."

This worked the hooks even deeper, pulling her to him, into his arms. "You'll protect me?" His hands went around her waist, resting with familiar affection on the swell of her hips.

"Yes, Miriam, I will protect you. You don't have to be afraid of him." This brought a hard knot of emotion into her throat and set her eyes to burning. Tears welled up, stinging salt running down her cheeks, all brought on by a simple statement, said as if it were obvious, like she should have known he would protect her. Like it was the most obvious thing in the world, and not a foreign concept.

Jack pulled her close to him, standing with his legs spread wide and his arms wrapped tight around her, her body pressed against him. She wanted to believe him. She really did. It would be so wonderful to just pretend that Jack could protect her from Ben if she were to do the unthinkable and break up with him. She laid her head against Jack's chest, imagining the scene: telling Ben, *I don't want to be with you anymore. Please leave me alone.* Oh, god, just the thought of it was frightening. He would be confused at first, then disbelieving, thinking she was joking. Then when he realized she was serious, he'd get angry. So angry. So violent. And Jack wouldn't be there, would he? He couldn't stand next to her as she broke up with Ben. How could he protect her then? But something told her he would find a way.

She looked up at Jack, her chin on his chest, her arms on the back of his shoulders. He smiled at her, a reassuring, tender smile that broke down her walls, one brick at a time. She was supposed to be slowing things down between them, but she couldn't quite figure out how to do that. And she found she didn't want to.

He leaned down and brushed his lips against hers, a hesitant, questioning touch, asking permission. The feather-light tingle of his lips against hers sent butter-flies trembling down her spine to flutter in her stomach, fanning the flames buried within her, bringing them to life.

She lifted up on her toes to deepen the kiss, putting her hands in his hair at the back of his head. This seemed to impassion him, turn him wild with desire. He slid his hand down to cup her backside and lifted her up, easily and effortlessly. She wrapped her legs around his hips, felt a rush of magic torch through her, trickling along her skin and setting the fine hairs to stand on end, filling her with a pressure needing release; the blaze of power expanded and burned hotter with every second that he kissed her, holding her aloft against him. She clutched him with her thighs, feeling eyes on them but not caring.

She was on the verge of detonation, the welling pool of energy demanding to be vented; she pulled her lips from him and breathed out, letting the power slip from her with an exhaled breath. Through half-open eyes she saw a stream of glowing golden particles flow from her mouth and spread out into a cloud, roiling and billowing in the air around them, floating, expanding, gathering force . People walked straight through it, not sensing anything. The cloud hovered in place for a moment, then burst apart and scattered throughout the stadium, darting here and there as if sentient.

Where the fragments of magic touched down, odd things happened: Cups of beer split apart to spill over their owners, cigarettes illicitly smoked flared into sudden torches, pop machines sent floods of soda pouring out of nozzles, beer taps opened and frothy beer scudded and splashed, light bulbs burst with a machine-gun *poppoppop*, and the stadium floodlights exploded with a shower of sparks and flying glass.

People screamed and scattered as the stadium went dark.

"Did you do that?" Jack whispered.

Miriam nodded her head. "I think I did." She heard herself giggle, actually giggle.

"No shit." Jack frowned, glanced around at the panicked, milling crowd. "Well, maybe we should get out of here?"

Miriam nodded again. "Sorry about the game," she said as they exited the stadium just ahead of the crowd.

She felt guilty, knowing she had probably just caused several hundred thousand dollars' worth of damage with that little display of...whatever it was. Jack drove her home, giving her his jacket to wear against the chill of the night wind, his hand on her knee. She left it there, toying with the zipper of his jacket, wondering what other chaos she would cause with the magic that seemed to be waiting all the time now just beneath the surface.

Jack kissed her goodbye, a brief brush of lips, too quick. She wanted to let the kiss ignite again, but he pulled away first, brushing her cheek with a thumb. "I'll see you soon?"

Miriam nodded. "I'd like that."

"Call me, text me. Something. Just...I need to know you're okay. If you see Ben, call me. I'll come get you. Okay?"

She nodded again. "I will."

Had she glimpsed a hint of fear in his eyes? She couldn't be sure, and she didn't want it to be there. But he would be prudent to be afraid of her. She was beginning to be afraid of herself.

Miriam had managed to avoid Ben for a while. When he did call, she ignored his messages. She switched shifts, and called in sick a couple of times. Larry knew the score and understood what Miriam wanted without her having to spell it out, for which she was grateful. She knew she'd have to face Ben eventually, but the longer she could put it off, the better.

He finally showed up at her apartment a few hours after Jack dropped her off. He pounded on her door so hard she thought he was going to break it down. She went out to him rather than letting him inside. She wouldn't bother Jack, though. She didn't want him to get hurt on her account, and this was her problem to solve anyway.

"Where the fuck have you been, Miriam?" Ben demanded. "You ignore my calls, avoid me at work? What the hell?" He was sober, but livid, a particularly bad combination. He grabbed her arm and dragged her to his car, shoved her in the passenger side, nearly bashing her head on the side in the process.

"I needed space, Ben. I still do." She moved to get out, but he locked the door and gunned the engine so she couldn't get out without hurting herself.

"Space? What the fuck do you need space for? You're the freak, remember?"

"Wow, Ben. Awesome. How loving and support-ive of you. I'm a freak now?"

He had the grace to look chagrined at least. "I'm sorry, okay? That was uncalled for. It doesn't excuse you avoiding me, though. What's going on?"

"I don't know, Ben. If I knew, I wouldn't need space, would I? And you being like this isn't helping." She found herself not caring what he did or said. She had decided, in that moment, to break it off with him, no matter what, and that freed her tongue. But she did expect to get hit at least once.

"Whoa! Where's this coming from?" He genu-inely seemed surprised at her outburst. In all the time he'd known her, she'd never talked back like that. Miriam was enjoying the sense of freedom she got from letting him know how she felt.

"It's the truth, Ben," she said. "I don't know what's wrong with me, okay? It's scary for me, and it would be nice if you could act concerned for once, and support me. Instead, all you seem to care about is yourself. You drive around in this stupid goddamn car like you earned it or something."

"What are you talking about? You're not making any sense, Miri." He never called her Miri unless he was trying to be all lovey-dovey.

"I'm talking about your new phone and this stupid car. Where the hell do you think they came from? Stuff like this doesn't just magically appear, Ben. Except it did, didn't it? Who do you think made that happen?" She knew she shouldn't make the connection for him, but her mouth was going faster than her good sense.

Ben jammed the brakes, skidding to a stop in the middle of the street, cars honking and lights flashing as they swerved around him. "You think YOU are responsible for this stuff?"

"I don't know, okay? I don't know. But it's the only thing that makes sense, and you know it."

"So you're a fucking…wizard now or some shit? Wow, Miriam. You've finally lost your actual damn mind."

"You know what, Ben? Fuck you. Let me out. I'm done. *We're* done."

Crack. She didn't even see his fist move. She felt it, though, like a ton of bricks. Her head snapped back and slammed into the car window. She felt a sticky warmth gushing from her nose and trickling down the side of her face. She pinched the bridge of her nose and peered at Ben through throbbing eyes, but he was driving again, knuckles white on the steering wheel. He jerked the car around corners, driving like a maniac.

He pulled the car into a deserted parking lot, threw open his door, and circled around to the passenger side. Miriam knew what was coming and tried to lock the door, but it was too late. He had her door open and yanked her out, and this time she saw his left fist flying at her so fast she had no time to duck. The impact connected with her cheekbone, toppling her backward. Madness burned in his eyes, an unseeing haze of hatred and violence seething within him. His fist bunched in her shirtfront and he held her up, the other fist crashing and bashing into her face and chest and stomach, over and over and over, an ocean of pain rolling over her, subsuming her, drowning her, burying her beneath its suffocating weight.

She retreated into herself, locked the core of her soul away and allowed the pain to scorch away what remained. One last blow struck her mouth, splitting open her lips and loosening a couple of teeth. At that moment the fires within her burst open and set her alight.

She was flame, she was burning, a living torch kneeling on the gravel of the parking lot. Ben was stumbling away, cursing and shielding his face with his arms. Miriam looked up through the flames erupting from her skin and saw Ben, his arms and hair singed and smoking, frantically patting the fire on his shirt.

Miriam held up a hand in front of her, marveling at what she saw: There was no skin, no bones, no blood, only fire, her hand carved out of flame. She sobbed, and she was extinguished. It was only a moment, and in an instant the flame was gone as quickly as it had come, so fast that she wasn't sure it was real.

Ben stared at her, shaking his head as if in denial. Whether he was denying what he'd done, or what he'd just seen, she wasn't sure. Both, maybe. She stood up and lurched toward him, glimpsing herself in the window of his car. She was unrecognizable, her face pummeled into a bloody pulp.

Ben threw himself into his car and tore out of the parking lot, sideswiping several other cars in the process. Miriam took another step forward toward the street, watching his taillights weaving through traffic. The sea of pain, momentarily pushed away by the ignition of flames, washed back through her, and she collapsed. She saw headlights sweep over her, heard voices speaking far away. Feet crunched in the gravel, and hands lifted her. The motion sent a lance of agony through her, and darkness devoured her.

She woke up to the smell of antiseptic. She felt an IV in her arm, and there were bandages on her face and wrapped around her skull. Hospital. Shit. Miriam hated hospitals. She had no health insurance, so this would ruin her financially. She moaned and tried to sit up. The attempt sent knives of pain throughout her body, and she slumped back to the bed.

"Don't try to move," a familiar and welcome voice said. Jack. She felt relief course through her at the sound of his voice.

She pried her eyes open, saw his face next to hers, worry etched on his features. "Is it really you?"

"Of course it's me," he said. He brushed her arm with his fingers, a touch gentle as a breath of wind.

"How are you here?"

"I went back to your apartment—I had a bad feeling. You weren't there, so I talked to Larry. He said you'd been in an 'accident.'" Jack made air quotes on the last word, rage in his eyes. "Apparently you have him listed as one of your emergency contacts, so the hospital called him when you were brought here.

"Jack, it's okay—"

"The hell it is! It's not okay! He nearly killed you, Miriam. What's it going to take?"

"I was trying to break up with him, and this is what happened."

"You did? You broke up with him?" Jack was holding her hand, fingers twined in hers, an intimate gesture that she found deeply comforting.

"I told him were done. He got pissed off, and then I got mad at him, and then he just...snapped."

Jack didn't seem to know how to respond. He let out a long breath, and then Miriam felt a finger brush away a tear. His lips touched hers, almost too gently to feel. She hesitated, confused, feeling the walls wavering, wanting to believe what she felt but unable to. His hand curled around the back of her neck, just below the bandage, pulling her to him, and she couldn't help but kiss him back.

Jack broke away after a moment and his eyes pierced hers, full of understanding and something frighteningly like love.

"It's not over, Jack." She'd seen the flash of love in Jack's eyes, and it scared her to death. She didn't know how to deal with that. She wanted it, but felt terrified by it at the same time. Her fear spoke through her. "He's going to come here. He'll apologize and be all charming. And, besides, telling him I'm breaking up with him doesn't mean he'll just go away. It won't be that easy."

"So have him arrested! Tell the hospital he's the one who beat the shit out of you and you don't want him in here."

"It's not that simple, Jack. He'll spend *one* night in jail, if that. Then he'll be even more upset. And PPOs aren't worth the paper they're printed on when it comes to actual protection. I know, I've looked into it. And besides all that, I have to leave the hospital. Like, now. I don't have health insurance, and every moment I sit here is costing me thousands of dollars I don't have, and will never have. And he'll find me, and...I don't have anywhere to go, Jack. I have no family, no friends except you. If I move, he'll find me. He'll follow me, and it'll start all over again."

"So you're just gonna stay with him? Just like that? You'll just let him beat the shit out of you? He's going to *kill* you eventually, Miriam. The beating he gave you last night *should* have killed you, according to the doctor." Jack was pacing, frustration eating away at him.

"I know, Jack. I know. I wish I had the answers, believe me. You think I *like* getting the shit beat out of me? You think I don't want—god, more than *anything*—to just run away with you? You're amazing, and you...you deserve someone who can love you back. I don't know if I can. Not with Ben in the way. And he'll *always* be in the way." She wanted to reach out to him, to touch him, but she didn't. "There's nothing you can do, Jack. This is my choice."

"It's the wrong choice!"

"I'm sorry, Jack. I really am."

Jack slumped down to the chair, frustration coming off him in waves. He took her hands in his. "So let me protect you. I can, and I will. I can take care of Ben. He's a bully, and he doesn't scare me. I can take him."

"No, Jack. I don't doubt that you would, or could. But I won't have you getting hurt over me."

He hung his head, cursing in a stream of hissed words under his breath. "You're determined to make this impossible, aren't you? You're afraid of what we could have, so you won't even try." The last was a statement, resigned and troubled. He met her gaze, squeezed her hands, kissed her lightly. "You can't get rid of me that easily, Miriam. I'm not giving up. There is a way for this to work, I know there is. If you'd just give me a chance…." He was nearly pleading, but silently. His eyes were begging her to give him the answer he wanted.

"Jack…please. Just stop."

All she could see was Jack in this same hospital bed, bruised and bloody and broken. She was already healing, she could feel it, but Jack wouldn't have that, and she couldn't deal with him being hurt because of her. She looked away from Jack's gaze, shook her head. Tears dripped from her chin, and she refused to wipe them away.

Jack did it for her, taking her face in both hands, wiping the tears with his thumbs, kissing her lips with a trembling intensity, struggling to be gentle but wanting to crush her with passion. Her cracked heart broke further when he walked away without looking back. When she opened her eyes, Jack was gone.

Alone, Miriam wept until there was nothing left inside.

Ben arrived at the hospital as she was pulling out the IV a few hours later. A nurse was standing at the doorway, looking on disapprovingly. Miriam had explained that she couldn't afford to stay, and that she was feeling better. Her doctor had come and examined her after Jack left, and was puzzled by how fast her bruises were fading. Her ribs were still cracked and sending lances of pain through her at every breath, but she refused to stay.

"Miriam," Ben began, "Look, I'm—I don't know what happened—"

She whirled on him, eyes blazing. "You don't know what happened? You fucking *snapped* is what happened, you bastard!" The nurse, still watching, gasped and scurried away, calling for security.

Two overweight security guards appeared at the door a moment later. "Is everything okay, ma'am?" one of them asked.

Miriam took a deep breath and waved them away. If she tried to have them remove Ben, he'd flip out, and Miriam was too tired and sore to deal with that kind of scene right then. "It's fine. It's not what it looks like."

The nurse, a middle-aged black woman, gaped in disbelief. "That's a bunch of bull, honey, and you know it. This A-hole here worked you over but good, and you can't try to tell me otherwise." Ben rounded on the nurse, and Miriam grabbed his arm, pushed him out of the hospital room, following behind him.

"It's none of your business, lady," Miriam said, wanting nothing more than to stay and make them take Ben away.

"Your funeral if you go with him," the nurse said, following them. "Foolish girl! He's gonna kill you sooner or later. I saw you when you came in, sweetheart. You were half-dead, and it wasn't no accident, neither."

"I'll be fine." Miriam knew it was lie.

"Your funeral," the nurse repeated. She didn't seem surprised, though. Perhaps she'd seen more than her share of battered women come through the hospital and leave with the men who'd put them there, denying the whole thing had ever happened.

Once she was out of the hospital and in Ben's car, Miriam felt the reality of what she was doing rush in on her. Ben was still seething, deep down. He was here because he felt bad on the surface, but she could sense his anger. She was being stupid, and she knew it. But she didn't care. It didn't matter. She was back to what she knew. This was familiar. This was easiest.

"I can't tell you how sorry I am, Miri. Really. I overreacted. I'm sorry." Miriam huffed a laugh but otherwise stayed silent. "Okay, fine, then. You don't have to talk to me. Are you hungry?" Miriam just shrugged. Ben rolled his eyes and checked his phone.

"Fine," he said. "Be that way. I said I'm sorry, didn't I?"

"Like that fixes it?" Miriam knew better than to expect true contrition from him.

"Well, what do you want from me? I said I'm sorry. It won't happen again, I promise." He was heading up I-75 toward Troy, going ninety-five in the fast lane. Miriam felt a wave of disgust as she realized where he was taking her.

"Whatever," she said. "Can we go somewhere else, please? Anywhere, literally *anywhere* but there."

"You love Ruth's Chris, don't you?"

Miriam wanted to laugh and cry. This was not the conversation she wanted to have. She was still fighting the agony of bruised ribs, and her eyes were still purple from his fists, but all he could think about was steakhouses. Nothing had changed, and nothing ever would.

Jack was gone, and she was back where she started.

She just shook her head, choking back a sob. "Whatever, Ben. Whatever you want is fine." The sense of entrapment washed over her, making her want to jump out of the car. It'd be so easy, wouldn't it? She watched her hand inching toward the door handle, helpless to stop it. This was one way out of this mess. Her fingers found the cool metal of the handle, and she pushed the door open. Blacktop and yellow lines blurred in the crack between door and handle; she heard Ben yelling next to her, but his words were buzzed and muddled and distant. All she had to do was jump, and she would be free. There was nothing between her and the freeway. The freeway. Free.

Free.

Miriam pushed the door open wider and leaned out, feeling the wind buffeting at her, snatching and tangling her hair. Freedom would come quickly.

CHAPTER 9

Carson

Present Day

CARSON SAT ACROSS FROM RHONDA GRIMES IN THE cafeteria of the Detroit Mercy Hospital. The Styrofoam cup of black coffee was hot in his hands, and he listened carefully as Rhonda spoke.

"She was beat senseless, Detective. I ain't kiddin'. I was just startin' a double shift when she was brought in."

"And when was this, Mrs. Grimes?"

"It was exactly a week ago today. I remember because it was my birthday."

"Can you tell me who brought her in?" Carson asked.

"Just some guy. I don't think she knew him. He said she'd just collapsed in front of his car, bleedin' all over the place. He said he thought she was gonna die in his car on the way to the hospital.

"Well, honestly, she shoulda died. Most of her ribs were broke, both eyes black, cheekbones cracked, back of her head busted open. She had a concussion, for sure. We were gonna do an MRI once she woke up, but she had to okay the procedure since she had no next of kin and no insurance. She was bruised all over, and I mean all over. I remember thinkin' when I first saw her, man, whoever done this to her hated her. I seen a lot in my thirty years at this hospital. I seen boys gang-beat and curb-stomped and hit with bats and stabbed and shot…shit, you're a cop—you know what happens. This girl was beat to death, only she didn't die."

Carson nodded, a grim expression on his face. He'd seen his share of awful things, of course. He'd seen a woman beaten to death by a jealous boyfriend before, and the image was one he would never be able to banish from his mind.

"Did anyone visit her while she was here?"

Rhonda nodded. "Mmm-hmmm. She had two visitors. The first was a nice boy. Handsome, too. Big blue eyes, lookin' at that girl like he couldn't get enough of her. Never left her side until she woke up."

This was new. "Do you know who he was? Can you describe him for me?"

"Maybe six feet tall, brown hair. He had a motor-cycle jacket and helmet. Jack, I think she called him. That boy loved her something fierce, although I'm not sure either of 'em knew it yet. Or maybe they did, but they didn't want to believe it." Rhonda wiped her fingers on a napkin and stood up. Carson followed her, fitting a lid to his coffee cup.

"Did they have an argument? Did she leave with Jack?"

"Oh, I think he was tryin' to convince her to, but she wasn't havin' none of it." Rhonda shook her head sadly at this. "They didn't argue, not like they were mad at each other, but eventually he did leave by him-self, and he wasn't none too happy about it. She cried for a long time after he was gone. Of course, this is just what I could see from across the hall. I wasn't tryin' to pry none…."

"Of course not." Carson took a sip of bitter, burnt coffee. "So then Ben showed up?"

"Ben's the other one, right? Yeah, he came as she was gettin' ready to leave. She was healin' faster than anyone understood. She didn't have insurance, like I said, and she was determined to leave. Don't blame her, poor girl. Hospitals are awful expensive, any way you slice it.

"Well, then the other guy showed up and was tellin' her how sorry he was, but she didn't believe him none. Neither did I. I been in her shoes, years past. They come to you with them sad puppy-dog eyes, actin' all sorry, buyin' you flowers and tellin' you how much they love you, but shit, you can't believe 'em 'cause they'll just do it again next time they get drunk." Rhonda fell silent for a moment, lost in bad memories of days gone by.

"But she left with him? Voluntarily?" Carson pulled a business card from his wallet, handed it to the nurse.

"Yeah, she did. I don't think she wanted to, but she didn't want a scene. That's as much of it as anything, you know. You don't want to draw attention. You don't want 'em to get mad in public, because they'll blame you for it when you're home, and that'll make it even worse."

"Well, I think I've got what I need for now. Thanks for your time, Mrs. Grimes."

"Oh sure, honey." Rhonda seemed lost in her thoughts, and Carson felt bad that he'd brought up memories she'd obviously worked hard to forget.

Carson knew all about memories that were best left forgotten.

Chapter 10

Miriam

One week earlier

Ben grabbed her by the hair and yanked her back in the car, holding her down as she screamed and thrashed. The car swerved, and Ben was cursing, trying to hold Miriam and drive at the same time. The exit appeared, and Ben pulled off the interstate, the car door swinging open, Miriam's leg dangling out, inches from the ground. Ben yanked the car over to the shoulder, slammed it into Park, leaped out, and circled around. He knelt in front of her.

"What the hell was that?" He was whispering, looking utterly baffled.

Miriam was numb, cold and rigid. She heard Ben speaking, felt him shaking her shoulders, trying to get her attention, but she had no energy to respond, no emotion left. She wouldn't fight, she couldn't. She felt Ben latch the seatbelt across her, close the door, get in, and continue driving. He got back on the freeway, but he took her to his place. But she didn't care. She followed him blindly, felt him lay her down, strip her clothes off, and cover her with a blanket. She felt completely empty. Nothing mattered now. She'd sent Jack away, and that was it.

She slept deeply without dreaming.

Hours later she was woken by Ben's hands exploring her body. Dim gray light filtered through the blinds, and Ben's lips kissed her shoulder, her neck, her ear. The fires within her remained banked and cold. His fingers caressed the curve of her hip, slid up her belly and tender ribcage to the swell of her breasts, cupping them, crushing them with unthinking strength.

This was his way of apologizing. She wanted to scream—she wanted to roll away and run. Part of her wanted to bash his skull in and watch him bleed out onto the pillow. Miriam was startled by the violence of that thought, but she let herself taste the idea, mulling it over in her mind. It didn't scare her the way it should. It excited her a little. It was the idea of fighting back that excited her, she realized, not the actual violence itself, and for that she was relieved. She remembered how free she had felt speaking her mind to Ben. The beating had almost been worth it for that brief moment of freedom.

His fingers were down between her legs and his mouth was on hers, and she let him do what he wanted, not resisting, not engaging. Numb and empty. Ben didn't notice the difference. He grabbed her hand and guided it to his semi-rigid manhood, and she did what he wanted. The sooner he finished, the sooner she could go back to sleep. The thought of another fight filled her with dread and exhaustion and fear: She wasn't ready to face him. Not yet. She retreated into the numb center of herself, letting the coldness wash over her as Ben straddled her, hands by her shoulders, his weight pressing her into the mattress. She focused her gaze into the middle distance, staring at the white expanse of the wall beside the bed.

Jack's face filled her thoughts, and she tried to push it away. The memory of his hands on her skin filled her, creating a breath of catalyzing wind on the banked fires inside her. No. She fought against it. If she let herself respond to the memories of Jack, it would encourage Ben. She refused to think of Jack when Ben was above her, grunting, every thrust bruising her pelvic bones with blind force. He neared climax, and the pain of his forceful thrusting sent Miriam deeper into herself. Her only escape was Jack, his face, his kindness the only positive memory she could summon to blanket the pain.

At that moment Ben pressed a palm against her broken ribs, leaning on her as he climaxed. The agony of his weight ignited her rage, took the fire inside her from warm banked coals to a burning inferno in an instant. She shoved him away with sudden strength, sending him flying off the bed to slam against the wall.

Heat washed through her, a now-familiar feeling. She felt power shuddering in her soul, felt it reach out and snake from her into Ben, latching onto him and vanishing inside. She'd never paid close attention to what happened in this moment before. She'd confused the rush of orgasm with the flux of power within her, but now, with her body's desires tamped and cold, Miriam sought to understand exactly what she was feeling within herself when the power—the magic— burst out of her soul.

She felt it leap from within herself and out to Ben, felt it wrap around him. She closed her eyes and imagined herself as a spirit, incorporeal and ethereal. She followed the magic on its journey, caught a fragmentary glimpse of a roiling ocean of energy inside her, a sea of magic boiling and raging like fire and magma. The glimpse was so brief, but what she saw took her breath away. Then, in the next moment, she was an invisible, nonphysical observer following the flow of magic, a jet stream of gold and silver sparks and coiling explosions of color spanning the spectrum.

The current of magic arced from her and into Ben, into his heart, digging into the core of his deepest desires, wrapping around the strongest element it found there within him. Suddenly, the image expanded and became a physical entity. There was a flash of light, and Miriam was thrown back into herself.

This was followed by a moment of disorientation when Miriam was still seeing the burst of magic like a shower of sparks from a bonfire, like stars falling in silver lines, like shafts from the sun refracting through a prism into shimmering rainbow light.

Then she was herself again, a woman physical and exhausted and hurting. Ben was lying next to her, moaning, but Miriam ignored him, trying to hold on to the sense of power she'd felt within herself.

A confused female voice spoke from the corner of the bedroom. "Wh-what the fuck is going on?"

Miriam started, gasping. She looked over to see a woman standing by the door, clad in black lace lingerie, huge, fake, pale breasts spilling out of the skimpy bustier, blonde hair teased out, full lips caked with bright red lipstick, eyes darkened with heavy makeup. The woman crossed her arms over her chest self-consciously, and looked over to the bed at Ben.

"Ben, is that you?" the girl asked. "What am I doing here in your room? What time is it? How did I get here?" She obviously knew Ben, and was familiar enough with his bedroom to recognize it.

Ben was getting to his feet gingerly, looking from Miriam to the other girl. "Rachel?" he mumbled. "What're you doing here?" He rubbed his eyes, as if to make sense of what he was seeing.

When the magic had latched onto Ben's deepest desire, it had woven itself around this girl, dressed in this lingerie. His desire was now flesh and blood, standing here in his room.

"Who *is* this, Ben?" Miriam demanded. She heard the anger in her voice, drawing confidence from it.

The girl, whom Ben had called Rachel, echoed Miriam's words. "Who is *this*, Ben?"

Ben looked from Miriam, naked and clutching the sheet to her body, to Rachel, standing in front of him in a sheer negligée. Ben's eyes and body revealed his desire for Rachel, despite having Miriam next to him. He struggled for words. "I—this, uh…shit. I don't know. How did you get here, Rach? Miriam, did you do this?"

Miriam leaped off the bed, pressing herself against the wall, holding the bed sheet in front of her. "We both know I did, Ben, so let's not play games. I'm a freak, I know. Now answer the *goddamn* question! Who the *hell* is this, Ben?" She repeated the question, yelling it this time.

Ben flushed, and she saw him searching for answers. "This is…this is Rachel. Uh, she's—she's a friend of mine."

Rachel planted a hand on her hip, angry. "A friend? I'm a *friend* now? What the hell, Ben? I'm your *girlfriend*. What is *she* doing in *our* bed?"

Rachel's high-pitched, whining voice grated on Miriam's nerves, and she felt the anger begin to burn again, ever hotter, threatening to reignite the magic. Now that she'd felt it, and seen it, Miriam could understand the power within her more clearly; she wanted to grasp it, let the anger set fire to her and burst through her and consume this irritating girl, and Ben along with her.

"Your *girlfriend?*" Miriam stalked around the bed and picked up her clothes, putting them on quickly and angrily. "Your *girlfriend*, Ben? If *she's* your girlfriend, then what the fuck am I?"

Ben opened his mouth to answer, but Rachel cut him off. "Oh, I know who you are. You're Miriam, aren't you?" Rachel smirked, cruelty and amusement glittering in her eyes as she pronounced the next words. "You're his booty call. Isn't that right, Ben? He's mentioned you before. You're the one he goes to for a little extra somethin' on the side when I'm busy. Isn't that right?" Rachel turned away and pulled open the bottom drawer of Ben's dresser, rummaged around, and produced a change of clothes.

She had her own drawer? Miriam's anger went cold for a moment, stung by the apparent truth in Rachel's words. Ben's mouth was flapping, for once at a loss for words. "I—It's not quite like *that*, Rachel…." he said. He wouldn't look at either girl, but instead he edged to the dresser, opened a drawer, and put on a pair of gym shorts.

"It's not, huh?" Rachel stalked up to Ben, poking a finger in his chest. "That's what you told *me*. You said Miriam was just a side-fuck. Is it something else, Ben? Is she something more serious? 'Cause that's not what you told me."

Miriam was disgusted. Not only did Ben obviously have another girlfriend, but that girl knew about Miriam and found nothing wrong with the idea of Ben having sex with someone else, as long as it wasn't "serious."

But she hadn't known anything about this Rachel. Although now that she thought about it, Ben *did* spend a lot of time sending text messages he never bothered to explain. Miriam had always just assumed they were to his Corps buddies or something.

"So what is it, Ben? Am I just something on the side?" Miriam asked. She was fighting tears, grasping desperately for anger to strengthen herself.

Ben looked from one woman to the other, caught between the two. Miriam watched him struggle for answers. Sure enough, his eyes glazed over, and the vein in his forehead started throbbing. He would retreat into anger now. It was the only way he knew how to deal with situations he couldn't control.

"Back off, both of you," he said, voice low and dangerous. "I don't owe either of you shit. Rachel, I'm taking you home. Come on."

"Why doesn't *she* go home?" Rachel whined. "I'm already here—I might as well stay. She can leave."

Ben growled and pushed Rachel out the door, snatching up his keys and phone with a string of curses. "Come *on*, Rachel. Let's go. Now." He turned back to Miriam and started to say something, but changed his mind.

Miriam watched from the window as Ben held the car door open for Rachel, kissing her as he started the car, laughing at something she said. Ben never held the door for *her*. Never kissed her, or laughed with her. So she was just "something extra on the side"? Miriam felt anger rush back with tidal force. She stuffed her feet into her shoes and stormed out of Ben's apartment, slamming the door so hard it shook the entryway windows.

Thunder rumbled, and a flash of lightning lit the night sky; drops of rain pelted Miriam, followed by a torrential downpour that soaked her to the skin in moments.

She barely noticed, lost in thought, consumed by rage. A *side-fuck?* Everything she put up with, and he was screwing someone else? *And* she had her own drawer in Ben's apartment? The drawer itself was beside the point; what had Miriam's breath coming in ragged, raging gasps was the fact that Rachel *knew* about Miriam. Ben had talked about her to Rachel. He'd probably told Rachel all about her, including everything Miriam had ever said in confidence. They probably laughed at her together, in Ben's bed, making fun of stupid, clueless Miriam.

The anger was hot inside Miriam, a river of fire in her veins. She could feel the magic boiling, ready to burst. Miriam had no thought for anything except Ben and his betrayal of her. Did he hit Rachel, too? Or was that just for Miriam? The way he'd held the door for Rachel: Even when he'd pushed her out the door he'd done it more gently than he'd ever treated Miriam in his kindest moments.

She was full of rage. White-hot, all-consuming rage. At Ben, yes, but at herself most of all for putting up with him for so long, for wasting so much of her life on him, for believing his lies, for never believing she deserved better. Especially when someone like Jack was waiting for her, wanting her, willing to fight for her.

There was a blinding light approaching, but so lost was Miriam that she paid no notice to it. She paid no attention to the fact that she was dry, despite the curtains of windblown rain still pounding down. She heard cars passing by, honking, but she ignored them too. Cars were swerving around her, people were yelling.

An odd hissing noise, the sound of water hitting a frying pan, somehow pierced through her daze. Miriam stopped and, for the first time, realized that the blinding light was *her*. She was glowing like the sun, lit up from within, and the rain was hitting her superheated skin and evaporating, turned to steam on contact. Billowing clouds of steam wreathed around her, trailed her, rose up and vanished and skirled in the thunderstorm wind. As she was walking down the middle of the street, another car appeared, honking and swerving around her, skidding on the grass, then disappearing into the rain-soaked night.

A single headlight penetrated the gloom and rain, approaching her like a freight train. She stopped in her tracks, unable to move. She could only stand and stare, rooted to the spot. The unnatural glow around her continued to burn bright, along with the rage still coursing through her.

The headlight wobbled, turned aside, and then Miriam realized it was a motorcycle, a red Suzuki like Jack's. The helmeted figure skidding the bike to the side looked like Jack, too. The rider fought for control, but the rear tire bounced and hydroplaned on the wet asphalt, and the motorcycle tipped over and slammed into the ground, sliding and tumbling, the rider rolling like a rag doll across the ground.

Miriam knew it was Jack. She ran to him, knelt beside him where he'd crashed. She pulled his helmet off, sobbed when she saw the blood spurting from his nose and ears and mouth. He moaned softly and tried to focus on her, but his gaze wavered, and he went slack in her arms, heavy and limp.

No. No.

Not again. No. She was suddenly eleven again, holding her daddy's head in her lap, watching him fight for breath, clutching his chest, gasping, trying to reassure *her,* plucking at her sleeve with weak fingers. And now, again, the man she loved was gasping for breath, limp in her arms.

The man she loved. Somehow it was true.

Jack coughed, blood dribbling down his chin, frothing as his lungs failed.

No. She refused to let it happen again. Not again. Not Jack, not like this.

"Oh, Jack, I'm sorry, I'm so sorry." She was pleading and begging, holding him in her arms, feeling the rage shift to desperation, feeling the magic burst open within her at her silent demand, burgeoning like an explosion. The magic was flushing through her, turning the heat to power, tendrils of magic licking at Jack's broken fingers, at his eyes and bleeding nose, filtering through his ears into his brain, eliciting a moan from him. The flow of blood slowed and his broken arm—the bone showing white through torn leather—healed in an instant.

Miriam sobbed and dove back into herself, closing her eyes and feeling the magic swirl around her, curling about her essence like a cat brushing against her legs, and she sent it back out, back through Jack, seeking out any cut, any scrape, any hurt on him, commanding the magic to heal it. She felt the magic obey her, and Miriam felt laughter bubbling up in her, a kind of wild joy at the power blazing within her.

Tires squealed and footsteps pounded the pavement, and Ben's voice boomed out, "What the hell are you doing, Miriam?" She felt his hands grasp her shoulder and yank her, toppling Jack to the ground in the process, striking his head against the pavement again. That sent Miriam over the edge. She jerked away, crouched at Jack's side and put his coat under his head, kissed his lips, stood up and turned to face Ben. She saw the anger in his eyes, the possessive jealousy at the sight of her with another man. She saw his fists clenched, and she didn't care.

"Who is that, Miriam? Is that who you've been with behind my back?" Ben had the gall to act outraged.

"Yes, Ben, it is. Do you remember when you were drunk and beating on me in your parking lot? Jack's the one who rescued me. He *rescued* me…from you."

She was full of magic and rage and bravado, and she didn't care what happened anymore. "He kissed me that night. Kissed me better than you ever have. One kiss from him is better than a *thousand* from you. He turns me on, makes me hot like you never could in your wildest dreams. You're pathetic, compared to him. I love him. I love him the way I've never, *never* loved you. The way I never *could* love you. You're nothing but a monster, and I hate how much of my life I've wasted on you. I hate how much pain I've let you put me through. No more, Ben. Do you hear me? I *will not* take any more from you. Never again."

That got Ben's attention. He stepped toward her, like a bull ready to charge. His eyes were full of the madness again, the same crazed blindness that had almost got her killed yesterday. Only this time, she was ready. She had the magic within her grasp; she had the rage in her grip. She squeezed it, felt the heat subsume her and turn white-hot. Jack was at her feet, moaning and coming to consciousness, and she wanted him to see her like this, to know who— what—he thought he loved. She wanted no secrets.

There was a *whoompf*, like a backdraft, like gas-soaked wood catching fire, and she was lit up from within, burning with sun fire; she *was* fire, her body a woman's body carved from living flame. She saw her features as clearly defined as if she were naked, her female form writ in tongues of fire hotter than the sun itself. She smiled, and she laughed, and the sound of her voice was the tolling of a thousand bells. Ben was transfixed, mouth agape, fear etched in his eyes. Jack was shielding his face with an arm, but not moving away, unburned somehow despite being mere inches from the inferno of her body.

Miriam took a step forward, and her footstep shook the earth as if she were a giant looming a hundred feet high. She opened her mouth to speak, to tell Ben to leave, but a gout of flame burst from her like dragon breath, forcing Ben backward to the ground.

"What the fuck *are* you?" she heard him ask.

"I'm over you, Ben, that's what I am," she answered, her voice echoing like thunder and tolling like a bell. She stepped toward him once more, and felt the asphalt beneath her feet crack and crunch with each touch of her foot. "If I see you again, I'll kill you. I'll burn you to a crisp."

Terrified, Ben scrambled to his feet, climbed into his car, and drove away, the terror still stark in his eyes as he looked back in the rearview mirror.

Miriam turned to face Jack, who was now on his feet.

"Are you afraid, Jack?" She was prepared for him to run as well, but what she saw in his eyes nearly extinguished her.

"No," came his whispered answer.

Jack lifted a hand, hesitant, as if testing the heat. A step forward, and he was close enough that the fire should have consumed him, but, impossibly, it didn't. The flames were licking at him, but he remained unburned.

She felt her magic arcing between them, saw it flowing around him, protecting him. He stepped closer to her, eyes shining with wonder. His hands rested on her waist, where they fit so perfectly; she felt his touch as soft and familiar as ever. She was kissing him, feeling the fire that was her essence washing through him, and he was gasping for breath, looking into her soul. She saw her own eyes reflected in his, glowing and flickering. His palms explored her body, pushing her even hotter, if that was possible.

"You're you," Jack said. It was cryptic, but she heard the meaning beneath the words.

"I don't know *what* I am, though," she whispered. It was true.

"Me, neither," Jack said, and his eyes showed curiosity, and a little fear, but even more love. Love that didn't scare her. "But I know *who* you are. You're Miriam. And you belong to me."

She wrapped her arms around him, reveling in the joy of belonging.

She thought of home, *her* home, her apartment. She felt the universe shift, tilt, felt something cold wash over her as she clung to Jack, inhaling his familiar scent. She felt power leaching out of her, tendrils of magic threading through her and touching the fabric of the universe around them; tilt and shift and cold and heat and fire and rain, all mixed and muddled, and then the rain vanished abruptly and she smelled home. Her eyes opened, and she saw her couch, tattered and ancient, saw her tiny TV, the small glass-and-brass coffee table.

Miriam didn't know how, but somehow they'd been transported instantly from the side of the road to her apartment. The magic inside her had taken over again, as she had wished. It had taken her home where she wanted to be, and it had brought Jack with her.

Jack reared back, his hands still on her waist, staring at her with a smile. He was waiting. She knew what he was waiting for: permission. Miriam breathed deep, closed her eyes, and searched her heart for reservations, for fear, for hesitation, and she found none, only desire.

Jack kissed her neck, slipped his hands under the bottom hem of her shirt, a habit of his she was growing to anticipate every time he put his hands on her waist.

Miriam didn't answer, at least not in words. She pulled away from him, led him by the hand to her bedroom, and then closed the door behind them. Her heart was pounding against her ribs: She had never, ever let anyone into her bedroom. Not Nick, or Ben, or anyone. Her bedroom was a sanctum, a place where she could let down her walls and just be herself. Now here was Jack, in her bedroom. He had gotten inside her walls, both physical and metaphorical, and she wasn't sure how he'd managed it, but she was glad he had.

"You're trembling. What's wrong?" Jack seemed to be attuned to every small detail, to every change in her mood.

Miriam wasn't sure how to answer. "I—it's nothing."

"No, it's not. Are you nervous? We don't have to do this, you know. I thought you wanted to, but if you're not ready—"

"No! It's not that. I want this. God, I do. It's just that—" She cut herself off, laughing in embarrassment. "It's stupid. I've never let anyone in my room before. I mean, like, no one. Ever."

"Not even your parents?" It seemed like an innocent question, but it reminded Miriam that Jack knew nothing about her. The one thing about Ben was that he knew it all. She didn't have to explain her past to him. He knew all about her parents. That might have been part of why Miriam was so hesitant to start anything with Jack: She didn't want to have to explain her life story.

"My parents are both gone, Jack. It's a long story." Miriam hated how much of a non-answer that was.

"I've got time." Jack sat down on the bed next to her, switching from passion to empathy with a speed that amazed her.

"Well, the short version is this," Miriam said. "My dad died of a heart attack when I was eleven, and my mom left when I was sixteen."

"Okay, so what's the long version?"

So Miriam told Jack about her mother's abrupt departure, living with Yanira, getting her first job, her first apartment. Nick. Waking up with a knife to her throat. Meeting Ben and thinking he was different.

Jack listened through it all, watching her attentively. When she finished her story and fell silent, Jack pulled her to him, and Miriam lay down next to him, placing her head on his shoulder, her hand over his heart, feeling it beat—*thumpthump-thumpthump.* She felt safe. Jack wasn't as big or strong as Ben, and he wasn't a combat-hardened badass like Ben, but somehow he made her feel safer than ever before in her life. Desire stirred in her stomach, and she slipped her hand under his shirt, tracing circles in the light coating of hair on his chest.

"I'd rather tell you all this now. Just have it out of the way. I've tried not telling guys about my history, but it never went well. I prefer honesty."

"Are we dating now?" Jack had his face buried in her hair, muffling his voice.

"I don't know, are we?" She craned her neck to look at him.

"Are you done with Ben? For good?" His tone was serious, and he propped himself up on an elbow, searching her face.

"I threatened to kill him if I saw him again, so I'd say, yeah, I'm done with him."

"That was awesome, by the way."

"What? The threatening to kill Ben, or the thing with the fire?"

"Both." Jack lay back down, and Miriam cradled her head against his chest again, touching his skin, greedy for his warmth, for the comfort of his presence. Jack let the issue drop, and she was glad. She wasn't ready to talk about that yet.

"So, I guess we *are* dating, yeah," Miriam said. There were several minutes of comfortable silence, and then Miriam said, "Jack? I have a question."

"What's that?"

"How is it you were there, on *that* road at *that* exact time? I mean, it seems like a crazy coincidence. You keep turning up exactly when I need you."

Jack didn't answer right away. "You know Gramps' second sight? He says I have it, too. I had a dream about you. I saw you walking in the rain, and I saw Ben show up in his car...and it wasn't just a dream, it became real. I had intended to go to your apartment, but that just didn't feel right, so I turned around and headed back to where I first met you, at the apartment complex. I assume that's Ben's apartment, right?

"Well, I knew I should've taken my Jeep, but I was in too much of a hurry. Something bad was going to happen if I didn't stop it. I just knew it in my gut. Just after I left home, it started pouring, and then I saw this glow. At first I thought a building was on fire, but as I got closer I realized it was you—the glow was coming from you. But I was going too fast, and I lost control on the slippery road...." Jack trailed off, shrugging. Miriam traced lines on his chest, waiting for him to continue.

Jack looked down at her, a thousand unasked questions glittering in his gaze. He rolled slightly so he was leaning over her, then dipped his head down and kissed her, his lips soft and gentle and questing. Miriam couldn't help her reaction. Any second thoughts she had were brushed away by the tenderness in his kiss, a gentility that was not at all lacking in passion or masculinity, but rife with affection and tenderness.

God, it was all so alien to her, but so wonderful. She couldn't help pressing up into the kiss to deepen it, tangling her fingers in the hair at the back of his head, her other hand on the hard muscles of his stomach. His strong arms curled around her and fanned the coals of her passion into burning flames. She was so hot she worried she might burst alight once more.

Miriam skated her trembling fingers underneath Jack's T-shirt, following the ridges of his spine, sliding the cotton upward with her touch. Jack broke their kiss briefly, tore the shirt over his head, and tossed it aside, and Miriam's breath was snatched by the beauty of his body—the hard planes of his chest, the sculpted perfection of his abs. And then she was lost even more as he leaned in to kiss her, stealing her breath all over again, making her heart hammer and her soul swell with joy and belonging and comfort and need. He palmed her ribs, pushing her shirt up, moving his lips to her throat as she wiggled out of the shirt. He continued pressing kiss after kiss onto her skin, down between her breasts. Miriam arched her back, roaming the broad expanse of his shoulders as he tugged her bra cups down one at a time, flicking his tongue over her rigid, hypersensitive nipples. His fingers sneaked under the arched bridge of her spine and released her bra straps.

She was bare from the waist up, and his mouth was roving over her heated flesh, his palms cupping her tits and his thumbs scraping back and forth over her nipples. His jaw was stubbled, and she loved the feel of it as his face rasped over her skin. She could only hold onto his shoulders as he kissed her side, her ribs, and then just below her navel, his busy, dexterous fingers hooking into the elastic waistband of her yoga pants and her underwear, tugging them down to bare more skin, his lips sucking and his tongue laving.

Her gasp turned into a moan as his stubble brushed over the soft skin of her inner thighs, his hands roaming upward along her legs, caressing the outside first, palming her thighs, her hips, and then sliding between her body and the bed to cup her ass. Miriam tangled her fingers in his hair as Jack lifted her lower half off the mattress, bringing her core to his mouth, his tongue parting her folds, tasting her essence.

Fire and magic blasted through her, pleasure igniting them to nova intensity, and then Jack let her down to the bed, sliding his fingers inside her, finding her G-spot and rubbing it in time with his lapping, circling tongue. Miriam cried out, feeling the heat billow off her, hearing the crackle of flames.

Miriam was seized by tremors, and an orgasm hurtled through her, shaking her, forcing her hips to lift off the bed. Wrenching moans issued from her throat, causing her to grind her core against Jack's mouth as she clutched his head, clinging to him, writhing and moaning. The fierce heat and power of her climax left her limp and wrung out, hypersensitive all over, and she pulled at Jack, tugged him up to her.

She opened her eyes and realized that her hair, tangled over her shoulders and splayed on the pillow around her head, was no longer plain brown locks but rather living flame, flames that coiled and flicked as if semi-sentient. Dancing bits of flame clung to her still-mortal flesh, running up and down her arms, bursting from her pores to evaporate, erupting in gouts to trip from her to Jack, running along his skin as well.

Jack leaned on his forearms above her, watching the flames play, then turned his gaze to Miriam's. She felt his body above hers, felt the thick presence of his arousal between them.

She wanted to feel him, to touch him. Miriam pushed at Jack's shoulder, and he rolled to his back, pulling her over him. She straddled him, her still enflamed hair trailing around her shoulders and hanging in flickering hot curtains around them both as she leaned down to kiss Jack's mouth, then his chest, then down to his flat, hard stomach.

Now it was his turn to groan and shift beneath her. Miriam ran her hands over his torso, learning him, feeling him, kissing his skin and tasting his flesh. She unbuttoned his jeans and tugged at the zipper, lowering it impatiently, pulling at his jeans and boxers. Jack kicked them away, and he was naked beneath her. They were flesh to flesh now, bodies poised to join. But Miriam wanted to feel more of him, taste more of him. She wanted to make him feel as good as he had her.

Lips stuttering over his skin, she kissed above his navel, then beneath it, and then she had his erection in her fist, hot and hard and thick and perfect. She stroked him gently, slowly, savoring the feel of him in her hand. She wrapped her lips around him, felt his soft springy head between her lips, took him in deeper and swirled her tongue over him, stroking his length with both hands, one and then the other, clutching and pumping and squeezing and plunging her fist around him, root to tip, sucking on him until he moaned and lifted his hips off the bed.

"Jesus, Miriam, you're gonna make me—" Jack began, but then groaned in pleasure as she brought him as deep into her mouth as she could.

Jack lifted his hips off the bed, writhing as she stroked him quickly with a loose touch. She pulled back to let his cock slip from her mouth, letting her saliva coat him, wrapping her palm over his broad head and smearing it down his length. Then she put her lips around his tip, sucking hard, moving her hands up and down his throbbing length.

Jack didn't stand a chance. He made one token effort to pull away, to bring her up, but she resisted, and now he tangled his fingers in her hair, which was flashing back and forth from coiling snakes of flame to her normal dark brown locks. He held on, gasped out a warning just before he released into her mouth. She took it all and kept going, drew another wrenching groan from him as he spurted again and again, groaning and cursing.

When he was spent, Miriam pulled away, intending to lie beside him, but she blinked, and in that instant, Jack's beautiful, naked form was replaced with a startling vision—a nightmare of bloodied features, and somehow she knew, she *knew*, Ben had done this.

Miriam blinked again, and Jack was himself once more, unhurt and staring up at her in confusion and concern. A sob wrenched through her, her passion and desire doused by the sudden and unwelcome vision, her eyes stinging with tears. She shook her head, trying to banish the vision, but it wouldn't leave her. The guilt of seeing Jack hurt because of her overwhelmed her every thought, taking over her emotions. Another sob wracked her, and she slumped forward, still straddling Jack, who sat up and wrapped his arms around her, cupping the back of her head as he kissed her temple.

"What's wrong?" he asked.

Miriam covered her face with her hands, not answering, not knowing how to explain what she had just seen. Jack tugged her hands away, gently but firmly, and brushed the tears from her cheek.

" I'm sorry, Jack, I just…I can't. Not yet." Miriam buried her face between his neck and shoulder, finding comfort in his hand wandering up to rub her back. "I'm so sorry, I know I told you—I know you must be so frustrated. I keep doing this to you. I keep backing off."

"Miriam, look at me, please?" Jack tipped her chin up, and she finally met his eyes. "If you don't want to, if you're not ready, I understand. Just tell me why, okay? I don't want to do this if you're not ready. I want you, yes. I'm...god, so turned on by you, so attracted to you. How could I not be? Look at you, you're *so* beautiful."

"No, I'm not. I'm not beautiful. And it's not that I don't want you. I do. I want you so bad. I want to do this with you more than I—more than I should, considering how short a time I've known you. It's crazy how badly I want this. So please, *please,* don't think it's that."

"Then what *is* it?" Jack rubbed her back, brushing her hair out of the way and massaging the muscles of her neck. He moved aside so that she was lying on her stomach, and he kneaded the muscles of her shoulders and back with a sensuality and affection that was in no way sexual, simply relaxing and comforting.

"It's Ben. I know I told you I was done with him, and I am, I promise. But I just...I don't think *he's* done with *me*. He won't let go easily. I—I just had this vision of you all bloody and beaten, and I knew Ben had done it, and that it was my fault. I healed you back there, but what if...what if he followed you to work and waited for you, jumped you as you were coming out? He would kill you, Jack. I've seen him do that before. Not actually *kill* a man, but close. With his bare hands."

Miriam shook her head, trying to push away the memory, but she couldn't. She went on, "We were out having dinner, and Ben had had too much to drink. We went out to the parking lot, and this guy was there, talking on his cell phone beside his car. He'd parked so close to Ben's truck that Ben couldn't get in, and the guy just ignored him when Ben asked him to move. Ben lost it. He just snapped. He attacked the guy and beat him into hamburger. He was unrecognizable before I managed to pull Ben away.

"It was…god, it was awful. And that was just a random guy who had ticked Ben off. If he knew we were doing this, talking, going out together…what we just did—I don't know what he'd do, but it'd be bad. He's not…he's not stable. I know I've said this before, and I know you think you can handle him. I'm not trying to insult you, Jack. I'm sure you can take care of yourself. But if anything happened to you because of me…I'd—I couldn't deal with that."

"Isn't that my decision?" Jack asked.

"I can't put you at risk like that. You deserve better than this." Her voice went quiet, almost inaudible. "You deserve better than me."

Jack stopped massaging her and looked at her with incredulity. "I know I didn't just hear that. Miriam… god, I can't believe you'd say that. You are…how do

I even say this so you'll believe me? You're the most amazing person I've ever met. Let's start with that. You're beautiful, I mean...gorgeous. I—there aren't even words for how sexy you are. You're smart, and kind, and strong...Miriam, you've got it backward. It's *me* who doesn't deserve *you*."

"Jack, that's stupid." Miriam rolled to prop herself up on an elbow. She loosely pulled her thick brown hair into a braid.

"It's not stupid. It's the way I feel. Listen. Let's not talk about who does or doesn't deserve what. The important thing is that you can't scare me away with stories of Ben beating people up. It doesn't scare me. Maybe it should, but it doesn't. I like you, okay? I like you a lot, and I won't be scared off by anything. Unless you tell me that you aren't attracted to me, and you don't want to be with me, you can't get rid of me. Everything else is just an obstacle."

Jack played with her braid as he spoke, his eyes intense. "I'll be honest here. I want you to be finished with Ben for selfish reasons—I want you for myself. But it's more than that. You deserve better than him. I want you to be with me because I think I can take care of you, and treat you right. I *know* I can. I can treat you like you deserve. I can protect you. I *will* protect you, no matter what. Ben will kill me before he hurts you ever again. I swear it."

Miriam felt his confidence, and she didn't doubt him for a second. "I believe you," she said. "And I want to be with you, Jack. In every way possible. I want to be your girlfriend—I want to kiss you, and make love to you. I just can't…not yet."

Jack cupped her face, a smile on his face that was so…complicatedly wonderful…that she almost lost her determination. "That's okay," Jack said. "I can wait as long as you need."

That kind of answer from Jack did nothing to help her efforts to resist him. She fought her desire, watching his liquid blue eyes drinking her in, admiring her. She had to look away from him before she kissed him. She lay down, rolled away from him, reached behind her for his hand, and pulled him close to her. She knew it wasn't fair of her to ask him to lie this close to her, pressed up against her, but she wanted it, wanted the comfort of his presence, even if she couldn't have him the way she truly wanted. His arm slipped over her waist, his hand on her stomach, his breath soft on her hair. She lay awake for a long time, trying not to imagine what it would be like to be loved, actually *loved*.

Jack's breathing evened out to a soft snore, and he cradled up against her in his sleep, holding her tightly, gently, protecting her.

It might feel something like this.

CHAPTER 11

Carson

The present

CARSON SAT AT HIS DESK, FLIPPING THROUGH FILES, NOT reading so much as staring, letting his mind wander, trying to connect the dots. The problem was, there weren't too many dots. An apartment, a job, an ex with a temper and a penchant for beating up girls. But that didn't necessarily make Miriam the primary person of interest in Wade's death The most *likely* candidate, perhaps, but not the only one.

He scanned her file again, looking at the names and dates and phone numbers he'd seen a thousand times already, waiting for that one detail to jump out at him.

Rachel Korolivycz, 4555 Gardenia Avenue, Royal Oak, 248-555-6545. Often seen at Woody's Diner. Another girlfriend, perhaps?

Definitely worth chatting with her.

"Yeah, Ben is—I mean...*was* my boyfriend," Rachel said, eyes red from crying. She'd obviously heard about Ben's death. "And yeah, I knew he was sleeping with—what was her name? Mary? Miri? Mara? Whatever the hell it was. That other girl." Rachel sat at the bar at Woody's, a sweating bottle of Michelob Lite in her hand.

"So you knew that, and it didn't bother you?" Carson tried to keep the disgust out of his voice, not entirely successfully.

Rachel shrugged. "She was just a booty call. Someone to take care of his urges when I'm working. She was nothing."

Carson shook his head, not quite believing what he was hearing. "Wait, so you *knew* your boyfriend had another girlfriend, and you didn't care?"

Rachel shot him a petulant look. "She wasn't his girlfriend. *I* was. He was *fucking* her, not dating her. There *is* a difference."

"So there was no jealousy at all?" Carson was pressing the point, trying to elicit a response out of Rachel.

"Not from me. He didn't care about her. She was just pussy for him. He *loved* me. He told me that all the time."

Carson's face crinkled in disgust, at both Rachel's language and her ideas. "So you have no idea who would want to kill Ben?"

Rachel looked at Carson in surprise. "I kind of thought it was an accident, or something? You mean someone…murdered him?"

"We have our suspicions," Carson said.

"But—" Rachel began, but fell silent. "I bet it was Miriam. She was pissed off when she found out about me. Stupid bitch."

Carson felt only contempt for Rachel, but he forced himself to remain blank-faced and professional. "So, did you know that Ben put Miriam in the hospital? He beat her nearly to death."

To her credit, Rachel cringed a little. "No, I didn't know that. I mean, I know Ben has a temper, but he's never hit me. He's gotten angry, and maybe screamed at me a few times, but…god, that's terrible." She seemed genuinely shocked.

As he drove back to the office, Carson had the feeling he'd just followed up on a lead that went nowhere. As much as he personally disliked Rachel, he didn't get the sense that she had had anything to do with Ben's death.

Carson sat at his desk late into the evening, facts and theories doing their endless tumble in his head.

Wade's death could still be the result of jealousy on Miriam's part. Maybe she found out that Ben had another girlfriend. That, combined with his penchant for abusing her, might equal a breakdown bad enough that she would kill him. But crimes of jealousy usually took the form of gunshots or stab wounds or poison, not murder by arson. A woman would have had to be pretty damn pissed off, not mention clever, to douse a man like Ben with fire propellant and torch him. Besides, if Miriam had poured accelerant on him, there would be other evidence at the crime scene, but there wasn't a thing to go on.

None of this made any sense.

The next day Carson got a break that came in the form of an abandoned vehicle report. A motorcycle licensed to Jack Byrne was found abandoned on the side of Eleven Mile Road near Crooks, scratched and dented as if it had been in a crash. A canvass of the houses in the immediate area produced one witness, Betsy Willis, a seventy-four-year-old widow living alone in the second-floor apartment across the street from where the motorcycle was found.

"Oh, my, that was quite a show!" Betsy exclaimed with unabashed excitement. "I was watching my shows—this was quite late, you know. I can't sleep much these days. And anyways, I saw this…oh, how would you describe it…it was like a *glow,* like something was on fire outside. So I went to look and see what it was, because if it was a fire I would have to find Mister Wiggles, my cat. He's old, too, you know, and he doesn't move around so good anymore." Pausing for breath, she continued, "Well, I'm sure you don't want to know about Mister Wiggles. I went to the window, this one right here, and would you believe what I saw? It was a *girl,* Detective. I swear I'm telling you the truth. I may be old, but I know what I saw. It was a girl, and she was on fire. Or no, that came later. When I first saw her, she was just…glowing. Her skin, I mean. And, my goodness, it was so bright, it lit up the whole street. It was raining something fierce that night, and I was worried about her. But she wasn't walking on the sidewalk, she was just strolling down the middle of the road, and cars were going around her, honking their horns and such.

"Of course, no one stopped to see if the poor girl was all right, and you know I would have gone out there, but at my age, I would have caught pneumonia, wouldn't you know? That's just my luck. Well, as I was watching, a motorcycle comes zipping down the street and almost hits her, but he swerved at the last second, and that wasn't the smartest thing to do, what with the pouring rain. His back tire went out from under him, and he lost control, and I was sure he was going to die, and I think he would have, if it wasn't for that girl.

"Now, this is where things get exciting, Detective, and I'm sure you won't believe me, but I saw what I saw, and it's all God's truth, so help me. She must have known the boy on the motorcycle, because she ran up to him and took him in her arms, and I could see her shaking her head. I think she loved that boy, that's my feeling, but you wouldn't be interested in that. He was hurt badly, and I wouldn't have believed what happened next if I hadn't seen it with my own eyes. She bent over him, and the glowing of her skin got brighter, so bright I had to look away, like…oh, like she had the sun inside her, as odd as that sounds. And wouldn't you know, that strange glow moved from her into *him* and spread out, and I think it must have healed him. And then a fancy red sports car comes squealing to a stop and this big guy with dark hair gets out and starts yelling.

"Oh, it made me so angry to watch how he treated that poor girl. My Frank, God rest his soul, would have gone out there and given that boy a piece of his mind, I'll tell you, but Frank has been gone these past ten years. Well. He grabbed that girl by the arm and yanked her away so that boy who was hurt hit his head on the street, and the girl, oh, she didn't like that one bit, I'll tell you. She was acting like she'd had just about enough of that guy with the fancy car, that's what it looked like to me, at any rate. She shoved him away, and they were arguing. She must have said something that made the boy with the dark hair upset, because he started after her like he was going to hit her, and then, if you'll believe it, the girl *burst into flames*. I swear, Detective, I swear on my very soul. She just went poof, and her whole body was on fire. But she wasn't burning, like someone had put a match to her, it was like…oh, goodness, like the fire was *part* of her, if that makes any sense.

"Well, that seemed to scare the angry one, because he got into his car and drove away. The other boy, the one who crashed his motorcycle, he was just fine, which shouldn't have been possible, because I've seen wrecks like that before, and people die from injuries like he must've had. Well, he and the girl were standing together in the rain and they kissed, and oh *my*, was *that* ever romantic.

"This is the weirdest part, though, because then the fire that was coming from the girl got really bright and then they both just *vanished,* just like that handsome magician, what's his name from the book… David Copperfield. Only, they were really gone. It was no trick, I swear. I watched out the window for a long time, but nothing else happened. They were just gone, and that motorcycle stayed there by the side of the road for a while until someone came and took it away."

Carson felt exhausted just listening to the old woman talk, because she never seemed to pause to breathe. But her story, however unbelievable it may have sounded, struck Carson as making a very strange kind of sense.

Another piece of the puzzle rattled around in his brain, and something told him the pieces were going to fall into place before long. He was so close; he just needed a few more facts, a few more witnesses. And, of course, he had to find Miriam and get her side of the story.

CHAPTER 12

Miriam

Five days earlier

MIRIAM TUGGED AT THE HEM OF HER DRESS, WISHING it were a little longer. She wasn't used to wearing dresses, especially not ones this...skimpy. She was most comfortable wearing her waitress uniform—a pair of black jeans and a bar T-shirt.

"Stop fidgeting, Miriam. You look amazing," Jack whispered in her ear.

"I look like a skank," she whispered back. The dress barely came to mid-thigh, and the filmy coral-colored material was cut low between her breasts, showing a strip of skin nearly to her navel, and was cut the same in the back. She had bought it for the wedding because Jack had really liked it. Modeling it for him in the dressing room and in her apartment was one thing. His hungry, admiring gaze had made her feel sexy and beautiful, and he'd spent half the drive to the church telling her how amazing she looked. But that hadn't prepared her for the looks she'd gotten from Jack's family when they'd walked in to take their seats on the hard wooden pews of the church.

"You do not look like a skank," Jack said, a little too loudly. "My cousin Shannon, now, *she* looks likes a skank, but then, she is one."

Miriam slapped his arm, shocked that he'd talk about his own cousin like that. She tried to spot who he was talking about, and he nodded behind them, at a short, voluptuous girl with elaborately coiffured black hair. She was wearing a red dress even shorter than Miriam's, her large, pale breasts pushed up to nearly overflowing. Miriam's eyes widened a little, and Jack sputtered, trying to contain his laughter.

"She's a skank, Miriam. She's my cousin, and I love her, but that guy she's dragging with her is the third boyfriend she's had in the last two months. She goes through men faster than outfits." Miriam was giving him a disapproving glare, so he lifted his hands in a defensive gesture. "I tell her she's a skank to her face and she calls me a fancy-nancy bastard, and we laugh. It's how we are."

"You insult each other?"

"Well, yeah. We tease each other. It's how we show love in our family." Jack shrugged. "I guess it's weird, now that I explain it out loud, but it's just the way we are. No one means any harm by it, and we all know it."

"I don't get it. Will they tease me?" They were whispering now, because the priest was rising from his seat and approaching the lectern. The organist played the "Wedding March," and everyone stood to watch Jack's younger sister Mary stride with slow, measured steps down the aisle.

Jack answered without taking his eyes off his sister. "Not right away, no. But the more time you spend with us, yeah, someone will probably tease you about something, just to see how you take it. It'll probably be either Gramps or my cousin Joe. Just remember they don't mean nothin' by it, and they expect you to rib 'em back. The better you can tease and be teased in our family, the better you fit in."

Mary was a beautiful girl, resplendent in a simple but stunning A-line dress and long veil covering her shimmering auburn hair. She took her place beside her fiancé, clasped his hands in hers, and fixed her eyes on him. Miriam, only a few rows back, could see the bride swallowing, fighting back tears already. Miriam wondered what it would be like to stand there like that, in a white dress, facing the man she loved, promising to stay with him forever. She just couldn't picture it. She stole a glance at Jack, who was watching his soon-to-be brother-in-law with an odd expression on his face. Jack turned to look at Miriam at the same moment, and their eyes met; Miriam couldn't help picturing Jack in a tuxedo, watching her walk down the aisle to him—

Miriam clamped down on that image with a ruthless ferocity.

He'd showed up unannounced at her door the previous day and had taken her to breakfast, where he informed her that his sister was getting married the next day, and he wanted Miriam to come with him as his date. She objected, saying that she didn't really have any wedding-appropriate clothes, and Jack had just shot her that knowing smirk of his that both irritated her and made her heart beat like a drum.

Ben had been mysteriously absent, and while Miriam knew things weren't over between them, she was acting on hope that she could attend this wedding with Jack and not have any drama ruin it. It was a vain hope, probably, but she clung to it tenaciously.

"I thought we could go shopping," he'd said. "I don't really have a suit, either, so we could make a day of it."

He wanted to take her shopping? What guy voluntarily did that? Of course she'd agreed, and then Jack had taken her to the Somerset shopping mall, following her into a dozen stores and watching her try on a thousand dresses, telling her he liked them all. Eventually she'd tried a dress on at Forever 21, and when she'd come out to show him, his jaw had loosened, and he'd approached her with adventurous hands.

"Get this one," he'd whispered in her ear, kissing the bare skin of her shoulder. She'd chosen that one, just because of his reaction. Then, just because guys could be so irritating, he'd browsed through the racks at the first men's store they'd entered, tried on one suit, and bought it. Of course, it fit perfectly, making him look like a model, with his messy hair and liquid blue eyes.

Now that they were actually at the wedding, she was wishing she'd worn a dress that wasn't quite so... revealing. She loved Jack's reaction to it, but she also felt the eyes of other men on her, and that was uncomfortable. A grab here and there by drunk customers at the bar was one thing, but to draw the attention of every guy within a twenty-foot radius was something different, especially when they were all Jack's family.

Jack seemed to sense her discomfort, for he told her, halfway through the long, unfamiliar Catholic service, "It's not just the dress that's making everyone look, Miriam. It's *you*. You're absolutely stunning. I wouldn't be surprised if a few of my cousins hit on you." He seemed to have an endless supply of cousins. "Don't worry, I'll fight 'em off."

"No! No fighting, Jack." Apart from everything else, she was worried that her magic—or whatever it was—would erupt if there was a fight.

He laughed and rolled his eyes. "Not *literally* fight them. Just keep them from stealing you. That thing with Jimmy, that was…an old argument a long time in the making." He didn't seem to want to tell her about it, and she didn't pry, although she was curious, having gleaned the basics from the argument itself.

The service finally ended, and Miriam gladly followed Jack out into the sunlight, stretching her legs after the long ceremony. She offered her congratulations to the bride and groom, and, holding Jack's arm, she shook hands with an endless bevy of cousins and aunts and uncles, most of who referred to him as "Jackie."

When they were in his car following the caravan to the reception, he remarked, "God, I hate being called Jackie. They all do it just because they know it drives me nuts."

"So I shouldn't call you Jackie, then?" Miriam teased.

"I'd rather you not, but if you really want to…."

She pretended to consider. "Hmmm. I think I like it, though. Jackie. It's cute." She pinched his cheek, and he batted her hand away.

"Yeah, you'll fit in, no problem." He laughed. "God, I never should've said anything."

The reception was enormous. There were at least five hundred people between the two families, all of them Irish, and they all had drinks in their hands, dancing and drinking straight through from cocktail hour to the dinner itself. Jack escorted her to their table near the wedding party, where they were seated with his brothers Jimmy and William, and the groom's brother and sister. He sat her down and vanished, reappearing with drinks in a few minutes.

He leaned in and whispered, "How do you want me to introduce you? My friend? Just Miriam?" His blue gaze was unnervingly intent.

She shook her head, her eyes not wavering from his. "I'm your girlfriend, Jack. Introduce me as that." If only he knew how much trust it took for her to say that.

He grinned, giddy as a schoolboy. "I was hoping you'd say that, but I didn't want to assume." He made the rounds of introductions, not quite but almost emphasizing the words "this is my girlfriend." He seemed proud of the fact that Miriam was with him, and that in itself was disconcerting. Ben had never taken her anywhere important except once, to a Marine Corps unit-reunion dinner, and he had seemed ashamed of her, never introducing her, barely touching her, always wandering away and flirting with other women—enough to piss everyone off and embarrass Miriam to tears.

She pushed away those thoughts, telling herself to stop comparing the two men. Jack was nothing like Ben, not in any way. She had broken up with Ben for good, and things were going to change. She drank freely, keeping up with Jack, who seemed to unwind a bit, getting a little tipsy. She felt her wariness increasing as the night progressed and Jack became looser with the drink. She was waiting for the shift, waiting for Jack to cross the line from pleasantly drunk to obliterated and mean, waiting for him to do or say something to hurt or embarrass her.

But he didn't. He stayed at her side, holding her hand all the while, introducing her proudly to his family and including her in all the conversations. He dragged her onto the dance floor, acting ridiculous and dancing with such abandon, if not skill, that she couldn't help but laugh and join him, letting her own buzz take over.

Halfway through the first slow dance song, Jack's grandfather tapped him on the shoulder. "Can I steal a dance with your lovely date, Jackie-boy?" Miriam took Séan's huge, callused, wrinkled hand in hers and allowed herself to be led away from Jack. "So, Miss Miriam, did you take my advice, then?"

"Yes, Mr. Byrne, I did, actually. I'm here as Jack's girlfriend this time, not just as a friend."

"Och, no one was fooled by that line, girlie. You may have been foolin' yourself, but not us. And call me Gramps, please. I'm old-fashioned that way, and I like you."

"I like you, too...Gramps." It felt odd but not uncomfortable to call this kind old man Gramps, having never known her own grandparents.

"Did Jackie tell you about my second sight?" Gramps asked.

"He did, yes. He didn't explain it much, though. What is it?"

Gramps guffawed and shook his head. "Oh, he was being coy, he was. He knows damned well what is. He's got it himself—he just won't believe it, damned stubborn boy. Second sight is like prophecy. Gettin' a glimpse of the future, you could say. Comes from havin' the Blood of the Niall." He looked down at Miriam, and his gaze was penetrating and serious. "I look at you, dear, and I see a girl who ain't what she seems. You don't know yourself, darlin', and that'll get you into trouble. You can't shy away from what you are, Miriam. I ain't sayin' I know, but it's plain as day that you're something' special, and that's God's own truth."

Miriam was strangely shaken by his words. They danced through the end of the song, and she stood still when it ended, still holding his hand. "I'm just me, Gramps," she whispered.

"No, child. You're more." He smiled and kissed her cheek, his whiskers scratching her face, whiskey on his breath. He handed her back to Jack, and took a seat.

"What'd Gramps say this time?" Jack wanted to know.

Miriam shook her head, not sure how to respond. "He…nothing. The truth."

"Which, then?" Sometimes, when his accent showed through, he sounded just like his grandfather.

"Don't worry about it, Jack. He just told me a bit about second sight."

A moment later Miriam felt something cold strike her chest, a sense of dread creeping through her. Suddenly, Jack's face was hard and angry. She turned around to see Ben in his full dress uniform standing less than a few feet away.

"I wasn't invited?" Ben's voice was low and heavy with threat. "That's insulting. Miriam is *my* girlfriend, after all."

Miriam wanted to take a step back, away from his jealousy-maddened eyes. Instead, she stepped forward, putting as much sharpened steel into her voice as she could muster. "What are you doing here, Ben? Don't you remember what I told you, last time I saw you?"

Ben flashed a humorless, arrogant grin. "You think you can sneak around behind my back without me finding out? You're not so hard to follow, you know. And as for your threat? You won't do anything.

Not here. There's nothing you hate so much as making a scene. And you wouldn't want to be *embarrassed* in front of all these people, would you?" He gestured to the crowd of people around them, some watching the unfolding drama, others remaining oblivious.

"Come on, Ben, not here, man. Not at my sister's wedding," Jack said, his voice calm but hard. "Trust me, pal, this isn't the wedding you want to crash." Jack stepped in front of Miriam, shielding her.

She was aware of Gramps and Jimmy and William all floating up to stand by Jack.

Ben didn't seem fazed. "You think I'm afraid of you? A bunch of drunk micks?" There were growls and grumbles and curses at the slur.

"You should be, boy-o," came Gramps' voice. "You're outnumbered by quite a fair margin." Gramps stepped forward to stand nose to nose with Ben. Miriam realized that even though Séan Byrne was stooped with age, he was still a large man, and that he had once cut a powerful figure.

"I know you, son," Gramps said, "I know what you done to this girl. And boy, if you know what's good for you, you'll get the fuck out of here before I knock your teeth straight down your goddamn bloody throat, y'fucking pig." Gramps' accent thickened as he spoke, and he seemed to straighten up, sagging muscles gaining firmness, leathery fists turning to chunks of granite.

Ben stared into Gramp's eyes, hate seething with every breath. "I don't hit old men," Ben said, "or I'd kill you for that."

Gramps huffed, mumbled a curse that Miriam didn't quite catch, and then rocketed a one-two punch combination that sent Ben to the ground, his fists moving faster than Miriam would have thought anyone, especially an old man, could be capable of. "Don't let that stop you, punk," he said, turning away. "Get 'im, boys."

Jack, Jimmy, and William darted forward, grabbed Ben by the arms and legs, and carried him out of the banquet hall. Ben was screaming and thrashing, and when the brothers launched him headfirst to the ground, he rolled away and scrambled to his feet, nose bleeding, and rushed the three Byrnes. William and Jimmy stepped aside and let Jack take the rush. Miriam watched as Jack ducked to the side, slapping Ben's initial punch away and sending a thundering right into Ben's face, spinning him around. Ben spat blood and scrambled backward, realizing Jack wouldn't be an easy target. Miriam recognized the look in Ben's eyes, and it terrified her. She'd seen him do horrible things when he was like this, and she wanted Jack to be no part of it.

"Gramps, please," she pleaded, "don't let them do this. Call the police."

The old man, draining a tumbler of whiskey, waved a hand in dismissal. "Oh, the boy'll be fine, girlie. The boys won't damage him too much." She realized he thought she was worried about Ben.

"No, you don't understand. I'm worried about *them*," she said as she gestured to his grandsons.

Gramps looked at her with incredulity. "Darlin', he ain't *that* scary. He's a big'un, sure, but you don't know my boys. They'll handle him just fine—don't you worry none."

Gramps wasn't going to do anything but watch, and if it were anyone besides Ben, he'd be right.

She ran into the melee, Gramps and Jack's mom calling after her. She pushed between Jimmy and William, who grabbed for her, too late. Jack was bouncing on the balls of his feet, fists up, body turned sideways. His nose was bleeding now, and one eye was purpling; Ben wasn't faring much better.

Just as Miriam reached Jack and caught at his sleeve, Jimmy wrapped his burly arms around her midsection and pulled her away, saying, "You're gonna get hit, you daft girl. Jackie can take him." Miriam tried to thrash free, but Jimmy held her tight.

Ben was biding his time, waiting for the right moment; she'd watched him bounce enough drunks out of the bar that she knew his style. He didn't just toss them out, he followed them into the parking lot and tore them apart. He'd stand his ground, let them hit him a few times, let them think they were winning, and then he'd explode in a fury of military-trained technique. Ben wasn't content to just break a nose or black an eye—he had a taste for snapping bones, catching a punch in one hand and using the heel of his palm to crush his victim's elbow.

She watched, helpless, unwilling to let her magic free in this moment, knowing she might accidentally hurt Jimmy or someone else, not to mention the spectacle of it all. But she knew she had no control over it, and she felt the fires burning, seeking release. She had to fight just to keep it in, keep it down.

Then, between one breath and the next, her fears came true. Jack threw a quick right jab and Ben blocked it, caught it, and flashed his opposite palm into Jack's elbow like a lightning strike. Miriam heard the bone snap, and Jack bellowed in pain. She screamed, twisting and thrashing against Jimmy with renewed desperation.

"Help him!" she shrieked.

Jimmy let her go and rushed in. A slow smile spread across Ben's face. He spat a gobbet of blood and kicked Jack aside, and turned to deal with Jimmy. William waited until Ben was tangled up with Jimmy, and then he joined the fray. William was a stocky man with a barrel chest and buzzed hair the same color as Jack's. He wrapped a thick arm around Ben's neck and squeezed, holding the larger Ben nearly aloft, bending backward to get the proper leverage. Jimmy backed away and slugged Ben repeatedly in the stomach. Miriam was at Jack's side, but he brushed her off until he realized who it was, and then he grabbed her around the waist and pulled her away, trying to get her inside. Other family members were crowded around the door at this point, watching. She heard someone in the doorway gasp, and she whirled to see that Ben had thrown William over his shoulder and was lighting into Jimmy with a wicked barrage of hammering blows to the kidneys and liver. William was on his back, moaning, struggling to his feet. Jack, cradling his arm, growled, and turned to rejoin the fight.

Miriam felt desperation run through her. These people had welcomed her as family, treated her kindly and with affection. She couldn't just stand by and watch as Ben tore them apart. Not over her. Miriam put her hands around Jack's broken elbow and channeled a tiny thread of the magic, felt it respond to her call and rush into Jack, healing him instantly. He looked at her, pain fading from his eyes, to be replaced by fear for her. He could tell what she was planning.

"Jack," she whispered. "I…"

She felt something inside her tear open. She had to stop this, had to keep anyone else from getting hurt because of her.

Before Jack could stop her, she kicked off her heels and darted in between Ben and Jimmy, pushing Ben away with her hands on his chest, meeting his crazed eyes with her own. "Stop, Ben," she said, "please stop. Leave them alone. I'll go with you. Just stop."

Ben backed off, and Jimmy staggered away, bleeding from his nose and cuts to his forehead and cheekbones. He was battered but enraged. He brushed the blood from his eyes and charged back at Ben, but Miriam held out a palm to stop him.

"No, Jimmy, it's okay. I'll go."

Jimmy looked down at her, shaking his head. "No, you can't—"

Jack was reaching for Miriam. "What are you doing? Miriam, talk to me! You can't! Don't do this!"

She only shook her head, turned away. If she looked at Jack, her resolve would weaken. These people would gang up on Ben if she asked them to, and they'd win, eventually, but the cost...too many people would get hurt. Jack's arm had been broken, Jimmy was gushing blood from a dozen places and clutching his ribs, and William was still gasping for breath and rubbing his neck where Ben had wrenched it nearly to breaking.

"Stop, all of you," Miriam pleaded, her voice catching. "I'm so sorry...I caused this. I shouldn't have come here, I shouldn't have—" Miriam saw Mary, the bride, standing next to Jack, the hem of her beautiful dress dragging through the dirt of the parking lot. "Mary, I'm so sorry I ruined your wedding...."

Miriam's voice broke then, and she turned to Ben, pushing him to his car. "Go, Ben. Let's go."

She heard Jack behind her, pleading with her, but she heard Gramps' voice raised over his, "Let her go, son. It's her choice. Let her go." Jack seemed close to sobbing, and she heard Gramps say, "If she loves you, son, she'll find a way."

Oh, Jack.

Miriam slid into the leather seat, hearing Ben's ragged breathing beside her. "I'm glad you came to your senses, Miri," he said, wiping blood from his chin. She wasn't sure this was coming to her senses, but she didn't know what else to do.

Ben was silent all the way back to his apartment, and that suited Miriam just fine. She had nothing to say. She had gone with him to stop the violence, not to be with him. The thought of letting him touch her, after what she'd experienced with Jack…no way. Not again. She would die before she let Ben touch her again. She delved inside herself for the coiled heat of the magic, seeking its reassurance, feeling it brush against her, reaching for her.

She followed Ben into his apartment, sat down on the couch, and rubbed her aching, dirty feet. She had kicked off her heels and was now shoeless. She desperately wanted to change out of the dress, but she had no clothes here. Except…she glanced at Ben, leaning against a counter in the kitchen, an icepack against his cheek, staring at his phone, ignoring her now. She padded on silent feet into Ben's room, dug in the bottom drawer of the dresser, and found a pair of gray U of M sweat pants and a long T-shirt with a picture of a long-eared, sad-looking donkey on the front. Eeyore? Really? Miriam hated the thought of wearing *her* clothes, but anything was better than being on display for Ben.

When she came out, Ben glanced up and saw what she was wearing. "What the hell, Miriam? You can't just go around wearing other people's clothes. Besides, I liked you in that dress."

He was acting as if nothing had happened, as if everything was normal.

She stood in the entry to the kitchen, letting her disgust and hate for him show in her eyes, letting her anger boil just beneath the surface. "I don't care what you like, Ben. I'm not here for *you*. Nothing has changed—you need understand that." She wanted to let the fire burst through her skin, send it out to consume him, but she reined it in. "I'm not your girlfriend anymore. I'm nothing to you. No one. I *fucking hate* you, Ben. I only came with you because those people didn't deserve that."

Ben shifted forward, placing his hands on her arms, acting as if he cared. As if he had a single kind bone in his body. "But you came, and that's what counts." He leaned in as if to kiss her, and she jerked herself out of his grasp, clenched her fist, and swung it at him with all her strength. She felt her fist connect with his jaw, heard a resounding *crack,* and Ben flew backward against the wall. He stared at her in shock, then spat a tooth out into his palm, along with gob of blood and saliva.

"What the *fuck,* Miriam?" He probed the gap where his tooth had been with his tongue.

"You do *not* get to touch me. You don't lay a god-damn *finger* on me," Miriam said.

Her anger was roused, her adrenaline pump-ing. She didn't care anymore. He could do what he wanted, say what he wanted. She'd had an amazing man, and she'd walked away from him. Now she was fearless.

He threw the tooth away, ripped a strip of paper towel from a roll hanging under a cabinet, placed a piece of ice in it, and held it against his gum. "I'll let that one go, but if you *ever* do that to me again, I'll—"

"You'll what?" Miriam interrupted. "Beat me half to death? Oh, wait, you already did that. Break my ribs? Crack my cheekbones? Yep, you've done all that, too. What's left, Ben? Or should I even ask? Are you going to actually rape me this time? Bring Rachel over here and screw her in front of me? Or maybe you want a threesome? Is that it? Want us both at the same time?" She slammed her palms against his chest, knocking him backward with more force than she'd ever possessed. "Or maybe I should drop to my knees and suck you off like a good little girlfriend? But then, I wasn't ever your *girlfriend,* was I? I was just a…what was it Rachel called me? A side-fuck? A piece of ass on the side?"

"It wasn't like that," he mumbled. "Seriously, Miriam, what the hell has gotten into you?" Ben pushed past her and retreated to the living room.

"What's gotten into me? I'm finally past caring what you do or say, that's what." She followed him, feeling invincible.

She knew he'd snap eventually, but she didn't care. She'd lost Jack, and nothing else mattered.

"You need to calm down." Ben sat down and turned on the TV, trying to dismiss her. She grabbed the remote from him and hurled it at the flat-screen TV screen, the glass smashing and splintering.

"Don't tell me to calm down! You've treated me like shit for a *year,* and I let you! You hit me and insulted me, made me feel like shit, and what do I do? Do I leave you, like any sane person would? No! I stayed with you, because I was weak and pathetic, and because I even wondered if somehow, deep down maybe, past all the bullshit, that you cared about me even a *little* bit. But then I find out that you've had another girlfriend *the whole time.* And she *knew* about me?" Miriam was pacing in front of Ben, seething with rage. The fire inside was nearly uncontainable, sizzles of heat and fire popping from her pores, her hair flickering and wavering as if alive.

Ben was speechless at her outburst, staring with comical sadness at his ruined flat-screen. "You crazy bitch," he finally said, "look what you did to my TV! That thing cost me two thousand dollars!"

"I don't give two shits about your TV, Ben!" she screamed.

"God, Miriam, you've really lost it, haven't you?" He shoved her out of the way, and she could see his anger starting to rise. He'd actually thought he'd won her back, as if she would just come crawling back to him like a little puppy dog.

"Yes! I've finally lost it, Ben. You crashed Jack's sister's wedding. You hurt Jack, Jimmy, and William, and you probably would've hit Gramps if he hadn't hit you first."

"Gramps? What are they, your family now? And he hit me. I don't hit old men."

"Yes, they're like family to me. And Gramps is more of a man than you could ever hope to be."

"You're starting to piss me off, Miriam. I promised myself I was done hitting you, but you're making it hard to keep that promise." Ben turned away from her, righting the TV.

"You think I care if you hit me? I'm used to it. Go ahead. Nothing matters anymore. I walked away from the man I love to keep you from hurting him or his family." She hadn't meant to say that, but it had popped out, and she realized how deeply she meant it.

"The man *you love?*" Ben whirled back to her, fist raised. Miriam didn't flinch. "You've known him for what, two weeks? Three? What about me?"

Miriam laughed, a harsh cough of sarcasm. "You? You think I ever *loved* you? I was afraid of you, Ben. The only reason I ever stayed with you, the only reason I ever let you fuck me, was because I was *afraid* of you. Because I didn't think I was worth anything else. And then I met Jack, and he showed me how a *real* man loves."

That one hurt him; Miriam could see the rage steeping in him, coming to a boil. "You little slut. You cheating little whore!"

She chose her next words with care, wanting them to dig deep. "Making love with Jack was the *best* thing I've ever felt. He knows what I want and how to give it to me. He's a bigger, better man than you in *every…single…way.*" She hadn't really, technically, had sex with Jack yet, but Ben didn't need to know that. Besides, it was the quickest way to hurt him.

Primal fury filled Ben's eyes, and his fists clenched, lifted. Miriam tilted her head back, keeping her hands at her sides. Let him do it, then. She didn't care. She could use the fire inside to protect herself, but why bother? She'd brought what was coming on herself with her words, and she refused to use her magic to protect herself. Miriam almost laughed out loud, thinking how easily the word "magic" came to her now. She had *magic*. She was a creature of fire. She didn't know where it had come from, or why it hadn't protected her before, or how she had gotten it, and that was a set of questions that needed answering.

But not now.

She waited, expecting a blow that never came. Chest heaving with anger, Ben grabbed Miriam by the shoulders, his fingers digging into her arms. He wrenched open his door and threw her out, hard enough that she slammed against the far wall.

"Get out of here. Get out before I kill you." The rage in his eyes was murderous, but he seemed in more control of it than she'd ever seen him. She didn't question it, though. She turned and fled, hearing the door slam behind her.

Some instinct in Miriam's gut told her this wasn't over. Ben wouldn't let this go, not this easily. Not after the things she'd said.

The walk home was long, and by the time she reached her door, her bare feet were bleeding.

She let them bleed. She didn't care.

CHAPTER 13

Carson

The present

JACK BYRNE'S APARTMENT WAS EMPTY, AND THE MANAGER had no idea where he was or how long he'd been gone. She did have his parents' address, though, so Carson went there next. He knocked on the door, and an old man answered it.

"Can I help you?" he asked.

"Yes," Carson answered. "I'm Detective Hale. I'm looking for Jack Byrne. Is he here?" Carson flashed his badge.

"No, he's not here. What do you want with Jackie?"

"Can we come in, Mr. Byrne?"

"I'm Jackie's grandfather. And you can tell me what you want right here."

Carson stifled a sigh. *Ornery old people.* "We just have a few questions for you, Mr. Byrne. We're investigating the death of Benjamin Wade."

"Don't know him."

Carson pulled out a folded sheet of paper with Ben's Marine Corps photo on it, showing it to the old man.

"Oh, that one. Right bastard, he is. Well, come on in, then, and I'll tell you what I can, but it ain't much."

When they were sitting down in the living room, Carson asked, "Did Jack have any reason to dislike Mr. Wade that you know of?"

"Well, of course he did. He hated the way Ben treated Miriam, and wanted nothing more than an excuse to rip into the bastard. He got it, too, only it turned out to be a bit more than he could chew."

"So Jack hated Ben?" Carson tried an obvious, leading question.

"Well, sure, but he didn't do nothing to him. Jackie's a good boy. They tangled at the wedding, and poor Jackie didn't come out of it none too well, I'm sorry to say. That boy, Ben? He was a rough customer. Took on all three of my grandsons and dealt with 'em handy, too. I coulda taken the boy down back in my prime, I'll tell you that for free."

"At the wedding? When was this?"

"Oh, 'bout two weeks ago now, I'd say. It was my granddaughter Mary's wedding. Jack brought Miriam with him. She's a lovely girl, that Miriam. Oh, she and Jack make quite a pair, they do, dancin' together. She was nervous, poor Miriam was. She don't have much family, I don't think, so bein' around a ruckus bunch like the Byrnes at a wedding…I can see how it'd make her nervous. Jack kept her calm, though, and she even danced with me, and boy, if I was younger, I might give young Jackie a run for his money. That Miriam is a fine woman, a damn fine woman, I tell you.

"Well, partway through the dancin' Ben shows up in a fancy uniform, just walks in like he was invited and starts arguin' with Miriam. Well, that girl don't deserve the treatment that animal gives her, so I stepped in. I'm the patriarch of this family, and it's a duty I take seriously. Started talkin' lippy, and I told him what for. He says, 'I don't hit old men,' and o'course, that did me in. Gave him a good left and a right, and there ain't a man alive who can stay up when I've hit 'em. Back in my day, there wasn't a man in Ireland who could stand against me, and believe you me, boy-o, they tried. They came from miles around to try their luck against Séan Byrne, and, by god, I took 'em all on. I may be old, but I still got a right hook what'll make your granddad feel it. I hit that boy, one-two, and he went tumblin' arse over teakettle."

Carson was unable to hold back a smile. "Wait, *you* punched Ben?" That impressed him. Everything he was finding out about Benjamin Wade led Carson to believe that knocking him down was no easy feat.

"Well, sure! He'd shown up, uninvited, at my granddaughter's wedding, and was talking a bunch of shite, tryin' to scare Miriam into leavin' with him. So I showed him how to behave." Séan's face darkened. "Only, he proved to be a damn fine fighter, I'll give him that."

"So what happened?" Carson asked.

"Well, he was doin' a number on my boys. We'd have taken him, but Miriam, bless her heart, she wasn't havin' none of it. I suppose when Ben broke my Jackie's arm, she just couldn't take it anymore. Her poor sweet heart was breakin', I think, and she was still all confused by everything. She didn't know what she wanted. Well, no, that ain't true, neither. She knew, she just didn't believe herself worth it. She left with him. With Ben, I mean. She didn't want to, I could see that, and so could poor Jackie."

"What did Jack do?" Carson asked..

"Oh, he wanted to go after her, take her back, but I wouldn't let him. She needed to face Ben, she needed to make her own choice, or she wouldn't ever be free of him. If Jackie kept rescuing her, she'd always be a slave to what she was afraid of. Jackie, he's got too kind a heart for his own good, sometimes."

Séan cocked his head, thinking. "You said you were investigating Ben's death? How'd he die, then?"

Carson shook his head. "I can't divulge that at this time."

"But you suspect Jackie?"

"We're pursuing every angle, sir."

Séan huffed. "Don't bullshit me, son. You wouldn't be here if you didn't."

"We think he may have something do with it, yes. I probably shouldn't say this, but I will. Personally, I don't think Jack killed Ben himself. He would be an accomplice at most. Can you tell me where he'd be right now, Mr. Byrne? So I can ask him for his side of the story?"

Séan shook his head, grunting a negative. "I'd tell you if I knew. Jackie's a good boy, and if he did have anything to do with it, it was only to protect Miriam."

"Have you seen her since the wedding incident?" Carson asked.

"No, I'm afraid not. I keep hopin' Jackie will show up with Miriam, but it never happens. Jackie went to work the next day, but I ain't seen him since, neither. I'm worried for him, to be honest with you. That Ben is a dangerous sort. He had the look of a man who could do murder, I'll tell you that much. My sight tells me they're both still alive, and that you'll find 'em when you're meant to." Séan looked as if he hadn't meant to say that last part.

"Your sight? What do you mean, Mr. Byrne?"

Séan didn't answer right away. He peered at Carson, who was staring at him, as if seeing into his soul, probing him, weighing him.

"I like you, lad," Séan said at length. "I get a good sense from you. I'll tell you somethin' I shouldn't, but you gotta listen and not interrupt. I'm old Irish, Detective. Grew up in County Cork, and my own mum, God rest her, had the Blood of the Niall, the second sight. Don't no one know what that is no more, so I'll tell you. It's visions of the future. But it's more than that. My grandson Jackie has it too, though he ain't accepted it yet. You're all tangled up together in somethin', and that is just the start of it. You ain't gonna figure this out till you accept certain things, though I can't see what. You're closin' your mind, and that's gonna slow you down and keep you blinded to the truth."

Carson wasn't sure what to say to this. No one he'd spoken to had seen Jack or Miriam in a few days, and he was sure he was going to find their bodies somewhere. The old man had had a vision of some kind, and that was supposed to mean something to him? This was a murder investigation, not a damned séance. He didn't say this to the old man, though.

What he ended up saying was, "If you hear from either of them, have them call me right away, please." He handed Séan his card and left.

He was starting to exhaust his leads. At this point, he would either find Jack and Miriam, or he'd find their remains. Carson was starting to worry that it'd be the latter. He was forming a picture of Miriam, and, despite his best efforts to keep a professional distance from her, he found himself liking her. He wanted her to be innocent. She had obviously made an impression on Jack's grandfather, and he seemed like a hard man to impress.

Besides, any eighty-year-old man who was capable of knocking down a thirty-year-old ex-Marine was okay in Carson's book.

CHAPTER 14

Miriam

Four days earlier

MIRIAM CALLED LARRY AND TOLD HIM SHE NEEDED SOME time off. He didn't like it, and liked even less that she wouldn't explain why, but he knew her well enough to grant it. She'd worked for him for a long time and had never taken a single day off, so to ask for two full weeks off meant something serious was going on.

"Hey, if there's anything I can do…." Larry said before hanging up.

"Thanks, Larry, I'll be fine. I just…need to figure some things out."

"Okay, if you say so. But seriously, Miriam, call me if you need anything. You know I'm here for you."

Miriam knew he meant well, but he wouldn't be able to handle the trouble she was in. He wouldn't know where to start. Neither did she, if she was honest. A million questions were banging around in her head like moths trapped in a lampshade, and she had answers to none of them.

Who was she? If she had all this magic inside her, where did it come from? This wasn't a book or a movie. Magic wasn't real. But the things she'd seen herself do were undeniable. What about her parents? Had her magic come from them? They'd never seemed anything but totally ordinary to her. Had they adopted her and never told her? But no, she'd seen her birth certificate from the hospital in Beirut with her parents' signatures on it. She'd seen pictures of herself as an infant in her father's arms—she looked just like him, got her dark brown eyes from him, her thin nose and full lips from him. If not from her parents, then where was this fire inside coming from?

She was going in circles, asking questions that had no answers. She had to leave. She couldn't stay in her dinky little apartment any longer. Besides, Ben would show up eventually. Or Jack would. And if Jack showed up, she'd go back to him, and then it would start all over again. Ben would do something else, hurt Jack again, or his family. He'd let her go for the time being, but she knew Ben wasn't done with her yet.

She stuffed some clothes in her tattered Jansport backpack, got in her car, and drove, not really going anywhere in particular, just driving to get away. She needed space from everything, from men, from her own fears and desires, from magic. She was hoping, somewhere deep inside, that she'd find answers to her questions somehow. Maybe the magic would provide answers on its own.

Maybe Jack would find her in spite of herself. She had her cell phone, and she'd heard it buzz a number of times, but she'd refused to look at it. There would be a dozen messages from Jack, all of them probably pleading with her to pick up, to talk to him, to tell him she was okay. She didn't want him to worry, but she couldn't talk to him, couldn't have any contact with him. The only way to protect him was to keep away from him.

Maybe if she stayed away, he'd forget about her. Find a girl to love who didn't come with so much baggage. The thought of him with another girl sent pangs of pain knifing through her heart, but she knew what he deserved. He deserved better than she could give him. She was damaged goods, and he was…Jack was perfect.

She felt tears dripping from her chin, but she didn't care. She wiped them away, let herself cry, allowing herself to grieve for what she could have had, what she had experienced, if only for a moment. But all that was gone now.

She was traveling north, away from the city on I-75, speeding faster than her car could really handle, but she didn't care. She passed Great Lakes Crossing without noticing, her thoughts spinning in circles, going from questions about the fire and magic in her blood, to thoughts of Ben and the man he had been before he went to Afghanistan, to Jack and how genuine he was.

So consumed was she in her own thoughts that she never even glanced in her rearview mirror. If she had, she might have noticed the red Maserati two cars back, and she might have noticed that it had been following her since she left her apartment.

Hunger gnawed at her stomach and thirst scratched at her throat, but she didn't stop. If she stopped driving, she might never start again. She might just curl up in the back seat and cry until she slept, and then she would sleep forever. She kept driving, paying no attention to mile markers or exits or landmarks. At some point she passed the Birch Run Outlets, and she realized she had driven a lot farther than she'd realized. It didn't matter. She didn't care where she was or where she was going, as long as it was away from Ben, away from the temptation of Jack, away from everything.

Miriam kept driving, mile after mile humming under her tires. She would need to stop, as the gas gauge showed she was perilously close to empty. She had no idea where she was; she hadn't been paying attention to anything but the road in front of her, driving on autopilot, lost in her whirling thoughts. The exits were few and far between in this area, and the trees were beginning to change from deciduous to conifer, oaks and birches and elms becoming pine and spruce and fir. How far had she gone?

She started watching the road signs, waiting for one that indicated a gas station. After another twenty minutes, she passed a blue sign advertising a Tubby's and a Sunoco, both just three miles ahead. She prayed she would make it that far; the gas gauge was faulty and often indicated more gas than was actually in the tank, something she'd learned the hard way more than once.

Miriam pulled off the expressway and turned left, cursing under her breath as the engine sputtered after less than a mile. It coughed, but caught again and kept going, and Miriam decided to throw caution out the window and gun it, hoping to get as far as possible before it died on her. She really didn't want to have to walk to a gas station and back, alone, way out here in the boonies. She glanced around her, real- izing how far out in the middle of exactly nowhere she was. Farmland spread out in every direction, row after row as far as she could see, the sprawling farms lined by distant walls of trees and dirt roads, dotted with farmhouses and barns. The road she was on lay in a perfectly straight line right out to the horizon, reminding her how far three miles actually was. The Volvo coughed again, guttered and sputtered, and then went silent. She coasted over to the shoulder and turned the ignition one more time, despite knowing it wouldn't start. The engine turned over.

Awesome. Now all she needed was some gas.

She got out, locked the door, and opened the trunk to get the red gas can—she'd run out of gas enough times that she always kept one in her trunk for emergencies like this. With a sigh and a curse, Miriam set off down the road, grateful that at least the weather was warm and dry.

Jack consumed her thoughts, her stomach a heavy pit of sadness. He had been so kind to her, so understanding. He didn't deserve this kind of jerking around. She had to at least tell him it was over, in so many words. She pulled her phone out of her purse, not surprised to see thirteen text messages, ten missed calls, and three voicemails, all from Jack.

She scrolled through the texts first. They started out simple enough: *Miriam plz call me…at least lemme know you're ok…I'm getting worried now. just send me a text so i know youre not hurt or anything….* Then the messages became more desperate: *im going crazy, Miriam!*

call me before i flip out, plz!...i swear to god if he hurts you i'll fucking kill him.... Miriam's heart contracted, filling her with guilt. He was worried sick. She desperately wanted to talk to him, to reassure him that she was okay. She dialed his number, something she'd never actually done before. He'd always just...shown up, been there, seeking her out. Her phone beeped and went silent, telling her she was outside signal range. She'd have to wait to talk to him.

She heard a car approaching from behind, and she moved farther over to the side of the shoulder, looking up from her phone to realize the sun was setting. She turned to watch the car drive by and felt her stomach clench. It was Ben, pulling up next to her, rolling down his window, pacing her. How had he found her? He must've followed her, she realized. She turned away from him and kept walking.

"What are you doing out here, Miriam?" He sounded sober and calm. Miriam ignored him. "Don't ignore me, baby, please. Just get in the car. I'll take you home."

"I'm not your baby."

"Okay, fine, *Miriam*, please let me take you home. Come on."

"I don't want to go home. I'm fine." She refused to look at him. He was looking at her with puppy-dog eyes, pleading silently.

"Look at me, Miriam. Just stop for a second. It's sunset—you'll be walking for hours. Anything could happen out here."

"I've walked home alone in the dark plenty of times. I can take care of myself. I'm a freak, remember?"

"I'm sorry I called you a freak. I've been an asshole. I know I have. I'm sorry, okay? I apologize. I can change, I promise. I'll stop drinking, and I'll treat you right. Just let me take you home."

"You've said all this before, Ben. Nothing has ever changed, and it never will." She hiked her backpack higher on her shoulders, tightened her grip on the gas can. "Go *away*, Ben."

"Miriam, this is stupid!" Ben said, frustration bleeding into his voice. "Come on. Just get in. I'll take you right home. I promise."

"Yeah, right. Funny how 'right home' always means going to your apartment so you can grope me. No, thanks."

Ben hissed, gunned the car, and pulled it over in front of her. He got out to stand in front of her, not quite touching her. "You're being fucking stupid, Miriam. Come on. Let's go. *Now*."

She stared at his chest, refusing to meet his eyes. "Get out of my way, Ben. You're wasting your time." She pushed him out of the way as she said this. Or tried to, though he didn't move.

"No. This is idiotic." He grabbed her arm.

Miriam wrenched her arm free and slapped him, hard. *"Don't* touch me."

"Listen, please! No, don't walk away. Just listen. Do you remember how we met?" Ben was walking beside her, his car still running, door open, on the side of the road. "You had just started at the Taproom. You were living in your car, and you thought no one knew. You didn't say one word the entire first day, just followed Beth around on your shadow shift, watching. You looked scared of everything. Your hair was braided down to your waist, and you had a *ton* of eye shadow on, making your eyes look big and even darker than they are. God, I was crushing on you from that first day. There was something mysterious about you. There always has been, actually, and that's part of what makes you so attractive, aside from your looks. There's this sense of…I don't know…mystique, something secretive about you. You refused to even look at me that first day. You'd come up to the service bar and you'd just stare at the liquor bottles, or out at the customers. You wouldn't look at me, and it drove me *nuts*. I thought you were so hot, and I just wanted to say hi, but you wouldn't cooperate. You barely glanced at Larry during your interview. Everyone wanted to know what your deal was, who you were, why you lived in your car, but you wouldn't talk to anyone. It was months before you even looked at me."

Miriam remembered. She had been trying to leave Nick. When she'd woken up with Nick holding a knife to her throat, she'd finally gotten desperate enough to run, but Nick had come after her, found her at the Taproom, tried to scare her into going with him. Ben had hospitalized Nick, protecting her, and after that he had acted like a friend and protector to her, going out of his way to talk to her, to make her laugh.

She had still been wary, keeping her distance from him for several months, putting him off at every turn. That had only made him want her more, though, made him chase her all the harder. Eventually she had given in, let Ben take her to his apartment, let him kiss her, let him touch her, let him sleep with her.

He was nicer than Nick…at first. He seemed normal. A bit quick-tempered sometimes, prone to outbursts about little things, but he'd never hit her, never treated her the way Nick had. His temper worried her. The ease with which he had ripped into Nick had sent warning flags waving in her head, but she ignored them. He was big and tough, promising to protect her, which was exactly what she thought she wanted after having barely survived Nick. Ben made her feel safe, or at least he provided the illusion of safety. She allowed herself to ignore the warning signs, one after the other.

Things had been fine for about six months, and then he told her he had enlisted with the Marines. She had just begun to get attached to him, so it hadn't been welcome news. He left for basic, and came back bigger and harder. He got drunk the day he received his orders sending him to Afghanistan, and he'd been rough with her that night. He hadn't been violent, just rough in the way he threw her to the bed and stripped her clothes off, rough in the way he had slammed himself into her, ignoring her whimper of pain. That should've been warning enough, but she'd shoved it down. For his sake, she told herself. Then he shipped out, and his letters and Skype calls got more and more infrequent over the months of his deployment, and the times he did call or write, he communicated in short, terse sentences.

He voluntarily signed up for a second tour, not even coming home in between, spending the time on a base somewhere in Europe. When he finally opted out and came home after the second tour, Miriam met him at the Detroit Metro Airport, and she'd seen the difference right away. It was in his eyes, in the way he assessed her, the way he hugged her. There was a distance somehow, a gap of a million years between them, a chasm ripped in his soul by whatever he'd seen or done over there, things he refused to talk about, things that gave him nightmares.

Miriam stopped walking finally, and looked up into Ben's eyes. She saw, for a moment, a glimpse of the Ben she had first met, and that weakened her resolve. He'd been a decent guy once. The things that had changed him hadn't been his fault.

"Fine, Ben. You can take me to the gas station. But if you lay a hand on me, or yell at me, I swear...."

"I won't, I promise." He was grinning happily, and she wondered if maybe he had changed after all. He opened the passenger-side door for her and closed it behind her, slid behind the wheel, and pushed the manual gearshift into First, but didn't release the clutch, just stared at her with a strange look on his face.

She never saw it coming. There was a flash of silver and a brief burst of pain at her temple, and then the gaping maw of unconsciousness swallowed her whole.

Jack sat in his apartment, idly flicking channels on the TV, a nearly empty bottle of Jameson next to him.

Empty, like his heart. The thought was melodramatic, but he didn't care. He had tried convincing himself there were other women in the world, but it hadn't worked. There weren't other women in the world, not like Miriam. Not because of the thing with the fire and the healing and all that, but because of who she was. Jack lifted the bottle to his lips and drained the rest of the Jameson in a long gulp, relish-ing the burn in his throat. A burning throat, a wild, dizzy drunk, those were feelings he could deal with. The cracking of his heart he couldn't.

She had just...walked away, gone with that pig, Ben. He didn't deserve her. She was so kind and so sweet and so beautiful, and Ben was...god, so awful. Jack had trouble understanding what she'd ever seen in Ben besides his looks. Sure he was, like, six foot four and 250 pounds of solid muscle, and he wore a uniform like he was born in it. Women loved men in uniforms. Stupid. Nothing that special about a uni-form. It didn't make the guy wearing it any less of a giant dick, did it?

Right now he wanted to get on his bike and go to Ben's apartment and lay into him, maybe bring Doyle and Jimmy with him and teach Ben a lesson. Jack stood up, wavered on his feet, and realized that maybe getting on his bike wouldn't be the best plan just yet. And besides, his bike was still missing. He shut off the TV and stumbled to his bed, fell across it sideways, wanting to crawl the rest of the way in, but somehow he just couldn't—his limbs wouldn't work, and the room was spinning in crazy circles. He passed out, managing to roll over on his side in his last moment of consciousness.

Jack didn't often dream. Or at least, he didn't usu-ally remember his dreams. This night, however, was different. At first he thought he'd woken up. He was standing in the doorway of his room, looking out into the living room; his stack of paintings was by the counter of his kitchen, and he turned so he could see them. That was the first hint that he was dreaming: The paintings not in their usual spot but were leaning against the adjacent wall. The next odd thing was that the painting he'd done of the candle flame was in front, when he knew for a fact it was near the back of the stack.

Jack felt drawn to the painting, pulled toward the candle flame as if he were a moth. His feet didn't move, the flame tugging him to itself with irresistible magic, and then he was standing in front of it, and he could swear the flame was flickering and giving off heat.

He stretched a hand out and felt a breath of hot air brush his knuckles, and yes, the flame was moving, twisting and dancing on the canvas, jumping and bending in hypnotic circles, sucking him into it, closer and closer, the form of the flame looking ever more like a woman dancing, graceful curves undulating, long hair waving and skirling like Miriam's hair.

The flame turned and grew and stood before him, taking on human form with shoulders and legs, hands and breasts, hips and eyes—glowing brilliant fiery brown eyes exactly like Miriam's. They were not "like" her eyes but were actually *hers*, boring into him with the tender affection so unique that it melted him every time.

He wanted to touch her, the fire-girl, the fire-Miriam; he tried to step closer to her, but his feet were frozen, his hand was outstretched, and she shook her head, curled a finger at him, beckoning. Jack would follow her anywhere, felt his spirit drifting after her as she floated away, the canvas now empty as the Miriam-flame coruscated in the midnight dark, blowing through the window and out over the silent suburbs, Jack pulled behind as if connected to her by a string.

The image of a string refused to leave Jack's dreaming mind, and suddenly there was a string between him and Miriam, a rope of luminous golden particles of sand stretching from his chest to hers, each speck brilliant as a miniature sun, shifting like billowing flames and radiating power. The skein of magic was a tangible thing: Jack wrapped his hands around it where it entered his chest, felt its familiar catalytic energy, brushing his soul with shades of Miriam.

The magic *was* Miriam, and he followed it even when she disappeared out of sight over the surrounding rooftops. His hands were coated with the magic, and before he knew what he was doing, Jack lifted his fingers to his lips and licked the magic from them. He tasted Miriam, saw her face burst into his

mind and fill his thoughts, not the fire-carved creature but the real, physical person, the flesh-and-blood
woman. She wasn't looking at him in this vision; she
was asleep, her face pressed against a car window, her
neck contorted in an uncomfortable position. Jack
focused on her image and realized she wasn't asleep,
she was unconscious, a thin trickle of blood weeping
from a scabbed gouge at her temple, thick strands of
brown hair escaping from her braid and sticking to
the blood. Jack reached for her, needing to wipe the
blood away, needing to cradle her in his arms. His fingertips neared her skin, and the vision broke.

Jack woke with a start. He was lying down, his
face pressed against a cold, hard, gritty surface. He
was shivering, the air around him chilled by silence.
He rolled over onto his back, his head throbbing, his
eyes crusted shut.

He was outside somehow. He pried his eyes open
to see the night sky above him, black shadows of
clouds illuminated by a crescent moon. Where was
he? Jack struggled to a sitting position and looked
around, a string of curses tumbling from his mouth.
He was on a rooftop, the flat, gravel-strewn surface
of an office building of some sort, twisting barrels
of air-conditioning fans sprouting from the roof and
cable TV satellites angling at the sky.

He stood up and brushed his knees and elbows
free of gravel, picking bits of rock from where they

were embedded in his face. He stretched his stiff muscles and went to the edge of the roof, looking for landmarks to indicate his position. The obvious question of how he had gotten there was nagging at him, but he refused to answer it yet. He suspected the truth, but wasn't ready to face that weirdness just yet.

Dozens of stories below him was an empty street, a few parked cars on the side, yellow lines stretching in either direction. Other office buildings rose up around him as far as he could see, except to the east, where he could just make out the Detroit River, sparkling in the moonlight. He was downtown.

He turned in place, examining the skyline, recognizing a few buildings. It was quite a view, actually, way up here. Jack cursed again and sat down with his back against the half-wall at the building's edge.

The dream hadn't been entirely a dream, then, it seemed. Miriam had demonstrated more than once that she possessed some rather unique abilities, but they'd always happened when he was with her. He'd dreamed about her before, but those dreams had been...different. He might have *wished* they were real, but they hadn't been. Those dreams were nothing more than lovesick wet dreams. Whatever he had experienced after he passed out in his apartment tonight had been far more. But what, and why?

He pushed aside his obviously mistaken ideas of real versus impossible and tried to reason through this conundrum with an open mind. There was something else. Something nagging and familiar, subtle, and just beneath the surface of the obvious. What was it?

Jack's mind wandered to the dream that had landed him here, thinking of the stream of glowing dust that had connected him to the dream-Miriam, and he realized with a rush of excitement what it was nagging at him: Beneath the flames, subsumed by the heat and the flickering fire and the glimpses he'd gotten of Miriam's glorious body, beneath all that was that same golden magic-sand, covering his whole body as if he'd bathed in it, a coating of dust that led from him to Miriam. He'd seen it before, too; once when he'd laid his bike down to avoid hitting her, she'd healed him. He'd been unconscious for most of it, but when he first came to consciousness, he'd cracked his eyelids open to see Miriam facing Ben, her body alight, and trailing from her to him, the skein of golden magic.

Maybe there was a connection between them all the time, present but not always visible? Jack's eyes popped open, and he looked down at himself, disappointed to see just himself, plain old Jack in ratty, paint-splattered, grease-stained jeans and an Irish Football Association T-shirt. He closed his eyes again, and this time visualized himself as he was at that moment, but with a river of glowing gold stretching out from his body, and he pictured that stream of gold reaching out over the city to wherever Miriam was.

Some instinct in Jack told him she was hurting, needing him. Maybe it wasn't instinct, maybe it was the connection that bound them, the as-yet unspoken love between them. He summoned the image of her magic again, envisioned it floating across the city to plunge into him, showing him Miriam.

He opened his eyes and breathed a sigh of relief: The skein was there at the center of his chest, stretching out across Detroit, skirting some buildings and spearing through others. He lifted a hand and waved it through the amorphous stream of particles, like sunlit dust floating in an afternoon window; his hand came away coated with it again, as in his dream, and he touched his fingers to his tongue and tasted Miriam.

He saw her again, in his mind. It was disorienting: He saw the city beyond him, a few streetlights flickering, silent streets like a maze, and over that he saw Miriam, still slumped against the car window, the trickle of blood now dried and crusted. Jack saw a male hand on a gearshift, caught glimpses of a neighborhood passing by through the car window. Something told Jack he was seeing Miriam in real time.

Gramps had always told Jack that he had the second sight, too. Perhaps that was the reason he could see the magic now. Jack never wanted to believe in

Gramps' visions of the future. It was freaky and unnatural, and Jack would rather just deal with what he could see and understand. Now, though, with all that had occurred with Miriam, he simply couldn't pretend everything was totally normal anymore.

He had to find Miriam and help her, and the only way he'd be able to do that was if he allowed himself to believe in the second sight, and that he had it, and that he could use it.

Jack closed his eyes yet again, and focused on Miriam's face.

CHAPTER 15

Carson

The present

CARSON WAS CLOSE. HE COULD FEEL IT. THE TUMBLING of facts and theories had slowed, and pieces were falling into place to create an image of a possible truth. He was still missing a couple of major pieces, but something told him he was closing in on those, too.

He had a report of an abandoned vehicle way up near Grayling, licensed to Miriam al-Mansur. There were no witnesses, although a farmer had reported seeing a girl walking down the road near dusk. She'd gotten into a red sports car, the farmer said. Carson crosschecked the motor vehicle files and discovered that Benjamin Wade was the newly registered owner of a red Maserati, but the strange part was that none of the high-end sports car dealerships in the Metro-Detroit area had any record of Benjamin Wade having purchased one. More phone calls and emails turned up nothing.

Wade owned a car he hadn't purchased, and a background check showed nothing to suggest it was black market, nor did he have the funds in his bank account that would let him buy so much as a tire for a Maserati. Carson set these odd details aside as not being immediately relevant. They were interesting, and set his suspicions to quivering, but they didn't feel as if they fit into the larger puzzle of Ben's death.

Carson was at his desk, staring at the file, turning the case over in his head, once again looking for something he'd missed, for the connection from one item to another. He read the facts again: Miriam's car was found way up outside North Branch, a long drive from her apartment in Royal Oak. What was she doing up there?

Séan Byrne had reported that Miriam had left the wedding reception with Ben to stop the fight. Where would they have gone? Ben's neighbors reported not having seen or heard from him since the day before his death, so they couldn't have gone there.

Carson pinched the bridge of his nose. He hated playing "what if" with cases. Carson hunted down the facts and put them together; he chased the bad guys and collared them.

What if Miriam had gone with Ben, as old Séan had suggested, just to stop the fight? According to what he knew so far, she wouldn't have gone with Ben to *be* with him. He wasn't clear on the status of Miriam's relationship with Jack, but it sounded like she had found someone who would treat her better than Ben. But that would make Ben jealous, wouldn't it? If Ben had showed up angry and causing trouble, Miriam might have gone with him just to keep the peace.

She'd known how mean Ben could get, and if the fight got nasty enough to where people were getting arms broken, then it just might send Miriam over the edge. Carson pictured her leaving with Ben, but only to remove him from a volatile situation.

Once she was alone with him, her own temper might flare. Maybe they argued, and this time Miriam really did try to get away from Ben, so she just hopped in her car and drove anywhere, headed north. Of course, Ben would follow her, being the jealous type. He'd be upset that she was at a wedding with another man. She ran out of gas, and Ben might have convinced her to let him take her home. Her car was discovered abandoned on a country road some two miles from the freeway, and the farmer had reported seeing her walking around sundown. Out in the middle of nowhere, alone at night, out of gas and upset? Even an angry Ben might seem like the lesser of two evils.

But then what? This was where Carson hit a wall.

It would have gotten ugly eventually, Carson figured. If Miriam was going to family weddings with Jack, she must have been pretty well done with Ben. The incident Mrs. Willis had described lent strength to the idea, as odd as some parts of her story might have been. So Miriam would have been in a car with an ex-boyfriend who'd put her in the hospital, which meant he'd definitely knocked her around before; the nurse's testimony confirmed that.

Carson flipped through the file. He had Ben's credit card purchase history, pulled when looking for a record of the Maserati. Now Carson looked through it again, not really knowing why, but ready to try anything other than more "what ifs." Ben had expensive taste, even if his budget didn't let him indulge frequently: upper-end steakhouses, cigar shops…and a room rental at the MGM Grand Casino and Hotel.

Bingo.

Carson grabbed his keys and went back to the casino.

CHAPTER 16

Miriam

Three days earlier

MIRIAM WOKE UP SLOWLY. FIRST CAME THE SENSATION of consciousness, accompanied by a wave of confusion, and then the familiar nausea and pain. Her head was throbbing, and she had no idea where she was. The last thing she remembered was getting in Ben's car, and then…what? She had a vision of Ben's hand lashing out, something silver in his hand, then nothing. He'd hit her, apparently, and knocked her unconscious.

Miriam stretched, carefully opening her eyes. She wasn't at her apartment or his, that much was clear: She was lying on a wide bed, an expensive flat-screen

TV hung on the opposite wall, and floor-to-ceiling windows ran the length of the adjacent wall. Thick carpeting, a leather couch and chair in a sitting area near the windows, a fully stocked minibar…she was in a hotel room. Miriam sat up, or tried to; her head swam, and she lay back down. When the dizziness faded, Miriam sat up again, much more gingerly this time.

She stood up just as carefully and realized she wasn't wearing her own clothes. She had left the house in an old pair of jeans and a hoodie; she was now wearing an expensive silver cocktail dress, scooped low in the front, the hem barely brushing her thighs.

In the forefront of her mind was the question of Ben himself: Where was he? She'd seen the madness return to his eyes just before he knocked her out, a blow worse than anything she'd ever experienced.

He'd appeared to be stone cold sober when he showed up next to her on the side of the road. Seeing her with Jack must have pushed him over the edge. Whatever the case, she knew she had to get away before Ben returned. She was barefoot, and the thought of running away on bare feet again didn't appeal to her, but it was better than being here when Ben got back. He had something planned, and she had no desire to find out what.

She managed to step away from the bed, but at that moment the door opened and Ben entered, wearing a charcoal three-piece suit with a pale blue tie. Ben was followed by a hotel employee pushing a room service cart. Ben took the cart from him, gave him a folded twenty-dollar bill, and shoved him out the door.

"Miriam, you're awake!" he said. He sounded cheerful, even excited, as if he hadn't knocked her out and kidnapped her.

Miriam moved to brush past him, thinking it was worth trying to just walk out, but he grabbed her, pushed her away from the door.

"What do you want, Ben?" she asked.

"What do I want? I want to spend time with you, baby. That's all." He pushed the cart over to the sitting area, laid the food out on the table, held a chair out, and gestured to it. There was a bottle of Johnny Walker Black on the cart, opened and already a quarter empty; Ben picked up the bottle and drank directly from it.

"Ben, you knocked me out," Miriam said. "You *kidnapped* me. I don't know what craziness you have planned, but it's not going to work. We're *done*."

Ben crossed the room in two quick strides, yanked her by the arm, and shoved her down into the chair. "It's *not* craziness," he said. "I just want to talk to you. I'm sorry I hit you. I know I promised I wouldn't, and I won't do it anymore. I really have changed, I promise."

Miriam tried to get up, but he held her down. "Let me go, Ben! I don't want to talk to you. You haven't changed! This is kidnapping. Don't you realize that? I don't want to be here. I want to go home."

Ben's voice hardened, and she caught a glimpse of the rage behind the mask of calm. "You'll stay here, and you'll listen to me. We're going to have a nice dinner together, do you understand?" Ben sat down unsteadily, unbuttoning his suit coat and taking a long swig from the bottle still clutched in his fist. The butt of a handgun peeked above his waistline.

The situation was now suddenly much more precarious.

Ben smirked, realizing she'd seen the gun. "You'll stay, and we'll talk," he repeated. Watching him, Miriam realized he was far beyond being merely drunk; that bottle of Johnny might not have been his first.

"Sure, Ben. That's fine." Miriam scooted her chair in, opened the cloth napkin, and spread it on her lap, knowing Ben wanted the ceremony, the process, the trappings of luxury. Ben nodded, approving.

He pulled off the plate warmers with a flourish. "I got you a salad, see? You don't like steak, so I got you a salad instead." He said this in a tone that almost begged her to see how much he'd changed, that he was paying attention to her, listening to her.

Miriam nodded, picked at the salad with a trembling fork. "Thank you, Ben. That was very considerate of you." She was too terrified to be able to eat, but she had to pretend— she had to keep Ben happy until she could escape.

"I'm really sorry I brought you here under these circumstances, Miri," Ben said between bites. "It wasn't how I wanted to do this. When that…thing with Rachel happened, and when you had to go to the hospital, it made me realize how special you are. I haven't been treating you very well. I know I haven't. I've been an asshole, and I'm sorry. You deserve better, and I'll give you better, I promise. This is a new start."

"Why are you doing this? This isn't you, Ben. You don't need to do this. Just let me go."

Ben froze, hands in the process of cutting steak. He didn't look up. Miriam watched his fingers tighten around the steak knife, watched his veins throb as the rage boiled to the surface. "You're mine! That's why! Because you can't just walk away from me like that. *You're mine*, Miriam."

"I'm not an object, Ben. I don't belong to you," Miriam heard the words rolling off her lips, but she couldn't stop them. Reckless honesty was flooding through her. "You can get help, Ben. There are therapists—"

"I don't need help! I don't need *therapy!*" he shouted. But then he subsided, and said more quietly, "I'm not crazy. I don't need a damned psychiatrist."

Miriam chose her next words with care, knowing she was treading on dangerous ground. "A therapist is different from a psychiatrist, Ben. A therapist would just talk to you, and listen to you. It's just a way of learning to deal with what's inside you, I think. Beth from work, she goes to one, and she was telling me about how much it helped—"

"I'm not going to a therapist, Miriam. I don't want to, and I don't need to." He took a drink from the now nearly empty bottle, slid his chair back, and tossed his napkin on his plate, clearly dismissing the subject. He came around the table and knelt next to Miriam, taking her hands in his. "Listen, I—I'm really, really sorry about the way I've acted recently. I really do love you, and only you. You belong to me. We belong together." He reached into his jacket pocket and pulled out a small black box.

Miriam's heart seized, realizing what he was about to do. "Ben, no, please don't—" She could barely choke the words past the coiled, throbbing knot of vomit in her throat.

Ben squeezed her hand with sudden, savage strength, and she went silent as he continued. "Just listen. I love you. I really do. I know I haven't been the easiest guy to be around, but I'll change that, I promise. I want to be with you forever." He opened the box, revealing a diamond ring gleaming against the black velvet. "Miriam, will you marry me?"

He said this with a pistol in his waistband, the butt poking out of his jacket, just inches away from her. Miriam was frozen, her breath coming in panting, ragged gasps of panic. She couldn't speak, couldn't even blink her eyelids.

He was completely serious, kneeling in the classic proposal position, waiting for her answer.

The bubble of fear trapping her in place popped, and she rose to her feet, calming her breath and steadying her trembling hands. "Ben…." She met his eyes, let the fires blaze up hot in her belly as she spoke. "No. I won't. I can't. I don't love you, and I don't think I ever have. I may have *wanted* to, and tried to, and convinced myself that I did, but…I don't. I needed you to protect me from Nick, but I never loved you. And you don't love me. Don't you see how crazy this is?"

Ben was shaking his head in denial. "What? What are you saying Miriam? I thought…."

Miriam backed away, edging slowly toward the door behind her. "No, Ben, I don't think you did think. Or you thought wrong. What I'm saying is that I will *not* marry you, not now, not ever." *A few more feet…just keep him shocked a bit longer….* "I don't know what had you convinced that this was a good idea, Ben, but it wasn't. For one thing, you've had Rachel

on the side for how long? And then you *kidnap* me…
and you *propose*? Can you see how that might be just
a bit…I don't know…contradictory?"

Ben closed the ring box and slipped it into his
jacket. His hand didn't quite reach for his gun, but
almost. "Miriam, I didn't kidnap you—"

"You knocked me out and brought me here
against my will! That's kidnapping, Ben!" Miriam was
breathless with panic, with the baking heat of her
anger, with reckless, mad fury. He had a gun and an
unhealthy dose of instability, yet Miriam chose *this*
moment to tell him the deepest truths inside her. "I
don't want to ever see you again. We're done! I broke
up with you that day on the road, when I told you
I'd kill you if I saw you again. Apparently that didn't
sink in. I can't stand you, Ben. You're selfish and abu-
sive and arrogant. You only care about you, and you
always have—you just disguised it when we first met.
I'm done, Ben. *Done*." The door bumped against her
back, and she grasped the handle in trembling fingers,
turned it, gave Ben one last glance, and ran out. She
heard him bellow a curse and fumble with the door-
knob, heard the door slam open, and he was behind
her, running after her.

Miriam ran, bare feet slapping against the car-
peted floor. She was running aimlessly, following the
endless hallway until she came to a bank of elevators.
Ben was close behind, so she threw herself against

the crash-bar to the stairs, noting with something like horror that she was on the tenth floor. She'd made her gambit; now she had to play it through. She could have stopped and let her magic burn Ben to a crisp, but the last time she'd let her magic out, she'd nearly destroyed Comerica Park. If she did it here, with the wild riot of emotions running through her, the entire hotel might very well go up in flames. She had no control over it, and there was no way of telling what would happen if she let it out.

No, Miriam decided. She had to deal with Ben without it.

Stairs flew under her feet with reckless speed, bruising her heels and sending lances of pain up her legs and into her back, but every instinct inside her screamed for her to run, run, run. Just before she fled, she'd seen the mask of calm on Ben's face slip, the façade of sanity crumbling to show the pounding rage and thundering madness that lay beneath. He wouldn't let her go, not without a fight. And a fight would mean destruction she wasn't ready to allow.

A stitch in her side stole her breath, slowing her descent. She heard Ben on the stairs above her, growling and cursing. After what seemed like an endless series of stairs, Miriam finally burst out into a lobby hallway filled with people. Most were heading in the same direction, so she darted in among the crowd, hoping to lose Ben in the crush of people. The crowd dispersed around her into the main floor of the casino, and Miriam was inundated with sound, overwhelmed by jangling slot machines and people chattering, card dealers jabbering their patter; she was choked by a thick haze of cigarette smoke, the cloud of nicotine rolling in a visible fog. People were everywhere, milling and chatting and drinking and smoking, playing slot machines and hunched over card tables.

Miriam glanced behind her to see Ben standing on his tiptoes, scanning the crowd. He saw her, and set out after her, shoving people aside, spilling drinks and earning hateful looks. Her dress made her stand out, she realized, the silver in stark contrast to the street clothes of the rest of the crowd. She'd hoped the bustle of people milling around her would be a hindrance to Ben, but it was just as much a problem to her as it was to him.

Ben was closing in, his suit coat buttoned now, concealing the weapon, but she could still see the butt distorting the line of his jacket. A rush of panic shot through her; she wasn't sure he wouldn't use the gun, even here. He was striding with bullish purpose through the crowd, eyes fixed on her, rage burning, jealousy and hurt and confusion stamped on his face. He hated her now, and he wouldn't stop until he had her. God knows what he would do if he caught her.

Miriam turned back to glance back at Ben, and in the process ran smack into a huge, sweating, pear-shaped man in overalls, dragging an oxygen tank with cannulae inserted in his nose, a pumpkin-round face covered in a thick beard that hung over his broad chest. Beady brown eyes glanced down at her, and he spoke in a gasping voice so deep it made her bones rattle. "You in trouble, little miss?"

She saw Ben a few feet away, shook her head, and pushed past the man. She heard him stop Ben, heard the man grunt in surprise as Ben shoved him to the side. It was enough of a distraction to let Miriam get farther ahead, and that enraged Ben even more. There was a clear area ahead of Miriam, a break in the crowd; she broke into a run, not caring about the stares she drew. Her hair was loose around her shoulders, flowing in brown waves behind her as she ran. She wanted to glance behind her to see if she was getting any farther away, but she was afraid of running into someone again and losing her momentum.

Miriam realized she had no idea of where she was going. She was running blindly, trying to get away from Ben. The casino was mammoth and expansive and maze-like, row after row of slot machines all lined up and marching off into the distance. Panic blinded her from seeing any directional signs. She passed by a darkened lounge with blue low-lights, people swilling booze from highballs, oblivious to her plight. She rounded a corner, glancing back as she did so to see Ben less than ten feet away, striding confidently, his hand on the pocket of his suit coat, holding the pistol, a smirk on his lips, a hungry smile offsetting the glittering anger in his eyes. He saw her glance at him, and his grin widened. He curled a finger at her, beckoning. She shook her head in denial automatically, not meaning to respond.

She slammed into yet another body, this time a smaller, softer one. Miriam was suddenly doused in drinks. She saw an attractive, Arabic-looking girl about her own age standing there in shock and outrage, an empty tray in one hand and a pile of foaming beer bottles on the ground, her skimpy black waitress uniform soaked.

The waitress was wearing a bodice that did little but prop her breasts up, and an apron that covered her thighs, and black tights, but little else. Miriam wasn't sure she was actually wearing a skirt at all, just a shirt and the apron. Despite the fear gripping her, Miriam felt a strange kinship to the woman, a connection she couldn't explain, a kind of familiarity, even though Miriam was sure she'd never seen her before in her life. The waitress was a little taller than Miriam, beautiful in an exotic way.

"Do I know you?" the waitress asked, curiosity written plain on her face.

The waitress reached up and touched Miriam's forehead with the tip of her index finger, and Miriam felt a bolt of electricity rush through her, felt her magic respond to the girl's touch, reaching out for the similar magic floating in a silvery tendril toward her.

Out of the corner of her eye, she saw Ben stalking after her, the pistol in his hand now, held against his leg. Slipping on the spilled beer, Miriam stumbled into a run, bounced off another man, barely hearing his yells of surprise.

A bank of doors appeared in the distance, and Miriam headed for them, Ben hot on her heels now. Miriam shoved an overweight older black woman out of the way and slammed into the door, felt it bounce off her as she careened into a wall. She was in the back area of the casino, an employee's-only section of white walls, white linoleum floors, and white drop-tile ceilings, clean, too-bright hallways startlingly silent after the clanging bustle of the casino.

Alone now, Miriam sprinted flat-out, her feet slapping loud, her breathing ragged. She heard the doors behind her bang open, followed by fragments of casino noise and shouts of "you can't go in there!" as Ben continued to pursue her. He had the gun out now, and he lifted it to point it at her, still walking with long strides after her, not running, not hurrying. Miriam heard her own panting breath mix with whimpers, smelled the pungent aroma of Pine-Sol from the freshly mopped floor. The hallway ended at a T-junction, and Miriam crashed into the wall and turned left, choosing arbitrarily, hurtled around another corner and another, each time at random, hoping to lose him. She heard Ben's feet pounding now as he ran to catch up; she heard the unmistakable ratcheting click of the pistol safety being pulled back and released.

She saw an exit sign bathing the hallway red and reflecting off the floor, and Miriam bolted through it to emerge into the low gray darkness of a parking garage, cars scattered between yellow lines, ramps leading up and down. Miriam headed for the downward ramp, hoping it would lead her outside. The door banged open behind her again, and she knew Ben had found her. At least she was alone out here. If Ben caught her, she'd use her powers. She might destroy a few cars, but no one would die.

No one besides Ben, that is.

Lower and lower into the garage she ran, fewer and fewer cars down here. By the time Miriam realized she'd trapped herself, Ben was already blocking the up-ramp, pistol out and held against his leg. He also stood by the only stairwell. Behind him was a concrete wall, blank and damp; a battered green Cadillac sat a few feet to her right, and beyond that was the dead end at the very bottom of the parking garage.

"Nowhere else to run, Miriam." Ben was gliding toward her like a lion stepping with careful paws through tall grass toward an unsuspecting gazelle.

His eyes betrayed him, as they so often did. He was hungry for her, fingers curling at his pants leg as if around her body, as if clutching her throat. Miriam backed away from him, grasping for the magic within her. Terror made her fumble, made the fire sputter. She was desperate, reaching for it, only to find it elusive now that she finally truly needed it. Ben was within arm's reach, and Miriam ran, only to feel his fingers close around her arm and yank her toward him.

"Ben, don't," she pleaded. She knew it was futile, but she pled with him anyway. "I'm sorry, Ben, I'm sorry...."

Ben didn't answer. He shoved her backward, sticking his foot behind her leg so she tripped backward to the ground, bashing her head against the concrete floor. She saw stars spinning above her, felt warmth spread out beneath her head. There was a dull glimmering spark of heat in her gut, and she struggled to remain conscious, reached for the guttering fleck of magic, felt it recede, buried by pain and drowned by terror. She wanted to scream with frustration, but the sound remained trapped in her throat in a hard lump, choking her. Her vision was wavering, spinning. Ben was straddling her, a black folding knife in his hands; the blade was between her breasts and slicing down her belly, ripping open her dress. Ben cut the dress off her arms and wadded it in his hand, pocketing the knife.

"I'm glad you ran, Miriam," Ben said. "You made this all a lot easier, and a lot more fun." Miriam thrashed and kicked and bucked, but Ben just laughed and rode it out, seeming to enjoy the fight. There was no Ben left in his eyes, only madness now, only desire and hate and anger.

"I figured something out, Miri," he said in a conversational tone. "The phone, the car, Rachel? That was all you. You made that happen somehow. I don't think you meant to, but you did. So I was thinking about it, trying to figure out how it had happened. Then you went all Human Torch on me, and it started to make sense."

Miriam tried again to buck him off, screaming and kicking. Ben shoved the wadded dress into her mouth, prying it open painfully wide. He shoved the cold barrel of the pistol against her forehead, and she went still.

Ben continued, "Once I got my head around the fact that I really did see you turn to flame, it was easier to think about how you made that other stuff happen. I was thinking about some stories I heard when I was deployed. Our translator had all these crazy stories about what he called 'djinn,' and the way he described them…it's you, Miriam. But what if you don't grant wishes, like, I just ask you for what I want, and you make it come true? What if maybe somehow you make what I want deep down come true? Like, the magic just works on its own. So then I kept thinking. When did those things happen? While we were having sex. Something about sex makes the magic happen, which is really fuckin' cool, you know? Ha, that was punny. So anyway. Here we are, and of course, you've got to do this the hard way, which is just like you. We could've done this all nice and comfortable up in the hotel room. You could've just...let go of all that other bullshit and realized that you belong with me."

"No, she doesn't," came a voice from behind them, just a few feet away. Jack. "Get off her, Ben."

Miriam tried to scream a warning: Jack didn't see the pistol. He didn't see Ben smile slowly, as if he'd been hoping Jack would show up. He didn't see Ben shift his weight, turn his head slightly to get Jack into his line of vision.

Jack might not have seen what Miriam saw, but he wasn't stupid. He lunged with sudden speed, throwing himself at Ben. Miriam watched it all as though in slow motion as Ben twisted, absorbed Jack's hurtling weight. Ben toppled away from Miriam to roll across the ground. Jack disentangled himself from Ben and scrambled to his feet, planted a kick into Ben's face and then another. Ben rolled away, and Jack followed him, fists first.

A pair of explosions filled the parking garage, the shots missing Jack as he threw himself to the side. Jack stood up and charged yet again; Ben fired twice more. This time, Jack gasped in surprise and stumbled backward, tripped, and fell to the ground. Miriam heard someone screaming, then realized it was her. Jack lay on his back, twin blossoms of blood spreading on his chest, froth bubbling at his lips as he struggled for breath.

CHAPTER 17

Carson

The present

THE CRIME SCENE HAD BEEN CLEANED UP AND THE garage reopened weeks ago, so the location itself offered no new clues up to Carson. He stood there anyway, looking at it again, with Miriam and the case as a whole in mind.

He pictured Ben bringing Miriam to the casino, perhaps as an attempt to woo her back. This was his turf, his territory. He knew people here. A buddy of Ben's from the Corps was a dealer at a blackjack table. The buddy hadn't exactly been forthcoming, wanting to protect his friend. The connection itself was enough: Ben would be comfortable here. His friend might be able to pull some strings, get people to ignore anything unusual, like a terrified girl running through the casino. There was a waitress whom Carson had interviewed before coming down here, a waitress who had left work by the time the body was discovered and reported, and thus had been unavailable for questioning at the time.

Nadira Nasri, a cocktail waitress on the casino floor, had seen Miriam, she said. Miriam had actually knocked into her and spilled a tray of drinks. She'd seen Ben, too, or rather, she'd seen a tall, angry-looking guy following Miriam, and had heard people screaming that he had a gun. That was all she knew, Nadira had claimed.

Maybe things had gotten…tense. If Miriam had tried to leave and Ben had chased her, they'd end up in the casino, almost by default. Carson prowled the casino, trying to think like a fleeing, terrified girl. The casino was huge and sprawling, the exits distant and not clearly marked. It was designed to keep you in. The confusion and chaos was intentional: no windows, no clocks, no evidence of passing time, no obvious exits. It was clever, almost diabolical, really. And if you were a scared girl, you'd have no way to know where to go.

Then he'd seen the bay of employee-only doors in the distance, and that had seemed an obvious choice. Doors meant *escape;* doors meant *away.* So he went through the doors, flashing his badge to employees protesting his presence. White hallways like an illusion stretching out in a further maze, silent after the chaos...Carson found himself disoriented, so he could only imagine how frantic and confused Miriam must have been. One random turn after another, and then suddenly he was in the parking garage. If she had gone left instead of right, maybe there would have been a different outcome. One direction would have led her to a break room, or a cleaning supply room, whereas she'd ended up cornered in the garage, where something truly unusual had taken place, a sequence of events that was still a mystery to Carson.

He had a clear picture of how events had led to the parking garage. He'd looked at the security tapes again, and had finally found a single, brief image of Miriam pushing through the crowd, obviously terrified, chased by Ben. The cameras had caught them in the casino and the back hallways, and entering the parking garage, but that was it. No footage of Ben's death. So how had Ben died? What had caused the fire? Had Miriam done it?

And again the question: Where the hell was Miriam?

Back at his desk, Carson stared at the casings, trying to piece the rest of the story together. The body had been burned, which meant it was likely that someone else had been shot. But there were no burn marks, no scorch marks, not even where the body had fallen, which suggested that the fire wasn't natural. If Miriam was able to…what? Manipulate fire somehow? That would explain the mysterious nature of the burned body. Maybe she had torched him somehow in self-defense. Maybe she had been shot in the process and run, or been found? But then, none of the hospitals had reported any gunshot victims that fit Miriam's description.

He had a pretty good idea of the people involved and the sequence of events, but it still left him stuck in the same place he'd been at the start: a charred skeleton, a missing girl who might or might not have been responsible for the burned body, a missing girl who might or might not be alive.

At his desk, Carson sat staring at the file. He *had* to solve this case. He had to know if Miriam had killed Ben, and how.

He hoped Miriam was still alive to tell him.

CHAPTER 18

Miriam

Three days earlier

MIRIAM FLASHED FROM COLD TERROR INTO FULL FLAME in a heartbeat. She moved toward Ben, unaware that her feet weren't touching the ground, unaware that she had relinquished even the slightest vestige of human form to become a pillar of raging blue-white fire pulsing and shifting and reaching out for Ben.

He backed away, stumbling over his feet and falling to the ground, scrambling away as she approached. She saw nothing but Ben, vaguely aware of Jack behind her, dying. She was reaching for Ben, seeking to grasp him with hating hands, but she had no form, no physical body. She reached for him, and she swallowed him, the column that was Miriam splitting apart like jaws, fiery teeth smashing together with a splash of fire and a juddering echo.

She heard him scream. He was wailing, his voice a horrified shriek of agony.

Then he was silent.

She was a woman again suddenly, mere weak flesh and blood, and Ben was a pile of charred skeleton bones on the ground behind her.

Jack was dying. His breath was coming in gasps, whistling past the holes in his chest, his eyes slack and rolled up into his head. She shook him, heard herself weeping, screaming, pleading. She kissed him, remembering the movies and the power of true love's kiss, but he stayed cold and limp and lifeless. There, a brief thud of a heartbeat under her hand, but it was faint, and slow.

Her stomach hurt, aching with sorrow.

She reached for the heat within, felt it in her grasp, and she pulled on it, forced it hotter, needing it not for herself, but for Jack. She let the rage at Ben come back, though he was dead, needing the anger to blow life into the magic. Rage fueled the magic, it seemed; rage, and desire.

She felt no desire in that moment, only desperation and pain. She needed Jack.

She couldn't live without him. Ben had tried to kill him, so Miriam morphed that into hate, into anger. The anger built, turned warm and then hot, and then burst into full and furious life in her hands.

She refused to let Jack go. He couldn't die. Her whole form wanted to turn alight, but she forced the magic to obey her will, forced it into her hands. She plunged her white-glowing hands into Jack's chest, through the skin and bone, through the blood and the cells and the mitochondria and electrons, into the smallest spaces of his body. She spread herself out, then dove willingly into the magic flooding from herself into him, became the magic itself, seeking out what was split and torn by the lead bullets and knitting the breaks back together, molecule by molecule, bridging the gaps with bits of herself, with fragments of magic, spanning with her own essence places where flesh had been not merely torn apart but dissolved and removed. She sought to erase all evidence of pain, all memory of hurt from him; she found the bullet holes and spread across them, sucked at them with all the force of magic she had, devoured them, absorbed them, took the pain into herself, took the wounds into herself.

Then, she could do no more. She fell to the cold concrete, exhausted, chilled to her very bones, hurting in every pore. She forced her eyes open, sought Jack and found him, sitting up and healed. There was no mark on him, no blood on his shirt, no blood pooled on the ground beneath him.

He saw her, clutched his chest as if remembering the wounds, found nothing, looked back at Miriam.

He scrambled over to her, knelt beside her, tears falling down his face. "Oh, god, Miriam, what did you do?"

She struggled to speak, to answer him. "Jack...." She knew she was hurt; even thought was difficult right now. But Jack was alive. That was what mattered. His hands were in her hair, caressing her cheek.

"No, no." He wasn't arguing, he was denying. "Please, God, no." This was a prayer, not an epithet, not a casual profanity, but a plea. "Holy Mary, mother of Jesus, please. *Et nomini Patri, et fili, et spiritus sancti.*"

He stripped his shirt off, wrapped it around her torso, pressed it against her aching chest and stomach. Why did she hurt so bad? She couldn't remember. There was only Jack, picking her up and stumbling into a run with her, spinning in circles, looking for an exit. Miriam didn't feel any of this, was only aware of Jack. She felt cold and faint. She pushed those sensations away so she could focus on him, on his features so etched with desperation and looking down at her, eyes welling with love...or was it fear? She didn't know. He was looking at her, holding her.

That was all that mattered.

"Stay with me, Miri," she heard him whisper. Miri. Only Ben had called her that, and she'd hated hearing him say it. But when Jack said it, it was different.

She felt the shortening of her name was like a verbal caress.

She thought of his words: *Stay with me.* Where would she go if not here? She was in his arms, and that's where she belonged. Then the fear in his eyes and the worry in the lines around his mouth brought her to awareness, and she realized he thought something was wrong with her.

Miriam tore her eyes away from Jack and looked down at herself. She saw Jack's shirt wrapped around her midsection, red and sopping with the blood now pooling between his arms and her flesh where he was pressed against her. She saw the blood welling from little holes in her body…where had those come from? She tried to count them, though the dizziness made it hard. One, there was another next to it…so two… and then two more above those, in her chest, oddly seeming to be exactly where the holes in Jack's chest had been.

She heard a female voice, a vaguely familiar voice nearby. Miriam tried to focus her eyes on the figure standing above her, seeing only a halo of black hair and piercing black eyes pinned on her, eyes brimming with worry. It was the woman from the casino, the waitress.

Miriam heard her tell Jack to put her on the ground, a sharp order that Jack obeyed. Warm hands pulled the shirt away, and she felt the woman spread her palms over the bullet holes. Miriam felt a humming vibration emanate from the woman's hands, her eyes erupting into a silver-blue glow, the color of a moonlit ocean. The warmth spread, and Miriam looked down at the hands, watching them sink into her flesh, seeking out the wounds and filling them, flooding Miriam with heat that cooled into blessed relief from pain. The bullet wounds remained, but the flow of blood was staunched, and Miriam felt less faint.

"We have to get her to my place," the woman said. "That will save her for now, but it's only temporary. Follow me." Jack picked her up again, and though the pain was less, it was still there, blazing through her in dizzying waves. He followed the dark-haired woman to her car, still pleading with Miriam to stay with him.

They got in the car, the woman behind the wheel, and sped out of the parking lot.

Miriam wanted to reassure Jack, to tell him it would be okay, that she was fine. But she didn't really feel fine, and she was cold, so cold. There was a waft of blessed warmth as something was thrown over her, pressing against her chest. Now they were moving, swaying this way and that, Jack above her, bracing one hand against a leather seat headrest, the other pressing a coat or a sweatshirt against her chest and stomach; he was looking down at her, tears on his face carving lines down his cheeks, and he brushed the tears away, but his hand was all red, as if he'd been painting. Where had he gotten so much red paint? It was all over him, smeared against his chest and heaving stomach. Some faint logical voice told her it was blood, not paint, and she wondered if he was okay. She had healed him, she knew she had. So where was the blood coming from?

It must be her blood. That made a kind of sense, only she didn't remember what had caused the injuries. But it didn't matter. She was here with Jack, and Jack was okay. She wanted to stay with him, though, and weakness was tugging at her, unconsciousness pulling at the edges of her vision. If she let Jack out of her sight, he might go away again, so she had to keep looking at him. He had asked her so many times now to please, please stay with him, and she would do anything for him. So she batted away the weakness, the urge to sleep. She couldn't sleep, not yet.

She didn't want him to be afraid.

I'm here, she tried to say, but the words faded in her throat. She felt for the magic in her belly, and she tried to remember how to use it. Maybe the magic would help her, just this once, without needing rage or passion to fuel it. She focused on Jack and tried, with every shred of strength she had left, to summon the magic for herself.

The magic responded, just a little. It was a trickle of warmth at first, like a warm breath of air, but then it grew, a little at a time. This wasn't really for herself, she told the magic. It was for Jack. He was so worried, so afraid for her. If she let the crouched beast of sleep any closer, if she let it take her, he would be so sad. She wasn't really making sense, even to herself. Lucidity was coming and going, but she kept the idea fixed in her mind. *For Jack,* she told the magic. *Keep me here with him, please? So he won't be alone, so he won't weep anymore.*

She felt the magic respond, filling her. She was still cold and weak, but the magic coiled like a serpent and lashed out, striking the beast of blackness, the hungry darkness, and banished it.

Then she felt herself being picked up and moved, and that hurt, sending pangs of pain bolting through her body. She might have whimpered a bit, or maybe screamed. She didn't know; she couldn't hear very well, for some reason. Then she was set down, and there was pressure and cold and warmth and hands doing things to her, and Jack's face above her, smiling through tears, a smile of offered bravery.

They were inside somewhere, not a hospital, but a home. There was a wood ceiling high above her with a spinning fan, and walls covered with paintings and posters. She was lying on a couch, a coffee table next to her, and the dark-haired woman was kneeling beside her, moving her hands over Miriam's body, not quite touching. Her eyes were closed, and she whispered words in a strange language. Every word the woman whispered sent bolts of cool relief coursing through Miriam's body, the woman's hands glowing in pulsing blue luminescence. The woman knelt next to Miriam for what might have been hours, or minutes, or days, or seconds. Time was flowing past Miriam without touching her; all she saw was Jack's face, looking down at her, worried and tender.

"I'm here, Miri," she heard him say. Did he say it, though? Or was it her mind speaking?

Jack...stay with me. She used his words, tried to say them, but they wouldn't come out, so she sent them to him across the bond of magic that connected them. *Don't leave me, please.* She knew he wouldn't, but she was so afraid of being alone, afraid of sleep coming for her before she was ready.

"I'm here, Miriam," he said, and this time it came both from Jack and from her mind. "I won't go anywhere. You're going to be okay, I promise."

She felt a powerful urge to sleep descend, despite her efforts to stave it off. She wasn't afraid of this sleepiness, the way she had been before, but she had to tell him. She *needed* to tell him, so he knew.

I love you, Jack. Had he heard her? He was silent, staring at her.

"I…I love you, too, Miriam." He said it back. He'd heard her. He loved her.

She slept.

Miriam awoke, snatches of memory flashing in her mind. She pressed her hands to her stomach, feeling for the injuries, the wounds, but finding nothing.

"You're awake." A woman's voice, cool and smooth and strong. Miriam opened her eyes, looked around her, saw the apartment that she had caught fragmentary glimpses of earlier. It was a large loft, simply but tastefully furnished and decorated. She was still on the couch, and the woman was sitting in a deep purple chair.

Miriam struggled to a sitting position, but found it painful and difficult. "I wasn't sure I would wake up," Miriam admitted. "Thank you for helping me. I'm Miriam." She was wearing a long black T-shirt that fell nearly to her knees.

The woman nodded. "You've been asleep for almost two days. I wouldn't move around too much right now. I've healed you for the most part, but you'll still be sore for a while. I'm Nadira."

"Where's Jack?" Miriam asked.

"He's out getting us breakfast."

"Oh," Miriam said. "Is he—is Jack okay?"

Nadira gave Miriam a questioning look. "Of course. Why wouldn't he be?"

"Well…he was shot first. He—he saved me from Ben—he stopped Ben from raping me, but he was shot, and I…I tried to heal him, but I think I ended up taking the wounds into myself somehow. I don't really know."

Nadira was clearly shocked. "Wait, what? Tell me what happened, from the beginning."

Miriam ran her fingers through her tangled hair. "Well, the short version is that my ex cornered me in the parking garage. Jack showed up in the nick of time—I'm not really sure how he found me, but he did, thank god—and in the process he got shot, and so did I. I didn't realize it at first, though. The magic or whatever it is had taken over, so I didn't feel anything until afterward. I saw Jack lying on the ground, and he was bleeding and…I couldn't—I couldn't just watch him die. I'd healed him before, but never from anything that serious. He was dying, and I had to do something. So I tried to heal him. I don't really know what happened—I was just so desperate, and I think the magic went too far."

Nadira shook her head, confused. "So you healed him, but you ended up with *his* wounds? I didn't even know that was possible. You're a healer? What's your element?"

"What? My what? What do you mean?"

"Your element. You and I are elemental djinn. My element is water."

Miriam shook her head. "I–I'm not sure what you mean. My element?"

"What form do your powers take? Earth, air, fire, or water?"

"Fire," Miriam said. "When all the weird stuff happens, it's always fire."

"Weird stuff? Wait, you don't…." Nadira tilted her head at Miriam, as if coming to a realization. "You weren't raised in your powers? You don't know what you are?"

Miriam shook her head and stammered, "No—I—no, I don't. It all just started happening a few weeks ago, and I thought I was…I don't know…a freak or something."

Nadira laughed, but came over to sit next to Miriam, hugging her in sympathy. "Oh, you poor thing. I've heard about people who didn't know, and apparently it can be pretty dangerous."

"Yeah, you could say that," Miriam muttered, thinking of what had happened at the Tigers game.

"Okay, well, let's start at the beginning, then. You need clean clothes, for starters."

Nadira stood up and helped Miriam to her feet, found her a pair of jeans and a T-shirt, which Miriam gladly put on, even if they didn't fit quite right. When she was dressed, Nadira led her to the kitchen and sat her down at a small round table. Nadira brought her a mug of coffee, which Miriam sipped gratefully.

"You are a djinni," Nadira said. "An elemental djinni, to be precise. There are a lot of different kinds of djinn, but that's a story for another time. What you need to know is that elemental djinn use one of the four elements as the basis of their power. You were probably born here in this realm to a human mother or father, the other parent a djinn. There are hundreds—if not thousands—of us on Earth, scattered around the world. Most are aware of who and what they are, but they prefer to remain hidden, for reasons I'm sure you can understand. Some are like you, with no idea of who or what they are. I'm guessing one of your parents was either absent or very difficult to be around?"

Miriam nodded, her head spinning with the influx of information. "Yes, my…my mother. When my father—when Daddy died—she just left. And even before then, I never really knew her. She was always secretive, closed off."

"She was where you got your djinn powers."

"So I'm half? Half-djinn?"

Nadira laughed. "No, it doesn't work like that. You're either a djinn or not. The magic that is the substance of a djinn is too powerful to be contained in halves. I don't know why—that's just the way it is. You were raised as a human, so this flesh-and-blood form is the most natural one for you to stay in, but it's not actually your native form. It's tricky to explain.

Djinn are shape-shifters, in a way. We can spend long periods of time looking and acting for all intents and purposes like a normal human being, but eventually the elemental magic will need a release. Have you ever gone full elemental?"

Miriam nodded. "Yeah, a few times. It's scary and wonderful. I feel so powerful, but it's scary because I have no real idea how to control anything. I almost destroyed Comerica Park because my powers got away from me, when I was...excited."

Nadira laughed again. Her laugh sounded like music, like a stream splashing over a rocky bed. There was actual magic in the way she laughed, Miriam realized, and she felt a pang of jealousy that this woman had so much control over her powers. "Yeah, if you're not in complete control, extreme emotions tend to make our powers go a bit haywire. I remember, when I was kid, my brother used to make me so mad, and I'd always lose my temper, and he'd end up soaking wet and crying to Mom. He still does that, actually, and he still gets a good soaking."

"You have a brother? And he's...he's a djinn, too?" Miriam tried and failed to fathom what it would be like to have a brother at all, much less one who shared her powers.

"Yeah. He's a water elemental, too, but he was a slow learner. He was twelve before he could use his powers at will. I was in full control by the time I was six."

"Can you teach me about mine?"

"To some degree. Every element is different in the way the powers work, but I can teach you the basics."

"What about the other stuff...the magic?"

"Well, that's the easy part," Nadira said. "You've just got to learn to bind them together. You're probably split right now, which just means the elemental powers and the magic are like separate entities inside you. You've got to learn to weave them together, and then you'll be able to control them both a lot better. I'll warn you, it's not easy. Even for me, and I've been in control my whole life. Keeping this form and using the magic *and* the element can be tricky. Everything wants to revert back to elemental form."

"So the magic and the fire, or the water in your case, I guess...they're separate?"

Nadira slowly shook her head from side to side. "Not exactly. It's tricky to explain, honestly. The magic stems from your element, but left unchecked and uncontrolled long enough, it can develop a...a mind of its own, I suppose you could say. And in your case, it seems you've somehow gone your whole life with your magic and your elemental powers bottled up inside you, which is probably why, when you do let them out, they go a little crazy."

Just then Jack walked in with two big brown paper bags full of carryout containers. "Miriam, you're up!" Jack set the bags down on the coffee table and rushed over to her, wrapping his arms around her, kissing her lips. "How do you feel?"

Miriam was overwhelmed by the joy and affection he showed. She wasn't used to such overt displays, and had to force herself to not shy away from him. She put her arms around him and closed her eyes, letting the emotions run through her. He loved her, openly and passionately, and that was something she'd have to get used to.

"I'm okay, Jack. Thanks to Nadira, I'm okay." Miriam let out a deep breath as Jack went back to the table and grabbed the bag of food.

He set out a spread of food from a local diner that made Miriam mouth water: everything from hot dogs and hamburgers and turkey clubs and french fries and cups of chicken lemon rice soup.

She glanced up at Jack. "Jeez, Jack, did you get two of everything on the menu?" she asked with a laugh.

"Pretty much," Jack said. "Nadira said you'd be pretty hungry and suggested I get a lot of food."

Nadira nodded. "Using your powers at all takes energy. Being magically healed as you were, well, that takes even more. So with everything you've been through, you should be pretty damn hungry."

Miriam realized she was ravenous, her stomach growling and rumbling, so empty it ached. "You've got that right." She grabbed a cheeseburger and began to eat.

As they all ate their meal, Miriam explained to Jack some of what Nadira had told her.

"So, you're a...djinn?" Jack asked.

"Yeah, it turns out Ben was right about that, at least." A shudder ran through Miriam as she said his name. She wanted to forget him, put him in the past and never think of him again. But he *had* been right about her, in one sense, at least.

"Who is Ben?" Nadira asked.

Jack answered for Miriam. "He was her ex-boyfriend."

"So...what happened? If you don't mind me asking." Nadira glanced from Miriam to Jack and back again.

Jack started to answer, but Miriam put her hand over his to silence him. It was her story to tell, after all. She had intended to only tell the basics, but found herself opening up to Nadira, telling her more and more as she spoke, going back to her childhood, to her first boyfriend and then to Nick and Ben and up to the present. It was a rush of words flooding out of her that she couldn't stop, couldn't slow or control. Miriam found it cathartic to unload everything that way, telling someone who would understand, relating events as she remembered them.

Nadira didn't interrupt, and when the flood of words finally stopped, Nadira said, "You've had quite a life, haven't you? You poor thing. Well, now you know what you are, and you've got Jack."

Miriam glanced at Jack, who'd been silent while she told her story, and she realized much of it was new to him as well. He was looking at her with something suspiciously like pity. "Don't look at me like that, Jack. It was my life. It was what it was. Don't you dare pity me."

Nadira glanced from Jack to Miriam, got up from the table, and retreated to the bathroom, giving them privacy to talk.

"It wasn't pity, Miriam," Jack said. "It was…sympathy. It was me wishing I could've been there for it all. I wish I could go back and be there for you through it all."

That put a knot of emotion in Miriam's throat, and she had to blink back tears and swallow past the knot to say, "Just be with me now, Jack. Just…promise me you won't change."

Jack took her hand in his and said, "I can't promise you I won't change at all, because life changes you. You're afraid I'll end up being just like Ben." Miriam nodded, not quite able to look at him, staring down at the limp leaf of lettuce in the bottom of the

Styrofoam container. "What I *can* promise you is that this is me. I'm not going to suddenly turn into somebody else. I love you."

Miriam couldn't contain the emotions any longer. She felt herself break open inside, pressure from years of being strong and keeping everything bottled in bursting out in a river of tears that she couldn't stop. It wasn't just Ben—it was her father's death, her mother's abandonment, the loneliness, the fear of herself and the confusion over her identity…it was so many things all bound up into a tangled mess of emotions that had no way of being expressed except through this river of tears.

Miriam tried to stop it, hating the feeling of vulnerability, the embarrassment, but it was no use. Jack handed her a box of Kleenex and held her against his chest. His presence both comforted her and made the weeping all the more embarrassing.

"I'm sorry, Jack," she said, when she could speak again. "I'm not…not usually like this."

Jack shook his head. "Miriam, listen to me. You don't have to be strong all the time. It's okay to be emotional. It's okay to let me see what you're feeling."

"No, it's not," Miriam said. "It's not how I am. I swear I've cried more around you in the last few weeks than in all the rest of my life. I hate crying. I hate being weak—"

Jack cut her off. "Stop, Miri. Stop. For one thing, crying isn't weakness. So much has changed so fast, and it's okay to feel overwhelmed. I'm overwhelmed, and I admit it. A month ago, I was alone, working in my cousin's garage, and that was about it. Now I have you, and I can't imagine life without you. Since I met you…I swear I can't remember what it was like when I didn't know you. I'm not perfect, Miri. I'll mess up, I'll make you mad and do stupid shit, but, whatever happens, I'll be here with you. No matter what."

She'd just met him, relatively speaking, but it felt like a lifetime had passed since Jack showed up to defend her from Ben in that parking lot. Now, like Jack had said, she couldn't imagine a day that didn't contain Jack. "Jack. Oh, Jack." She put her hand on his cheek, kissed his lips. "You've saved me, so many times. Not just from Ben, but from myself. I wasn't sure love existed until I met you, honestly. "

Nadira came back, showered and dressed in her waitress uniform. "God, are you two done yet? You're making me sick." She was laughing as she said it, but something made Miriam think she wasn't entirely kidding. "I've got to go to work, but you two are welcome to stay here as long as you want. Your handiwork in that parking garage won't go unnoticed for long, and there'll be cops looking for you. When I come back, we'll talk about the best way to proceed, because explanations in cases like this can be…tricky.

Just stay here, and make yourselves at home. I'm scheduled to work till seven tonight, so I'll be back not too long after that. Stay inside, don't make any phone calls, and just wait for me."

After Nadira had left, Jack and Miriam lay down on the couch, holding each other. Miriam felt a sense of peace steal over her as she listened to Jack's heartbeat. But there was one question burning in her mind.

"How did you find me?" Miriam asked.

Jack didn't answer right away. "Well…it's a bit strange," he admitted.

Miriam snorted a laugh, "Stranger than everything else that's happened?"

"I was at home after the wedding, pissed off and still half-drunk. After you left, things were weird—don't apologize, it's not your fault. Mary doesn't blame you, I promise. She wants you to know that her wedding was wonderful. She just wished you could've stayed. That's her way of saying don't feel bad.

"So anyway…I might've kept drinking after I got home. I was never mad at you, Miriam. Okay? You hear me? I was hurt that you had to make that choice, and that you felt going with Ben was the only way to solve the problem. My family would've defended you, no matter what—"

"But it's not your family's battle to fight, Jack. I know you would have kept fighting, and you would've won eventually. But too many people would've gotten hurt in the process, and I—I just couldn't let anyone else get hurt because of me. I'm not worth it." She hadn't meant to say that last part out loud, and she knew how Jack would respond.

"Miriam, don't be stupid. You *are* worth it. You're worth everything." Jack lifted up on his elbow and stared down at her, his eyes intense. "Miriam, you have to hear me now, okay? This is important. You have to believe in yourself. I know, that sounds like a stupid self-motivational tape or something, but it's true. If you don't think you're worth the best, neither will anyone else. It doesn't matter if I think you're the most amazing woman I've ever met if *you* don't think you're worth anything. I can't believe in you for the both of us, Miriam. I need you to believe in yourself. I need you to see the worth in yourself."

Miriam looked away from Jack, wanting to retreat behind her walls, but she couldn't. He was inside her walls. This was getting too close, too deep. Trusting Jack was fine, but letting him all the way in, to where her most secret doubts and fears were…that was too hard.

"Jack…" She didn't even know where to start, what to say. "It's not that easy. You can't just undo a lifetime of conditioning in one conversation. My mom never loved me, Jack. She never believed in me. My dad may have, but I lost him. And after that, any man I've ever been with has treated me the same—"

"Like shit," interrupted Jack. "Worse than shit. I know. And I know that I can't make you feel your worth just by saying so. Have you ever heard the phrase 'fake it till you make it'? Maybe it's like that. Maybe you have to start by telling yourself you have worth, even if you don't believe it."

"That's stupid, Jack. I'm not going to argue with myself—"

Jack shook his head, "No, Miriam, that's not what I meant. I'm just saying, you have to—"

Miriam cut him off. "Jack, listen. If you believe in me, if you treat me like you have been, and keep telling me I'm worth it, eventually I'll start believing it."

She wasn't sure that was true, but she had to get him off this subject. It was making her insides churn. She wasn't ready for that kind of vulnerability. Not yet.

Jack nodded. "Okay, Miriam." He wasn't acquiescing, merely realizing that she wasn't ready for this conversation.

"You still haven't told me how you found me."

"You know Gramps' second sight?"

Miriam nodded. "Yeah. He told me you have it, too, but you don't believe in it."

Jack laughed. "Yeah, he does say that to anyone who'll listen. But I may believe him now. After I passed out, I had a dream. Or at least I thought it was a dream. 'You were there, and you, and you,'"

Jack said in a strange, high-pitched, sing-song voice. Miriam looked at him blankly. "No? *Wizard of Oz?* Nothing? Okay, whatever. Anyway. I woke up—in the dream, I mean—still in my apartment, and I saw that painting of the candle flame, and there was something about it, like it was real." Miriam couldn't help a ripple of shock going through her, and Jack clearly noticed it. "What?" he asked.

"Oh, it's nothing," Miriam said. "When we were at your apartment that one time, I was looking at your paintings, and that one stood out to me. There was something…hypnotizing about it. I was staring at it, and the magic seemed to kind of reach out to the flame on the canvas, and it turned real. I swear it did. I could see it moving and flickering, and I could feel heat from it."

"I believe you. And that makes all the more sense now. I think something about your magic connects us. Maybe because you've used it on me before? I don't know. If you used your magic on the painting, maybe there was still some left on it, residual magic, you know? I don't know." He shrugged and waved a hand.

"Whatever. Anyway, in the dream, the flame turned real, like you said, and then the flame left the canvas entirely, as weird as that sounds. But it gets weirder. It started to change shape, started to look like a woman…like you do, when you're all"—Jack waved

his hands vaguely, searching for the right words—
"made out of fire. Or whatever that is.

"The point is, the candle flame from the painting turned into you. It *was* you. I knew it somehow.
You floated out the window and beckoned to me.
There was this...rope, of magic. I don't know how
to describe it. It was made out of little golden specks,
like glowing dust, and it was coming from my chest
and went to you, in the dream. I knew it was connected to you somehow. I just knew it. You flew away,
pulling me with you, so I followed you, and then I
woke up. But when I woke up, I was on a rooftop in
the middle of downtown Detroit. I knew, in my gut,
that you were in trouble. During the dream, I'd seen
you somehow, like...the real you, the non-dream you.
I had to find you. I guess I tapped into Gramps' second sight or something, because I was suddenly able
to see that magical connection again, in real life."

Miriam was intrigued. "Can you see it now?"

Jack tilted his head, thinking. "I can see you, normal you...but there's this fire rushing just beneath
the surface of your skin. It's like fire in your veins
instead of blood, but I can see it. I can see the magic
too. It's...a cloud around your body like...how do I
describe it? Like a glowing golden ghost. It's moving, too. Not in random motions, but like something
almost alive in, animal-like. Like the way a bird swoops
and soars. Maybe that sounds stupid, but it's the best

I can describe it." He turned his palm up, then down, wiggling his fingers as he dragged his hand through the air in front of his chest. "Can you see this?"

"See what?"

Jack reached out and took her hand in his. "See it now?"

"No," Miriam said, frustrated.

"Close your eyes," Jack instructed. "Now picture us as we are right now. Then imagine there's a curtain in front of your eyes, and it's stopping you from seeing the world as it really is. If you can move the curtain, you'll see the magic."

Miriam was silent, her eyes closed. "I don't feel anything," she said.

"Use your magic," Jack suggested. "Use your magic to *see* your magic. Sounds ridiculous, but try it."

Miriam shook her head, a hesitant negative. "I'm afraid to. Every time I use my magic, something gets destroyed. The magic does what it wants. When I use it on purpose, it's always destructive."

Jack seemed stumped for a moment. Then he said, "But maybe it's just that you weren't being specific enough. You're a genie…a djinn. Everything I've ever heard about those legends says that you have to be specific, or the wish will turn against you. Maybe you're being too vague."

"I can't use my magic on myself. It doesn't work that way. And I don't think it has anything to do with wishes, exactly."

"Okay, well we can work on terminology another time. For now, we have to find out how you can use your magic without blowing up sports stadiums." Jack was teasing her, but he was serious as well. "Just try. Be specific about what you want the magic to do."

Miriam took a deep breath, closed her eyes, and delved down inside herself. She felt the magic there, a constant presence now, a familiar sensation of waiting power, but it was slippery, elusive. Miriam calmed her frustration, imagined herself to have mental fingers, grasped the magic with a firm grip, and when she did so, something invisible *popped* inside her, and suddenly she was holding a writhing snake of burnished gold, glowing with power and struggling in her grip. It didn't want to be held, didn't want to be controlled. It had been free for too long, doing what it liked. Miriam felt its presence, nearly sentient, definitely alive, if not in the organic sense, then in some way Miriam couldn't quite describe even to herself. The magic was a *thing*, a being. It was part of her, it dwelt within her, but it wasn't synonymous with her identity; it was separate somehow. But it wasn't supposed to be separate, and that was the problem. Miriam held the serpent of magic in a tighter grip, watching it thrash furiously, seeking escape. If it were to have a voice, it would be shrieking. It had never known control, so it was bucking like a wild stallion trying to shake off a rider.

Miriam felt the fire within her as well, the heat poised beneath her skin, guttering in her belly. As she thought of the fire, she realized she was comprised of three distinct parts: the magic, the fire, and the soul. They should all be one, a single entity. Until then, she would never have control.

Miriam pulled up the fire, called on it, and drew it to herself, built it higher, let it rise up inside her like a flood of flames. When it reached critical mass, Miriam seized it and held it, now trying to keep under control both the fire seeking vent and the serpent of magic seeking escape. She needed both, for they were both part of her, both present and tangled up into her identity. She was not just Miriam any longer. She wasn't just a cocktail waitress; she was something else, something greater. She was flame, and magic; she was heat, and power. These elements within her, they weren't meant to be disparate creatures; they were intended to be braided strands of a single entity. Just as Nadira had described.

Using every ounce of her mental strength, every shred of control that she could summon, Miriam wrapped the fire and the magic together, tangled one around the other, forcing them to her will, joining them so they formed a helix around the core of her soul, weaving the three together. They resisted, straining against her, but she refused them freedom. The fire burned her and the magic bit her, sending pain bubbling throughout her, so intense she wanted to cry out, but couldn't.

She was unaware of anything around her, jerked out of reality, out of time and space. There was no Miriam, no Jack, no Ben, no past or present, only the struggle of wills, all of it internal. The fire was threatening to burst her alight, to spread from within to devour all that stood beyond her; the fire was her anger personified, her anger at Ben, anger at her mother for failing to love her and for abandoning her, even anger at her father for leaving her too soon. That last thread of anger, at her father, that was the most potent, burning the hottest within her, and she hadn't even known it was there until she tried to identify the nature of her own rage. It had always been there, she knew, a pooled ocean of it inside her, usually buried beneath a mountain of fear. The fear fed the anger, in a strange way, Miriam realized. She hated being afraid, and she'd spent so long fearing Nick, fearing Ben, fearing herself. She'd been afraid of what would happen if she let her anger out. And now she knew.

She'd let her anger out, and she'd killed Ben with it. She was no longer afraid of herself. She knew what she could do, and she knew she could control it. She had to, or it would break free and destroy everything around her.

The magic was a different story. It was an alien within her, and she'd just realized it had always been inside her. Maybe it had been hiding, or waiting. She didn't know which, but now that she had it in her grasp, she wasn't going to let it free.

She'd felt pain before, and she could take it. The fire burning her insides was a familiar feeling, not exactly painful, but distracting. She absorbed the burn, let it percolate through her, pushing her adrenaline into full flood. The biting of the magic-serpent was a different pain, a new kind of agony, like venom spreading in her blood. Miriam saw the stain spreading, and she dipped herself into it, tasted it, felt it, allowed herself to fully experience the cold stinging touch of magic.

She took that as well and consumed it, letting it spread and mingle with the flames, letting it feed them. Together, the flame and the magic became something new, the yellow-orange flames changing color, becoming even more intense, turning from yellow and orange to blue and purple and red, shifting and morphing and coiling about itself like a serpent eating its tail in a never-ending ouroboros. The flames formed a veil across her mind, dancing like an aurora borealis across her internal vision, and Miriam felt the power within her growing, deepening from a pool into an ocean, a bottomless void filled with energy waiting to be used, needing to be given expression.

Miriam opened her eyes. Jack was pressed flat against the far wall, holding his arms in front of his face as if to shield his eyes. She looked down and saw that she had assumed the fire-form, the flames no longer natural orange flames, but flickering bolts of multi-colored lightning, dancing with ethereal grace, blazing into nova brightness, flickering and wavering in the small room. But the flames also burned beyond the four dimensions of the Earth, burning somewhere beyond, stretching up and away into somewhere else, somewhere far past Earth, past mortal flesh and oxygen and sunlight and soil.

She reached for Jack, took his hand, watched him tentatively allow her to touch him, recoiling at first, and then with confidence as he realized the magic was cocooned around him and protecting him. She smiled at Jack, kissed his lips, felt the surge of passion take the place of flames. She wanted nothing so much right then as to be alone with him, to hold him, sleep in his arms, kiss him as he woke and let him show her what love really was.

Soon, but not yet. Not here. Something still held Miriam back. They were in Nadira's apartment, and that was a large part of the hesitation; she didn't want making love to Jack to just *happen,* one thing leading to another as had happened in the past with other men.

Jack was different. He deserved more. She wanted to be with him intentionally, when the moment was perfect.

She wanted to say this to him, but the words stuck. Jack placed a finger across her lips, pulled her next to him, his chest against her back, curled together, his arm across her belly, his breath on her neck.

At some point, the flames cooled, and she became flesh and blood once more.

As she fell into sleep, she realized the fires that made up her being hadn't devoured the building, hadn't destroyed anything.

She was taking control.

CHAPTER 19

Carson

The present

CARSON WAS AT THE OLD SHILLELAGH, A GIN AND TONIC in hand, the Benjamin Wade case on his mind. He thought about it all the time, eating, driving, showering. It was turning into an obsession. There was so much to it, so many factors to consider.

He was skirting around the edges of the most crucial element, the manner of Ben's death. It just wasn't natural. No matter which way he looked at it, there just was no rational explanation that made any damn sense to him. He'd spoken to an expert on burn patterns and had been informed that for a human to have been so thoroughly consumed, the fire would have had to be more than just a casual, accidental blaze. There was no evidence of accelerant anywhere on the scene or the body. Just...nothing. Only the remains, which couldn't even really be properly termed a "body." He didn't get it. It didn't make any sense. There should've been evidence of fire, evidence of the extreme, destructive heat. The only way the body could have been destroyed beyond a simple fire was if it had been cremated. But there was no such evidence. And no matter where he looked, there was no Miriam, either. He'd looked for her everywhere—gone to her apartment and Jack's, he'd been to Jack's parents', to his grandfather's....

Neither Jack nor Miriam was anywhere to be found.

Carson sighed in frustration, slammed his drink back, and crashed the glass onto the bar..

"Bad day?" Leila asked. She was stacking pint glasses, highballs, and shot glasses into a dishwasher behind the bar.

"Sorry," Carson said. "Tough case. I can't crack it. It just...doesn't make any sense. I've looked into every angle, thought of every possibility, but it still doesn't add up."

Leila shrugged. "Well, sometimes we overlook the most obvious answers simply because they're so obvious. I don't know if that's true in your line of work, detecting and all that, but it's what I've noticed."

Detecting. Carson laughed at that. "No, that's often how it is in cases. This one is different. There is no obvious answer. It just seems…impossible."

"But if it happened, then it's not impossible, right? I mean, you just don't know *how* it happened. I don't even know anything about this case, and you probably can't tell me, but when people say something is impossible, they usually mean they just can't accept the actual answer." Leila snapped her fingers. "Isn't there a quote about that? Something about eliminating the impossible?"

Carson nodded. "Yeah, from *Sherlock Holmes*. 'When you have eliminated the impossible, whatever remains, however improbable, must be true.'"

Leila nodded. "Exactly."

Carson sighed. What was the "improbable" answer? Imagination wasn't his strong suit; his mind just didn't work outside the boundaries of reality. He connected dots and added one fact to another to arrive at a logical conclusion. Leila had hit on his problem exactly, and yet he just couldn't make himself seriously consider the impossible scenarios, which were all that he really had left. Everything now sounded ludicrous and silly. Could Ben had spontaneously combusted? Could Miriam have attacked him with a flamethrower? Yeah, right. What else made people burn? Carson's mind kept feeding him the logical solutions that he already gone through a hundred, a thousand times.

He tossed enough cash onto the bar to pay his tab and leave a sizable tip, forcing himself to leave before he ended up drunk again. He liked Leila, and he didn't want to embarrass himself in front of her any more than he already had.

"Thanks, Leila. I'll see you around."

Leila smiled at him, waved a hand. "Sure thing, Carson. Hope you figure your case out."

Carson laughed, a bitter, sarcastic laugh. "Yeah, me, too."

He had meant to go home, but he found himself back at the precinct, sitting at his desk, staring at the folder and wishing he were still at the Old Shillelagh.

He heard Leila's words again, about not being able to accept the impossible. His gut told him Miriam had something to do with Ben's death somehow, that she had caused his death...and that it had been in self-defense.

But how had she done it?

Chapter 20

Miriam

One day earlier

NADIRA ARRIVED HOME AROUND 8 P.M., SMELLING OF cigarettes and beer. She waved hello to Jack and Miriam, heading straight back to the bathroom for a shower. She re-emerged in men's boxer shorts and a tank top, her long black hair tied up in a sloppy bun.

"Listen up, kids," she said. "We have a problem. There was a detective sniffing around the casino tonight. I didn't tell him anything, but I think you should go in and talk to him. He's...I've got a sense about him. He's part of this somehow. He's tied to you, and to me, in some way. I know that doesn't make any sense, but just trust me. I have gut feelings that are never, ever wrong. You need to go in and talk to him, and you need to tell him the truth. It sounds crazy, but I think he'll believe you."

Miriam shook her head, "No way. He'll arrest me on the spot if I tell him the truth."

"I know, that's what my instincts tell me, too," Nadira said. "But I've also learned that these feelings about particular people are never wrong. Carson, the detective, is important to us somehow."

"Us?" Miriam asked.

Nadira just shrugged. "Well, you need me to teach you how to use your powers, right? And Jack is with you, so…us. I like you. You've been through things most people can't fathom. I know what that's like, all right? I've had have my own issues. But aside from that, djinn aren't really social creatures. We don't often gather together in groups. Like, ever. There's rarely more than one djinn in a particular city, or if there is more than one, they don't overlap their geographical or social circles. So for you and me to encounter each other like we did…there's something to that, some purpose. I have a feeling that detective has something to do with it."

"I believe what you're saying, Nadira, but I just don't know if I'm capable of doing it," Miriam said.

Authorities, hospitals, all made her wary. She'd just gotten free of Ben, and she wasn't about to put herself in the hands of the police. Jack hadn't said anything, and he was sitting on the edge of the couch, staring down at the carpet, still as a statue.

"Jack?" Miriam said, touching his shoulder. "Are you okay?"

Jack shook himself, but when he met her gaze, he had a strange, distant look in his eyes. "I think we should go," he said. "I just...I have this image of us talking to that cop, a tall guy with blue eyes, right? Brown hair, blue eyes?"

Nadira stared at Jack with suspicion. "You know him?"

Jack shook his head, a frown on his face. "No, I just...I can see him. And I think we should talk to him."

"His grandfather has what he calls second sight," Miriam explained to Nadira. "He sees things. Jack has it, too, and I guess he's seeing something right now."

Jack shrugged uncomfortably. "Yeah. It's weird, and I'm not sure I like it. It feels like a memory of something that hasn't happened yet. But I feel like the cop will listen to us."

"I guess if both of you are having the same idea, or vision, or whatever, then I should do it," Miriam said. "But I don't like it."

"I'll go with you," Jack said, taking the detective's business card from Nadira.

The next day, Jack and Miriam met with Detective Carson Hale at the precinct. He was sitting at his desk with a mug of coffee, an open file folder in front of him and a frustrated expression on his face.

"Detective Hale?" Miriam approached him, holding out her hand. The detective stood up, towering over Miriam, shaking her hand gently.

"Yes?" He sounded tired.

"I'm Miriam al-Mansur. I wondered if you might have a few moments to talk?"

The detective looked shocked. "Yes, yeah, uh, lemme just—uh—hold on." He gathered the scattered papers and stacked them neatly, then placed them in the folder. He gestured at the chairs in front of his desk as an invitation to sit down, which she and Jack both did. "So, Miriam. I have to admit I wasn't sure I'd ever see you. You're an elusive woman, Miss al-Mansur."

"I hadn't planned on coming in, honestly, but I…."

"Well, I'm glad you did," Carson said. "I've got a few questions for you."

"I'm sure you do, Detective," Miriam said.

He rummaged through the papers in the case file and clicked his pen several times. He opened his mouth to speak, and closed it again. "I'm honestly not sure where to start. I have so many questions, but…." He waved his hand, trailing off.

Miriam scratched the tabletop with a fingernail, watching Carson closely. "I don't know anything about police work," Miriam began, "but I imagine you've had some trouble trying to figure out what happened to Ben—"

Carson nodded. "Perfect. Let's start there, Miss al-Mansur. Why don't you tell me what happened to Ben?"

Miriam took a deep breath. "And that's the thing, Detective. It's a bit of a difficult story, and I'm not sure you'll believe me."

"At this point, I'm ready to believe just about anything. I can't make heads or tails of the crime scene." Miriam winced. *The crime scene*, he'd called it. Carson continued. "So, please, just try telling me your version of events, and let me worry about what to believe."

Miriam searched Carson's eyes, not sure what she was looking for. She should be scared stiff, sitting in a police station, about to tell a complete stranger the truth of what had happened to Ben. She wouldn't believe it herself, if it hadn't happened to her. Strangely, though, she wasn't afraid. She didn't get a sense of threat from this detective. Curiosity, skepticism, exhaustion, those were all written on Carson's face, but she didn't feel as if he wanted to arrest her, or cause her trouble.

She took another deep breath and prepared to tell her story yet again. She started with how she'd met Ben, and their difficult relationship, her fear of him, the escalating physical abuse, and the odd occurrences that had started not too very long ago.

Carson didn't interrupt, only took a few notes here and there, listening intently. Jack was silent next to her, holding her hand. Then Miriam came to the incident in the parking garage, and that was when she began to falter. Jack picked up the tale.

When Jack told of being shot, Carson asked his first question. "Wait, Ben shot *you,* Mr. Byrne? You were there?"

"Yeah," Jack answered. "I just had a feeling that she was in trouble—"

"What, you have superpowers too, now?" Carson asked. He winced, realizing how harsh that had sounded. "Sorry, I'm just having trouble keeping up with all of this."

"No, it's fine," Jack said. "It's a crazy story, and I don't blame for you not believing it."

"I didn't say I don't believe it, just that I'm having a hard time accepting it."

"I experienced it, and I am, too," Jack said. "So, yeah, Ben shot me. How I found them doesn't matter. I did, and I stopped him from hurting her, but he shot me in the process."

"You don't look as if you've been shot," Carson said, skeptical.

"That's because Miriam healed me." Jack shrugged, inviting Carson to believe what he wanted.

"Go on." Carson didn't give away his thoughts.

"Miriam healed me. But Ben had shot her, too, by accident, I think. He meant to shoot me, but missed, and he hit her instead."

"She doesn't appear to have been shot, either."

"That's because someone else healed her," Jack said, realizing how absurd it all sounded. "The identity of the person who healed her isn't relevant. The point is, when Miriam realized I'd been shot, she—"

"I defended him," Miriam interrupted. "And I killed Ben. I used my powers and killed him for what he'd done to Jack, and for everything he'd done to me. Ben was completely out of control. We'd both be dead now, if it weren't for—"

"If it weren't for your...powers. Yeah. I can see *that*." Carson was openly skeptical now, arms crossed, leaning back in his chair, spinning his pen around a finger. "Look, just explain to me how you killed Ben, because that's the part I don't get. You said you killed him. But how? What did you use? Your superpowers?"

"They are not *superpowers*, Detective Hale," Miriam said, letting an edge of frustration creep into her voice. "You said you were ready to believe anything. Are you? Really?"

Carson sighed, pinched the bridge of his nose, and leaned forward to look Miriam in the eye. "I don't know. Just tell me what happened."

"I'm a djinn, Detective. And I can turn into...I don't know what to call it...a fire elemental, I suppose.

I still look like…me, but I'm made entirely out of fire. That's how I killed Ben." Miriam could tell Carson wasn't convinced. She would have to show him. She needed him to understand. He wanted to believe, something told her, but he couldn't. He needed proof.

Miriam closed her eyes, fell into herself, and grasped at the woven column of magic and fire within her, holding it in her invisible hands. She visualized herself opening her eyes to show not the brown irises of a human, but the fiery orbs of a djinn. Miriam cracked her eyelids open slowly, and saw the world through a distorted filter, saw whorls of magic skirling around her body, streaming from her to Jack and back in a constant flux. She had succeeded, she could tell.

Carson was frozen in his chair, the pen dropping from his fingers, fear and wonder in his eyes. Miriam touched the table with a finger, letting the tiniest trickle of flame escape from within her core to travel up the length of her body and down her arm to crawl from her fingertip along the surface of the desk, a dancing candle-flame figure waltzing in graceful, flickering steps toward Carson. The flame jumped and gyrated in the middle of the desk, living a brief life of its own before leaping from the table onto Carson's hand, where it stood stock still, as if staring at Carson, who was transfixed, his hand trembling, his mouth agape, his eyes wide.

"What…? What is this?" Carson's voice was an amazed whisper.

Miriam felt triumphant, overjoyed at having made her powers follow her commands. "I told you, Carson. I'm a djinn. That's just a small example of my powers. Ben tormented me, beat me, abused me emotionally, cheated on me, kidnapped me, chased me through a casino, cornered me in a parking garage and tried to rape me, and probably would have killed me. He shot the man I love in the chest, and me in the stomach." She felt her anger heating her up from within, felt the fires inside start to boil. "I got…angry."

Carson shook his head as the miniature flame figure twisted on his palm, fluttered, gasped, and died. "I…I can see how that might not have gone well for Mr. Wade," Carson said.

"No," Miriam whispered. "Not well at all."

Carson was silent for a long time, staring at his hand where the dancing candle flame had been. Miriam was starting to wonder if he'd heard her. "Against my better judgment, I think I believe you, Miriam. I'm not sure anyone else would believe *me* if I told them, however, and that's the problem I find myself facing, here. What do I do with you? According to your own story, you're guilty of manslaughter, however justified it may have been. You might be able to classify it as self-defense, which personally I think it is. But in technical terms? There's no evidence for *anything*.

Neither you nor Jack show any signs of having been shot, and, at the same time, there's no evidence tying you to Ben's death. I just don't know what to do about any of this."

Miriam met Carson's eyes, pleading with him. "Just let us go. Like you said, there's nothing connecting anything. Can't you just…let us go? Let the case go…cold, or whatever?"

Carson didn't answer. He picked up his pen and doodled, thinking. He drew the flame that had danced on his palm. "I think you may be right." Carson stood up, gathered his files and notepad. "Thank you for coming in, Miriam. I know it couldn't have been easy. And thank you for showing me…the truth." He stuck out his hand, and Jack and Miriam shook it in turn.

"You have my card, so if you ever need anything, just call me," Carson said.

"Thank you, Detective," Miriam said, and then she and Jack left the station.

Nadira didn't seem surprised that Carson had let them go. "I told you," she said, "he's going to be coming back into our lives, I think. And soon."

Jack had that faraway look in his eyes that Miriam knew meant second sight. "This is the beginning of something," Jack said, his voice deep and echoing with preternatural energy. "There are more coming, to complete the circle."

"What circle?" Miriam asked. "More what?"

Jack shook himself, "I don't know. It's…hazy. I can see us, the three of us and Carson, and more, but they're just…shadows. I don't know what it means."

"Prophecies and visions are like that," Nadira said, shrugging. "They create more questions than answers, and often you don't know if they've come true or not until afterward. That's my experience, at least."

"Your experience?" Miriam asked.

Nadira shook her head, her eyes staring into the middle distance. "Oh, nothing. Just…the past. Prophecies are a pain in the ass. Don't worry about it." Nadira wouldn't say anything else, and Miriam didn't push it.

Later that night, after they'd had dinner, Nadira sat down with Miriam, and asked her if she knew how to shift. "Shift what?" Miriam asked.

"Guess that means no," Nadira said. "I can tell just by looking at you that you've managed to bind your element to your magic. Am I right?"

Miriam nodded. "Yeah. How can you tell?" She looked at her hands and touched her face, but it all seemed normal.

"You look more balanced. Your energy, your… aura, I guess you could call it, is more focused. Before, you were all out balance and disturbed. Anyway. Now that you've done that, you should be able to do some basic manipulations. That's what we call it when we use our powers: manipulation. Try to do this."

Nadira held up her palm and focused on it. Her dark eyes turned the blue of the ocean, glowing from within as if lit by the sun, wavering like liquid. A pool of water formed in her hand. It was flat at first, cupped in the dip of her palm, but then it grew, stretched up, and lengthened, twisted into a helix, looped and bent, spun and bounced, animated as if given life.

"That's kind of like what I did to convince the detective," Miriam said, amazed to see someone else use the kind of power she'd thought only she had.

Miriam held out her palm, pulled on the magic within her, and summoned the trickle of flame to dance on her palm, mimicking what Nadira had done, only with a fragment of fire.

"That's the most basic manipulation I could think of," Nadira said, "so if you can do that one easily, then you're well on the way. Let's try something more difficult, just to test your limits."

Nadira took several deep breaths, and her eyes once again assumed the liquid, shifting light. Her lower torso seemed to waver and distort and then become less solid somehow, as if melting from ice into water. Within moments, Nadira was only an upper torso that faded into a column of storming ocean water. She hovered in place for a moment, and then the jet of liquid that was her body from the waist down coiled to spring her forward in a serpentine motion. Miriam was hypnotized, incredulous. She didn't think there was any way she'd be able to duplicate that, but even as the thought crossed her mind, Miriam realized she did know how. She'd watched the way the magic shifted around Nadira, braiding with the elemental power to obey the djinn's will.

Miriam did as Nadira had, focusing her mind on breathing while delving down within herself and grasping the fire-magic. With a quick visualized command, Miriam felt her legs buzzing and humming and growing hot, and then suddenly she was floating several feet off the floor, supported by a gout of roaring flame. Jack was laughing in amazement, and his approval filled Miriam with pride, even more than the accomplishment itself.

"Good, very good," Nadira said, returning her lower half to human legs. "One thing you have to remember is that you're not omnipotent. You can be hurt and killed in your elemental form—it just takes a lot more to do it. We're particularly susceptible to magic, so if you find yourself around other djinn, you'd best be on your guard. And one other thing: The more of your magic you've used, the harder it will be to retain your human form, so don't go around using magic for every little thing. The key to staying under the radar and fitting in is to act human as much as possible, and never use your powers around normals if you can possibly help it, because there can be side effects if you're not in complete control of your magic."

"That's what's weird," Miriam said. "When all this first started, the magic made Ben's desires real."

Nadira bit her lip, thinking. "Well, I don't know the specifics of how your magic works, but…I think that was your magic needing to get out. It had been building up your whole life, and it reached max capacity, you know? It needed to be used, so it reached out for the first thing it found, namely, the desire of the person you were with. By desire, I mean things inside, unspoken things. That's how the old legends got started, you know. Our magic has a tendency to work not so much on what is spoken, but on what's inside."

Nadira stood up, and took Jack and Miriam's hands in her own. "Now, listen…I'm glad things worked out for you, and I'm glad I could help you, but I want my apartment back."

"Yeah, about that," Jack said. "We have no way back home. Neither of us have our cars."

Nadira laughed. "All right, well, I guess I have to teach you one last trick." She faced Miriam, suddenly serious. "This is hard, and dangerous, so pay attention. We can location shift when we have to. If you don't do it right, you can end up literally anywhere, and if you try it with a normal, like Jack here, and you don't keep your destination clearly in your mind, you can kill him."

"Location shift?" Miriam asked.

"Yeah, like teleporting, I guess. It takes a huge amount of power to accomplish, so when you arrive, you'll probably be in elemental form, which is why you can't just do it whenever you want. You won't have any control over your form until you've rested a bit, so it only really works if your destination is somewhere private. Basically, you're just ripping open a hole in the fabric of reality between where you are and where you want to be. This realm is fragile and delicate, and easily manipulated, but that's as much a danger as anything else. Again, you have to be intentional, and careful, or things can go seriously wrong. Location shifting is something I only use if I have no other option." Nadira took a few steps back. "I'll show you how it works, just because explaining it is damn near impossible."

Miriam watched Nadira summon her magic, pulling until she was all but obscured by the blinding glow of magic roiling around her. Jack seemed able to see the magic glow as well, for he was squinting and shielding his eyes. Miriam was watching carefully, studying Nadira's movements and the way she performed the manipulation. Nadira placed her palms together in front of her chest to form a knife and lunged forward as if spearing the air with her hands.

In the moment before her lunge, Nadira had gathered the magic together into a single column grasped between her palms. When she lunged, the magic pierced the air and vanished; as Nadira had explained, the magic had ripped a hole in reality itself, it seemed, so that when Nadira's hands followed the magic into the gap, she spread her palms apart to enlarge the rip enough to allow her to step through. The moment her body was through, the hole closed silently behind her and Nadira was gone.

The bathroom door opened a few moments later, and Nadira reappeared in full elemental form, a woman made from living water, each motion sending ripples throughout her body. "You can go anywhere you can visualize," Nadira said. "But you have to have a mental image of your destination, and you can't let it go, no matter what. Did you catch how I did that, Miriam?"

"I think so," Miriam answered. Nadira had made it look easy, but Miriam had a feeling it wasn't. "Should I try it on my own before trying to bring Jack with me?"

Nadira nodded. "Yeah, you wouldn't want to vaporize the new boyfriend."

Miriam took a deep breath and closed her eyes, and, holding her hands as she'd seen Nadira do, she pulled deeply from the magic boiling just beneath the surface. She felt the magic respond, billowing out of her in a cloud. Miriam brought the raw power together into her hands, again mimicking the way she'd seen Nadira do it, and then held an image of her apartment in her mind, her living room with the faded couch, the small, little-used TV, the half-counter separating the living room from the kitchen, focusing on all the little details, the chip in the Formica counter, the threadbare tan carpet with the age-old stain beneath the window.

When she had the image firmly centered in her mind, Miriam stabbed forward with her hands and the magic simultaneously, picturing the magic as a sword slicing open a curtain. She felt a resistance, which dissipated as she thrust forward even harder, realizing how much force it took to fully pierce through. She felt the gap widen, saw it in front of her, a tiny speck of darkness and distortion a few feet in front of her face.

With one last push, Miriam was through and grabbing the edges of the hole she had made. It was a strange sensation, holding in her hands something invisible yet tangible, slippery and hard and flexible and cold. The gap wanted to close, and she had to shove her hands apart using all her strength. She saw her apartment beyond the gap, and she contorted her body through the hole and found herself in her dark, cold, and empty apartment. Jack and Nadira were watching her, Nadira with approval, Jack with mixed amounts of pride and wonder.

When the portal closed, Miriam's body burst into flame, and it was several minutes before she had enough control over her power to reassume her.

Miriam decided to make use of the fact that she was home, and packed a backpack with a few changes of clothes, her phone and charger and some makeup. She would return eventually to pack up properly, but for now Miriam didn't want to be here, didn't want to be alone in her apartment. She'd spent enough time alone, sitting by herself in her living room, waiting to fall asleep, waiting to go to work.

She didn't want to be alone. She wanted to be with Jack, and she had no intention of spending another night alone in her bed.

Miriam reopened the portal, calling to mind the details of Nadira's apartment, and stepped through, finding it much easier the second time. Jack and Nadira were waiting, sitting side by side on the couch, chatting. As she stepped through, Miriam felt a pang of jealousy at the sight of them talking together. It was stupid, she told herself. But telling herself to be reasonable didn't get rid of the feeling, the unreasoning desire to tell Nadira that Jack was *hers*. Miriam forced the emotion away, forced herself to be logical. They were just talking.

The moment the rip opened and Jack saw Miriam appear, he jumped up and went to her, taking her hand and helping her step through.

"You packed a bag," he remarked, taking it from her and slinging it on his shoulder.

Miriam let him take it from her. She felt possessive, wanting to snatch it back, but she forced herself to let him have it, to trust him. Trust started with the little things.

"I went to my apartment because it was the first place that I could see clearly in my head," Miriam said. "But once I was there, I…I just didn't want to be there. I've got so many memories of that apartment, and not all of them are bad, but I just don't want to relive them, you know?"

"Yeah, I totally understand," Jack said.

Miriam turned to Nadira and hugged her. "Thank you *so* much…for everything. I don't want to think what would've happened if you hadn't helped us."

Nadira waved her hand dismissively. "I couldn't *not* help you. When I saw you in the casino, terrified and running for your life, I just had a feeling. Our lives are joined now."

"Good." Miriam had always wanted a sister, and now she had one.

Nadira seemed as flushed with emotion as Miriam, holding it in, keeping it down, under control. Nadira squeezed Miriam's hand and hugged her again.

Gathering the magic one more time, Miriam called up a memory of Jack's apartment: stacks of paintings, a canvas on an easel, the smell of paint and turpentine and engine grease. She opened the portal and pushed it as wide as it would go, wrapped her arm around Jack's waist and ducked through. When the rip closed and Nadira was gone from sight, Miriam felt the flames escaping to consume her and was suddenly exhausted, unable to stand.

The weight of memory crashed down on her. She felt herself swaying in place, Jack's arms around her, felt the magic reaching out to Jack and enveloping him, protecting him from the flames until they subsided and she was able to bring herself back to her human form.

He carried her to his bed, set her down, and covered her with a blanket.

Miriam felt peace mixed with the exhaustion. Sleep stole over her, and she let it take her, Jack's arms wrapping around her and pull her close.

Chapter 21

Miriam

The present

She woke fully clothed, the sun streaming in, peeking above the windowsill to limn everything in the room with a soft yellow glow. The light fell across Jack, who lay on his back, an arm flung across his forehead, his mouth slack. She smiled, as she looked at him, admiring the planes of his face, the stubble on his cheeks and chin, his oft-broken nose.

A memory thrust itself into her mind, brief and sharp, an image of Ben above her, madness in his eyes, his knife cutting away her dress. She remembered the fear and helplessness all too well. But then she remembered Jack showing up in the nick of time, fearless in the face of Ben's violent rage. He'd faced Ben down without flinching, without hesitation. He'd kept his vow.

"Ben will kill me before he ever hurts you again," Jack had said, and in that parking garage, Jack *would* have died, shot twice in the chest. He'd come for her, and he'd saved her. She'd always felt safe with him, but it had been an emotional thing, a feeling of security that she got from being in his presence. But now, having seen him literally risk his life to protect her changed things. She *knew* she was safe with him, and that was a new feeling. Miriam snuggled close to him, and he automatically wrapped his arm around her, which struck her as funny somehow. He held her close, even in his sleep.

She'd never felt safe before, not really. There'd always been the threat of danger, of someone out there being able to hurt her. But Jack...she trusted him, which was also new for her. So many new feelings, she didn't know what to do with them all. She searched herself, and found her walls were gone, at least in terms of Jack.

They'd never be truly gone, not completely, but Miriam discovered that at some point she'd let Jack into the innermost places of her soul, and she wasn't afraid of his presence there. He would protect her, and love her. That was the feather that tipped the scales. She felt a butterfly in her stomach, the whisper of wings inside her, the breath of desire stirring within her. She'd resisted him for so long, it seemed. In terms of actual time, it was only a matter of weeks, but to her, with all that had occurred, it felt like a lifetime.

He was still sleeping, but he was stirring a little, waking up. He cracked an eyelid, glanced at her sideways through half-awake eyes, and smiled groggily. He groaned, stretching, and Miriam's hunger for him ignited as she watched him, his powerful arms stretching and descending to pull her against him, his arms that had carried her bleeding to a hospital, his arms that had held her as she slept and had never let her go. She pressed herself against the length of his body, finally giving herself permission to have what she'd wanted since the moment she met him.

Jack was awake now, his hands exploring her body, running from her shoulders down her back to cup her backside, sliding up her side along the soft curve of her hip, along her arm to her elbow and fingers. His lips were brushing her cheek, feather light, then her forehead, then her chin, then the corner of her mouth and her neck and just above her breasts. She wanted to feel his lips on her breasts, his hands between her thighs. The fluttering of desire in her belly was quickening, no longer the gentle beat of sparrow wings but the wild soaring of something more powerful, a predator hungry for him, this man who had somehow become so important to her.

She kissed Jack's jaw, his neck, his cheekbone, and last his lips, touching his teeth with her tongue, pushing up his shirt and pressing her palms against his soft skin and hard muscles. Jack responded with fervor, ripping his shirt off and tugging at hers, lifting it over her head, unclasping her bra and slipping the straps from her shoulders, brushing her breasts with eager hands. Her nipples hardened, and she arched her back to press her breasts into his hands. Jack was kissing her with desperate desire, leaving her breathless.

Miriam lay back, watching Jack with glittering eyes as he unbuttoned her pants and rolled them off, ran his lips down her body, kissed her ribs, her belly, her hips, looping his fingers through the band of her panties and pulling them off. She was bare against him then, the heat of his skin igniting sparks in her soul and fire in her belly, making her delirious with need.

Miriam guided his fingers to slip inside her, breathing in quick, panting breaths as he stirred the fires even hotter with his touch. She reached down and unbuttoned his pants, slipped them off, and tossed them aside, kissing him all the way down as she went. She wrapped her fingers around his hard, silken length; Jack gasped at her touch, pulled her up to straddle him, crushed his lips against hers with an intensity of passion that stole her breath. Miriam pressed her body against his, reveling in the delirium of at last being naked against him.

Jack's hands were all over her, cupping her breasts, and tracing the ridges of her spine, the curves of her ass. She pressed her hips against his, felt his cock hard and throbbing against her opening. Miriam needed to feel him inside her. With a low moan, she pressed her face against the flesh of his shoulder, lifted her hips, reached between their bodies and guided him into her pussy.

She moved slowly, so slowly, savoring the hardness of him in her softness, gasping against his panting mouth, scraping her nails against his shoulders. Miriam had waited so long for him, needed him, wanted him, and now she had him, and she couldn't get enough. She matched his rhythm, a slow glide, deep, gentle thrusts. This only sated her for a few seconds, and then she needed more. Miriam rocked her hips to push him deeper, pulled his body against hers, needing more of him, all of him, needing him harder, faster, deeper. Her own desperation surprised her, feeling a driving hunger, a crazed passion awoken within her that she hadn't known was there.

Jack whispered her name, a breath in the stillness. She loved the way he said it, as if the taste of it was sweet in his mouth, pronouncing each syllable with a clarity of affection that bound her heart a little closer to his.

"Miriam."

It could have been spoken directly into her mind, or it could have been said out loud. Miriam wasn't sure which, and in the passion of the moment, she didn't care.

They were moving together now, synced in a rhythm of passion, breath coming in quick gasps, kissing gently with trembling mouths, his hands in her hair and on her hips, pulling her against him harder and harder as their passion rose to a climax. She felt the magic within her exploding and roiling around them, rushing through them both, enveloping them and consuming them.

She felt her skin heating up, burning, becoming fire; runnels of flame licked out from her skin and ran up Jack's arms and down his chest and across his legs and back, and then more tongues of fire arced from Miriam to Jack until they were both torches of living fire.

Jack was unafraid. He rolled over so she was beneath him, but he didn't put his weight on her, instead holding himself aloft. Hesitating a moment, Jack stared down at the pyre of woman-shaped flame that was Miriam lying beneath him. Then he pulled almost all the way out, poised at her trembling entrance, and pushed himself back in, eliciting a gasp from her. She felt secure there with Jack above her, not hemmed in, not trapped, but held tight and close and exactly where she wanted to be.

Miriam wrapped her legs around his back, pulling him down, and moving her hips up against his to press him deeper, clutching him with shaking hands. She bit his shoulder, rocked with him, moaning and gasping his name. They were both afire but unconsumed, and the flames didn't spread but stayed contained to them. As they neared orgasm together, the fire that was the combined entity of Jack and Miriam roared hotter and higher with every motion, billowed stronger with every wave of ecstasy washing through them.

They exploded together, and time stopped.

In that moment Miriam felt a portion of her soul reach out and span the molecules between them, tracing along the path of magic binding her to Jack, felt that bit of her heart, that fragment of her identity collide with Jack, delve into him, into the secret core of him. Miriam, eyes closed and mind merging with her magic, watched the detached part of herself glowing like an ember, like a star, as it neared the sun of Jack's soul and combined with him, their merged brilliance going nova, brightening in exponential increments until Miriam had to retreat back into her physical self.

When she opened her eyes, she and Jack were lying on her bed, twined together, sweat mingling, breath still coming in long gasps; her fire was still wrapped around Jack like snakes, flitting and flicking, jumping and tangling together.

"This is so cool," Jack said, watching the fire play on his arm. His voice was strangely loud, deafening, ringing in her ears and in her mind. Miriam found that odd, the way she could hear his words in her mind.

She decided to try something, as foolish as she felt thinking about it. She spoke Jack's name, not out loud with her physical voice, but in her head. *Jack? Can you hear me?* She focused the thought at Jack, who seemed startled, confused.

"What the hell was that?" he said aloud.

"Try it," Miriam said. Jack seemed to feel the same strange, painful volume and confusing echo of mental and physical words.

Try it, Miriam said mentally. *Think the words at me.*

Jack seemed skeptical, but he tried it anyway, frowning as he focused on her. *Miriam? Can you hear me now?* Jack was grinning as if he'd told a joke, and Miriam seemed to remember seeing a commercial for cell phones with that tagline. She rolled her eyes at him. *What is this? How is this happening?* Jack asked.

I don't know, Miriam said. *I think it's the connection between us, the way the magic reaches out for you and protects you from the fire. When we made love, I felt—I actually watched a part of myself become part of you.*

Jack nodded. *I think I felt that, too. Like a second orgasm, but inside both of us...or not inside both of us, but between us?* Jack shook his head, not satisfied with that explanation. *That's not right, either. It was…we were one entity for a moment. I don't know, I can't explain it any better than that.*

Miriam ran her toes up and down his leg, rubbed his chest with her hands, loving the feel of his muscles, the comfort of his presence, the desire for him now as much a presence just beneath her skin as the magic was.

I don't think the explanation matters, she said, *as long as we both understand it. I think what it means is that we belong together.* She twisted her head to look into Jack's eyes, watching for his response.

That's because we do, he said, tangling his fingers in her hair.

They were silent for a while, drowsy in the quiet and the stillness of the morning.

*Why didn't I make your wishes come true? Always with—*Miriam cut herself off, not willing to even speak the name in this sacred place—*always before, the magic granted the wish at climax. But just now, with you, the magic didn't make your wish come true. I felt the magic reach for you, I saw it wrapping all around you, so it should have granted your wishes….*

Jack smiled, kissed her gently, and said, *You did make my wish come true: my heart's desire is for YOU. My only wish has always been for you, just you. The magic can't give me something I already have.*

Miriam's passion for Jack was roused even hotter by that answer, by the sweetness inherent in it, and by the obvious truth of it. Ben hadn't truly wanted her, not ever. But Jack did, and that made all the difference. She wouldn't forget Ben, not entirely, because he would always provide a reminder of how perfect Jack was. She knew he wasn't actually perfect. She knew there would be times he would make her mad, and he would annoy her in some way, but even those worst of times with Jack would be minuscule in comparison to the best moments with Ben.

She breathed deeply into Jack's presence, smelling him, feeling him tangled skin to skin with her, his eyes drooping and his lips pressed against her shoulder as he drifted off to sleep.

An infinite time later, Jack was next to her, snoring lightly, one arm thrown across her stomach. Late-afternoon sunlight streamed through the window above her bed, turning the dusting of stubble across Jack's jaw to flecks of gold.

Miriam smiled, running her fingers on his jaw, admiring the hard lines and soft contours of his face, relaxed in sleep. She didn't want to move, feeling an almost overwhelming contentment in that moment. Suddenly, she couldn't remember anything. Her entire life up until that moment, in bed with Jack, was a haze and a distant memory. She closed her eyes and brought up a memory of the night before, feeling the sparrow wings of desire flutter in her stomach.

Jack stirred, rubbed an eye with his palm, and glanced at Miriam. "Mmmm, it was real?" he mumbled.

Miriam laughed and burrowed closer to him. "Yes, it was real. Should it not have been real?"

"No, I mean, yes—argh! I don't make sense without coffee." Jack slipped his knee between her legs, ran a hand along the line of her body from knee to breast and back down to her hip, where it came to rest. "I may have dreamed about you a few times. I always woke up afterward, and it was always a dream. This time I woke up, and it was real. That's what I mean."

"Oh. You dreamed about me? Really?" Miriam said.

"Uh-huh." Jack grunted his answer, kissing her neck where it met her breastbone and slipped downward to her breasts, kissing in quick soft pecks the skin underneath her breasts, first one and then the other, his fingers splaying across her nipples as they hardened, rubbing his legs against hers. Miriam arched her back, pressed herself against him, luxuriating in the feel of his lips against her flesh.

"What kind of dreams?" she asked, reaching down to caress the tip of him, the length of him, delighting in the way he gasped softly and pressed himself into her hand.

Jack didn't answer, not with words. He rolled over on top of her, and showed her.

THE END

Author's Note

Domestic abuse features heavily in this story, and it is a subject that has affected me personally—there is a reason the hero in this story is named Jack.

I could fill this note with statistics on domestic abuse, I could give my own story, I could do many things. Instead, what I will say is that I chose to write this story because abuse is something that affects people all over the world, from every ethnic, religious, and socioeconomic background. It is a real and tragic problem, and it deserves attention. I've received criticism regarding Miriam before, people saying she's weak for sticking with Ben for so long despite the abuse. But that, sadly, is a reality. You start to think you have no other choice. You start to think you've earned it, you deserve it, that no one can help you. That there is no escape. That every man will treat you the same way.

I escaped. It took a lot of courage, but I did it. And I found a man who, like the Jack in this story, treats me with the love and affection that I deserve.

That I DESERVE.

Do you hear that? If you've experienced anything like what I did, you know how hard that can be to believe. And if you know anyone who is in the middle of such trauma, you know how impossible it can be to convince them of it.

There is always another option. No one has the right to treat you or anyone you know with cruelty, with emotional or physical violence. Seek help.

There are any number of websites dedicated to the topic, but here are a couple to get you started.

www.womenhelpingwomen.org/what-is-abuse/domestic-violence/

www.thehotline.org/

abuseintervention.org/help/friend-family/

Continue reading for a sneak preview of

DJINN AND TONIC

By
Jasinda Wilder

Coming Soon

DJINN AND TONIC
CHAPTER 1: A BREATH OF WIND

DETECTIVE CARSON HALE WASN'T SURE HOW HE ENDED up at the Old Shillelagh again, a highball of gin and tonic in hand, watching replays of the Tigers beating the Rockies. He had left the station after work, but hadn't felt like going home.

He was watching the TV screen, but not really seeing the action. It was more of a distraction than anything. He was trying not to think about the case. Or, as Carson thought of it in his own mind, The Case. It was one he'd not forget any time soon. Miriam al-Mansur remained stuck in his head somehow. It wasn't like he was attracted to her in a sexual way. She was beautiful, sure, but it just wasn't there for him, and she was with Jack Byrne, anyway. No, there was something else about her that kept her on Carson's mind, and he knew perfectly well what it was.

How could he just...let it all go? Just write off the murder of a man as...what?

It wasn't self-defense; Miriam had admitted that much herself. At least, partially. She had been defending Jack. Or, more accurately, exacting revenge because he'd shot Jack. Two bullets to the chest, she'd said. But you didn't survive that kind of injury, you just didn't. A sucking chest wound was, by all accounts, one of the most painful ways to die, next to being shot in the gut, and Miriam had had both wounds...and survived.

According to their account, Miriam had been shot in the stomach, and then somehow she'd taken Jack's wounds into herself. Which, if that was at all believable, meant that she had had four gunshot wounds to the chest and stomach, and she'd survived. Either she was inhumanly tough, or she healed like Wolverine. There was no other explanation.

Carson finished his first drink, raised the glass, and clinked the ice at the bartender—what was her name? Leila? Yes, Leila. That was it. She filled a clean highball glass half-full with ice, then tipped a bottle of Bombay Sapphire to pour a generous two fingers' worth. She smiled at Carson, a quick, flirting glance.

"Nice to see you again. Do you want me to start a tab?"

"Yeah, sure," Carson answered. "Thanks."

"You seem preoccupied," she said by way of making conversation, setting down his drink.

She leaned on the bar in front of Carson, toying with a book of matches. Her T-shirt was a low-cut V-neck, and when she leaned over, Carson found it hard to keep his gaze from straying to her spilling cleavage. Carson had spent enough time in bars and on patrol to know the various ways women leaned over. He'd categorized them: There was the absent-minded lean, in which the woman was simply assuming a natural, comfortable position, either not realizing or not caring about how she was displaying herself; then there was the flirt-lean, where she was more aware of the spillage, but not necessarily trying to accentuate it; last was the overt seduction-lean, where she squeezed her arms underneath her breasts to prop them up and leaned over so they all but spilled out. Carson was pretty sure Leila was somewhere between number one and number two.

The way she was looking at him, combined with her body language, hinted at flirtation, but certainly not seduction. He was kind of glad for that, actually. He'd been seduced on any number of occasions, mostly by women trying to get out of a speeding ticket or a DUI arrest. He'd come across the occasional witness hoping to sway the outcome of an investigation, and he'd met his share of drunken badge-chasers. The ones who were into serious seduction, he'd found, were not the kind of girls he was interested in, at least not long-term. He'd like to be able to say that he'd turned them all down, but he hadn't. Not all of them. He never took favors *on* the job or *for* the job— he drew the line at that—but if a girl threw herself at him off the clock, what was the harm?

Carson realized he'd not responded to Leila's comment. "Sorry, yeah," he said. "I guess I am a bit preoccupied, at that."

Leila laughed at him. "Delayed reaction, much? I was starting to wonder if you'd heard me."

"No, I heard you, I was just…."

"Lost in la-la land?" Leila teased. "It's okay. I imagine your job takes up a lot of brain space."

"You have *no* idea," Carson said. "Today especially."

The bar was dead, Carson one of only three patrons in the place, so Leila had time to chat. She was a beautiful girl, tall and willowy, with thick black hair tied back in a neat ponytail, and wide, dark eyes that held a wealth of expression. She seemed to like him, and that made it even better. Carson could use a distraction.

Leila grimaced, somehow making the expression look attractive. "You must see a lot of unpleasant stuff, huh?"

Carson finished his drink, and Leila poured him a third without asking. "Yeah," Carson said. "Part of the job, I guess. Most of it I can block out, some I can't. There are some things people just aren't meant to see."

"I bet. So is that what's preoccupying you? A bad case or whatever? I hope I'm not being too nosy."

"You're not being nosy. And, yeah, it's not one of those gruesome cases that'll give you nightmares, it's just…confusing. I'm not sure what to believe, you know?"

Leila just nodded, her attention fully focused on him. She had her chin propped on her palm, listening, watching him. Carson found himself talking about the case out loud, which he knew he shouldn't do with a stranger, but Leila seemed different somehow, trustworthy. And the gin was clouding his judgment enough that he didn't care.

She was pouring them stiff, more gin than tonic or ice, and Carson wasn't protesting. He heard himself telling her about Miriam, how odd things were, how so many elements to the case seemed unbelievable, if not impossible.

"Unlikely, sure," Leila said, "but impossible? Didn't we talk about impossibilities before? From what you're telling me, this isn't one or two odd little things. It's several big things, almost too big too ignore, or to pretend it's not what it looks like."

Carson nodded and drank. "Yeah, that's what part of me says, too. And I shouldn't be talking about this with you."

"I won't tell anyone. Promise," Leila said, smiling.

"Better not. But if something goes against everything you know to be true? What then?" Carson felt himself slurring a little. He should slow down on the drinks, but he didn't want to. He liked the warm muzziness, the gentle floating of his mind. He liked not feeling as uptight about the whole business. Leila was easy to talk to, and easy on the eyes. It was past two in the morning at this point, and the last customer was walking out the door.

Leila considered before answering. "Well, it depends, I guess. If you can't deny it, if it's just *there* and obvious, despite the apparent 'truth' of things, then you can't really keep insisting on what you think is true, can you? I mean, isn't that just being obstinate? There's so much about this world and about life that we can't see, you know? Just because we haven't seen something before doesn't make it impossible."

Leila came around from behind the bar and started lifting chairs onto tables. Carson stood up to help her, a little more unstable on his feet than he'd expected to be. Leila rolled her eyes, pushed him back to his stool, and sat him down. Her hands on his back were warm, the feeling of her touch was electric, sending thrills through him. He wanted her to keep her hands on him, but she moved away to finish putting up the chairs.

"Yeah, you're right," Carson said. "But that doesn't make it any easier to accept what you've always thought was impossible." Leila had moved back behind the bar, wiping bottles with a rag. Carson watched her move, admiring the easy grace of her motions. She was light on her feet, every step smooth, every twist of her body as she performed the closing ritual flowing into the next. There was something airy about her, Carson thought. The idea seemed odd, even to Carson in his tipsy state, but it stuck with him as true all the same. She moved as if blown by a secret wind, like she was a leaf. She had a dancer's body, he realized. Maybe that explained it. She must be a dancer.

Carson watched raptly as she took her hair out of its ponytail and shook it out to fall in glinting waves around her shoulders. But being a dancer didn't explain the way her hair floated and fluttered as if blown by a breeze. There were no open doors, no windows, no fans, but her hair was definitely fluttering. That was the word, too, Carson thought. Fluttering.

She was standing at the bar counting the register drawer, her hands peeling bills in quick, sure motions that spoke of years of practice. She was standing still, but her hair was moving. Carson felt himself repeating his thoughts, but he couldn't help it. He was watching her, mesmerized, and he couldn't deny what he was seeing. It was weird, all this talking about the case and

Miriam and the strange facts, and now Leila was part of the mystery. He considered asking her about her hair, but the words wouldn't coalesce into a sentence that didn't sound stupid. *Excuse me, Leila, but your hair is being blown by a wind that doesn't exist?* That was just stupid.

Carson finished his drink, handed his credit card to Leila, and signed the slip with a sloppy signature, accepting one last drink. He'd lost count again. There may have been one or two he'd tossed back so quickly that he forgot to count them. Either way, the room was wobbling a little as Leila shut off the lights in the kitchen and locked the drawer in the office, sitting down next to Carson with a Styrofoam cup of Coke. Carson could smell rum in the Coke and on her breath. She was sitting close to him, her shoulder brushing his, her thigh nudging his as she bounced her knee absently. He was acutely aware of every point of contact between them; her presence grounded him, in some indefinable way, keeping his spinning world centered.

"So, what are you going to do about the case?" she asked, toying with a matchbook. She lit a match, watched it burn down toward her fingertips. Before it could burn her fingers, it puffed out as if blown by an unseen wind.

"I don't know. Legally, technically, what she did was manslaughter. She should've reported Ben to the authorities and let them deal with him. But, speaking *as* one of the authorities, by the time she did that, there's no telling where he would've gone. He might've disappeared before we could catch him, and, in reality, there are just too many other cases to investigate. To be honest, I doubt we'd have spent much time chasing him. I investigated his death, but along the way he turned out to be an asshole who deserved what he got."

Carson drained the last of his drink, chewing an ice cube as he spoke. "I know what I *should* do, according to the specifications of my job, but I just don't think I can. I became a cop to get justice for people. There were other reasons, but that was one of them. Miriam did the only thing she could do in those circumstances, and I can't make myself arrest her for it. And even if I did, proving anything at all, for her or against her, would be impossible anyway. But...it's like—it's ethics versus morals, you know?"

Leila nodded, bumped her shoulder against his. "Hey, all you can do is what you think is right, you know? For what it's worth, I think you're making the right choice."

"Thanks. That does help, actually."

"So you're gonna close the case?" Leila had a ring on her right hand that she twisted absently. It looked like a keepsake of some kind—perhaps something that had emotional value to Leila, and Carson found himself wondering what the story was. He remembered the first time he'd met her, the way she'd paused before answering a question, and how much of a back-story he'd sensed in her.

"Yeah, I guess I am. I'll tell the Captain it's a cold case, that there's not enough to go on. And technically, there's not. There's no physical evidence tying Miriam to Ben's death, and even if there might be plenty of motives, I don't think there's a way to make the charge stick. It would waste everyone's time and money, and just cause more trouble for Miriam. And she's had enough of that."

"Good," Leila, said. "I'm glad."

Carson hesitated for a moment, then asked, "So... what's your story? You said last time I was here that you needed a fresh start, so you came here. What's all that about?"

Leila glanced at him, took a deep breath, as if wishing he hadn't asked that. "Oh, it's a long story. Not very interesting, especially if you weren't there."

"Oh, you never know what I'd be interested in." Carson reached over the counter, grabbed the soda gun, and filled his glass with water. "I'm interested in you, for example."

Christ, he hadn't meant to say that. He drank his water to cover his flush of embarrassment. Leila had turned on her stool, regarding him with several emotions written plainly on her face: surprise, embarrassment, curiosity, maybe a little fear.

"You are, huh?" she said, a slight smile on her lips, chewing on her straw. Curiosity was winning, apparently.

Carson laughed, an awkward chuckle. "Yeah, that just kind of slipped out. Sorry. But it's true."

"A Freudian slip? What else are you thinking about me that you're not saying?" She had inched over on her stool so she was just at the edge of his personal space.

Carson hoped he was reading her body language right. He wanted to believe she was expressing interest.

"Oh…I don't know," he said. "You're hot." Shit. That hadn't come out right.

Leila laughed, an infectious, musical sound that made him not feel so stupid. "Is that right? Keep going." She crossed one leg over the other, facing him.

"Um…." There were a lot of things going through his mind. Her lips looked soft, a slight glimmer of lip gloss on them, making him wonder what they would taste like. He'd only met her a couple of times. It would be reckless to act on that thought. "I'm wondering what flavor lip gloss you have on. What your lips taste like." Carson heard himself speaking the words as they entered his mind. "God, I have no filters suddenly," he said.

Leila arched an eyebrow. "Filters are a nuisance anyway," she said. Was it Carson's imagination, or was she leaning into him, ever so slightly? "I've always believed in saying what you mean."

Carson was leaning toward her, thinking how ridiculous it was to be considering kissing a girl he'd met a handful of times here, in the bar, at her place of work. "Yeah? So what are you thinking? Now that I've embarrassed myself completely."

"Oh, so it's my turn now, huh?" Leila was definitely closer than she had been a moment ago. Her wide eyes were inches from his, sparkling with amusement, and secrets, and something he wanted to believe was desire. "You haven't embarrassed yourself at all. I'm glad you can say what you're thinking."

"You're avoiding my question," Carson said. Leila was sitting facing him, her feet on the rungs of his stool, her knees resting between his legs. His hands were on her knees, and she wasn't pulling away.

"You caught me," Leila admitted with a mischievous tip of her lips. "Okay, so what am I thinking? Hmmm. I'm thinking…you're cute, in a rugged sort of way. I'm thinking you're a little drunk."

Carson nodded. "Keep going."

Leila's fingers were plucking at a loose string on the collar of Carson's shirt, and then they were playing with a lock of his hair at his neck. She was definitely moving into his personal comfort zone; touching someone's hair was a strangely intimate thing, yet he didn't mind. "I'm thinking…I like you, and I'm hoping you'll ask me out. There. How's that for embarrassing myself? Admitting you're interested in a guy goes against every rule of the dating game I know."

"I've never been too interested in the dating game anyway," Carson said.

"Me, neither. That's part of the reason I moved up here," Leila said. "I know I'm avoiding your original question, but…I don't want to talk about that just yet."

Carson nodded. "Fair enough."

"Do you have a girlfriend?" Leila asked. "Or a wife?"

Carson shook his head. "Nah. Would I be here, talking to you like this if I did?"

"You'd be surprised what some guys will do even though they're with someone."

Carson shrugged. "You'd be surprised how much it takes to surprise me. I'm a homicide cop, remember? I've seen just about everything. What I should've said was, I wouldn't be here like this, with you, if I was with anyone else." Carson had been about to kiss her, but the moment seemed to have passed with the turn in the conversation.

"Well, that's good. I wouldn't like to have any surprises come up later on." She glanced down, saying, "If there *is* a 'later on.'"

"Why wouldn't there be?"

"Well, I left you a pretty big opening to ask me out, but you didn't." Leila bit her lip, chewed on it, scratched at a stain on the leg of her jeans.

Carson cursed himself for being so dense. "Yeah, I guess I missed the boat on that one. Is it too late?"

"You'll never know until you ask," Leila said.

"So…do you want to go out with me? For dinner? Sometime?" Carson was fumbling. He took a drink of water and tried to clear his head. "Sorry, that didn't come out right. Lemme try again. Leila, would you like to have dinner with me?"

Leila shook her head and rolled her eyes. "You're funny," she said, a teasing grin on her face. "Yes, Carson, I would. I'm off this Tuesday."

She was slipping forward again, touching her lips with her tongue, an invitation in her eyes. Or at least Carson hoped it was an invitation. He swallowed his nerves and allowed himself to lean forward, touching his lips to hers, slowly and hesitantly, giving her every chance to pull away, to tell him he'd misunderstood her. But she didn't. Instead, she moved her hand from her leg to his, the other to his shoulder, and, moving toward, pulled him closer to deepen the kiss.

Her breath was cold, like a winter wind, and her lips tasted like cherry lip balm, and a hint of rum and Coke. He felt a rush of excitement run through him at her response, an absurd joy that she was kissing him back. Carson would have sworn that a breeze had kicked up to blow through his hair, ruffling his shirt and skirling Leila's long raven-black hair to tickle his face.

Then he felt a quick, sharp pang of pain blast through the back of his skull, and darkness leaped up to swallow him. As he faded into unwilling unconsciousness, he heard Leila shrieking and cursing, and he fought to keep his eyes open, but it was no use.

The world went black and silent.

Djinn and Tonic: Coming soon!